Shady Park Panic

Rea Keech

ISBN 978-0-9983805-7-5 Hardback
ISBN 978-0-9983805-9-9 **Paperback**
ISBN 978-0-9983805-8-2 **Ebook**

Library of Congress Control Number:
2018946765

PS 3561 .E333 S53 2018

Published by
Real
Nice Books
11 Dutton Court
Baltimore, Maryland 21228
www.realnicebooks.com

Publisher's note: This is a work of fiction. Names, characters, places, institutions, and incidents are entirely the product of the author's imagination or are used fictitiously, and any resemblance to actual persons, living or dead, or to events, incidents, institutions, or places is entirely coincidental.

Cover by Robert Mansfield.
Cover photo: Africa Studio/Shutterstock.com
Set in Sabon.

Shady Park Panic is
Book 2 of the Shady Park Chronicles

Also by Rea Keech:

First World Problems (Book 1 of the Shady Park Chronicles)

"Keech (*A Hundred Veils*) takes on a literary classic in this novel, which follows the romantic and social trials and tribulations of Emma Bovant and her husband, Charles.... This tale should please readers who enjoy romantic drama, and may be of interest to fans of Flaubert." — **Kirkus Reviews**

A Hundred Veils

Publishers Weekly BookLife Prize: General Fiction Finalist 2017

"Set in the lead-up to the Iranian revolution, *A Hundred Veils* is a rich portrait of cultural and personal discovery and forbidden love. Keech uses both humor and drama, as well as finely chosen details and rich description, to bring the characters and their world to life."
— **Eleanor Brown**, best-selling author of ***The Weird Sisters***

BookLife assessment of ***A Hundred Veils***:

Prose: The writing is as economical and succinct as a film script. The narrative moves along swiftly, and yet it's studded with evocative detail.

Originality: This gripping book is a romance with humor and cultural insights that readers will find original and intriguing.

Character Development: The characters here are well developed and fully formed. Marco in particular feels vivid and real.

Maryland Writers' Association: Best literary/mainstream novel 2017 awarded to *A Hundred Veils*.

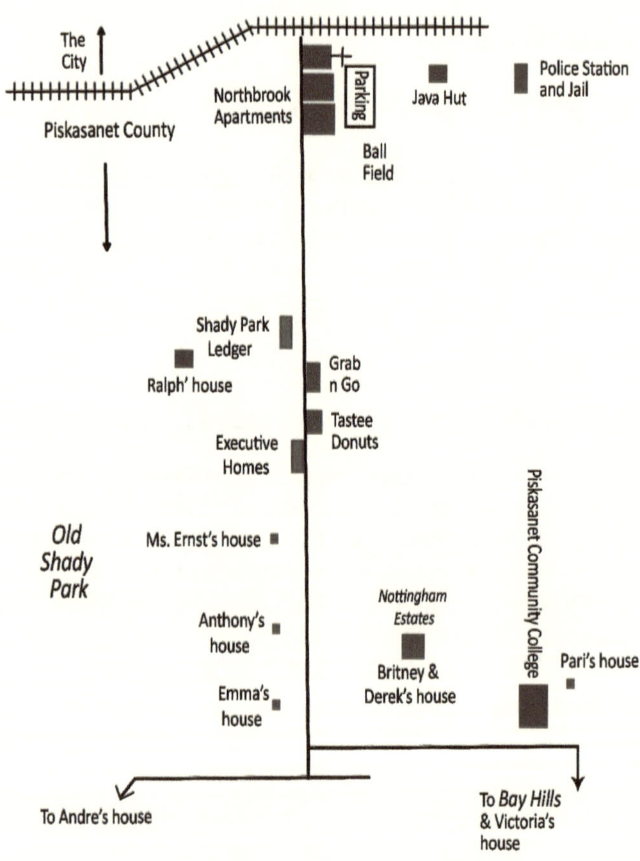

Shady Park and vicinity

Riverside Village

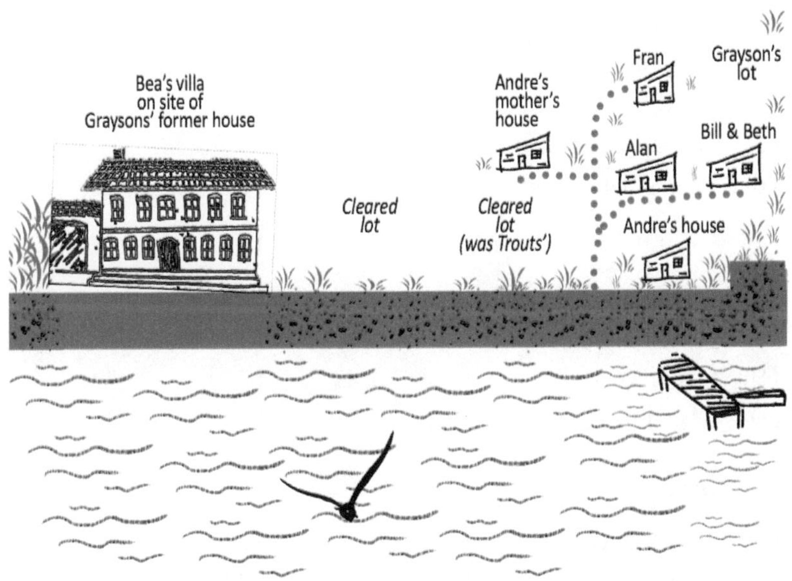

Piskasanet River

List of Chapters

I

SHADY PARK LEDGER

Panic in Shady Park

Special edition

Reports by
Anthony Mansfield
and Pari Shandule

INSIDE

1

Armed for protection

In the first place God made idiots. This was for practice. Then he made school boards.

—Mark Twain, *Following the Equator*

The odor of teenage perspiration hung heavy in the high school multi-purpose room as the parents filed in. Wooden folding chairs scraped the tile floor, concerned citizens and community leaders fighting each other for seats. Anthony stood with the overflow crowd, leaning against the clammy yellow wall at the back, taking out his notebook. He heard grumblings: "They ought to air condition these schools." A man in a checkered sport coat chided from the platform in a high-pitched voice, "You want even more taxes?" Anthony recognized Andrew Mauer, the County Executive.

The young reporter had been sent to cover this meeting as a kind of punishment. His articles about Riverside Village residents losing their homes to corrupt developers had annoyed his publisher at the *Shady Park Ledger*. "You're not a detective," Pop Whitman had grumbled. "Your job is to cover Rotary dinners, store openings, bridge tournaments. The *Ledger* doesn't need a nosey reporter stirring things up."

Anthony flipped to a new page in his notepad. The Board chairman—Anthony could never remember his name—had trouble making himself heard above the racket and looked for help from a beady-eyed man on the platform next to him, the Northbrook High principal, Anthony assumed. "All right.

All right, now," the principal called out. Unfortunately, this wasn't an assembly of students who feared his authority. The shoving and grousing continued. Anthony heard the word "foreigners" several times.

Only a few years ago, most of the foreigners in Piskasanet County had come fleeing from violence and corruption in Central America. County Executive Mauer was running for re-election on a platform that echoed the demands of national politicians to send all the illegals back, keep them from taking Americans' jobs. Recently a new trickle of refugees from war-devastated Syria had begun to appear. To county residents, these seemed even more threatening. They were from, well, from somewhere over there in the Middle East, the place terrorists came from. Seated in the back row in front of Anthony was a woman wearing a black hejab.

A shapely woman stepped forward on the platform in a silky dress that looked more appropriate for a nightclub than a Board of Education hearing—Beatrice Doggit, Anthony knew, the newest member of the county Board of Education. Bea tossed her head, flicking her bleached blond hair aside, and took a breath deep enough to challenge the straps of her plunging neckline. Her bare arms outstretched, she turned her palms up. "Lord," she intoned, "Lord Jesus, we seek your guidance." The room settled to a hush.

"Mmm-mmm. Look at that," a bald man near Anthony quipped.

"I could do with a piece of that," the guy next to him said. "Tell you what!"

With a timid cough, the Board chairman circled his finger for Bea to get on with it. Ignoring him, she called out, "What a wonderful turnout on this Thursday evening. What a wonderful show of support for the policies the Lord has moved us to bring to our schools."

The room gave a round of applause—although Anthony

also noted one or two timid boos.

"I apologize for taking up your time with the subject of this hearing," Bea said. "As you know, there has been a complaint."

A chorus of "Nooo" rose up.

"Yes, a complaint against requiring our children to use textbooks that teach the basic truths of our Christian heritage."

This was a new, doctrinaire side of Bea, whom Anthony had previously exposed in a series of *Ledger* articles detailing her fraudulent Riverside Paradise scheme. He licked the tip of his pencil.

"This complaint," Bea raised her voice. "Please, listen. This complaint is from a woman who is with us here this evening. The Board has asked her to stand in front of the other parents and describe, if she can, what harm our new curriculum could possibly be doing to her child."

The woman in the hejab half-rose, waited for a signal from Bea, then made her way to the platform. She wore a paisley skirt over dark, loose-fitting trousers, and she was gripping a book in trembling hands.

From one of the seats, a female voice shrieked, "*Her* child? It's *our* children who are in danger." New murmurs.

Bea nodded dramatically. "These are dangerous times, we all know. Times when our values are under attack." She went on, "But the Board of Education is determined to hear out any opposition to its policies." She stepped back, motioning for the doe-eyed young woman to turn and face the crowd. Anthony snapped some pictures with his phone.

"I am Shahnaz," the woman began. She raised her voice over some jeering. "My son is in the tenth grade at this school. Like you, I want our children to get the best education possible." She held up her son's social studies book. "But when our U.S. history books talk about an 'immigration of workers' from Africa and never use the word 'slave,' our children's education suffers. When Islam is not mentioned as one of the world's religions but appears in a chapter called Political Ideologies, my son, a Muslim, is confused. And yours should be, too."

Anthony wrote fast: *Shahnaz (sp?) Get last name.*

The Board chairman dabbed his forehead with a handkerchief. "Thank you, Ms., uh, Shanitz. The Board of Education will consider what you say and—"

"I'll tell you what the Board should consider." A woman in a bulging leather skirt jumped up from the front row. "The safety of our children. What they need is protection from the terrorists threatening our country."

A murmur of approval encouraged her. "Let me tell you, my husband and I are armed, armed for protection." She tapped a beaded handbag hanging from her shoulder. "Just like the teachers and staff at our schools should be." The man beside her, presumably her armed husband, stared down at the floor. Anthony recognized him as Derek Grosbeck, a developer involved in Bea Doggit's Riverside Paradise scheme.

A few shouts of "Yeah!" and "Right!" rang out.

A heavyset woman sitting in a group of teachers near the door stood up with her hands on her hips. "No guns on school property," she shouted. "It's the law."

"For now it is!" a man in a red baseball cap shouted back. "We're going to see about that."

The teacher called out, "School is no place for guns."

Chairs scraped the floor. A woman in jogging pants and two men in baseball hats waved their fists. Anthony pulled his phone from his belt, set it to video, and steadied himself against the wall behind him. The chairman's calls for order could barely be heard.

Anthony smiled to himself, imagining his publisher's reaction to the report he would write of this Board of Education hearing. Previously, he hadn't mentioned the publisher's golfing partner Grosbeck in any of the articles exposing Riverside Paradise, not being totally clear about Grosbeck's connection. But Anthony had a thing about guns. He would quote Grosbeck's wife, if he could confirm that was her, saying she and her husband were carrying guns to the meeting. Pop was sure to have his editor take that out, of course. Anthony knew it was foolish to irritate Pop, but facts were facts.

Bea Doggit stepped forward on the platform holding up an arm, and the racket slowly began to settle down.

The next moment there was a scream. A stubble-headed teenager in a camouflage T-shirt stood blocking the doorway, waving an automatic pistol across the room. The gunman's arm, tattooed with a large black cross, came to a stop with the gun pointed at Shahnaz, the woman in the hejab. He narrowed his eyes.

A deep, reverberating pop silenced the room completely. Bea sank to the platform, motionless. More screams and shouts rang out.

Anthony ducked, shrank to the ground. The memory of what happened to his little brother had never left him. He wanted to run, but he was a reporter now. And, besides, there was nowhere to run. Still stooping, he held his phone above his head, recording.

The back door behind the platform squeaked open, and Anthony saw Derek Grosbeck's wife bolt out, clinging to her beaded handbag, nearly knocking the principal down on her way. Others followed, including her husband and the County Executive.

Just then a folded chair slammed the gunman behind the knees, doubling him over. The heavyset teacher who had yelled "No guns on school property" grabbed him around the neck from behind. "All right, now, young man," she said. Her powerful arms held him in a chokehold. The gun slid away over the tile floor, nobody venturing to pick it up.

Anthony was afraid of guns, but he warily made his way towards it and flicked it out of the gunman's reach with the toe of his shoe. The attacker was proving too strong for one teacher alone, and two more teachers threw themselves on top of him. Anthony snapped pictures of the women holding him down.

He looked to the platform. Bea Doggit was sitting up now. Apparently, she hadn't been shot. She'd fainted. But a slender teacher was lying on the floor, holding her lower leg. Anthony recognized her from a science fair he'd covered when she taught at Shady Park. It was Ms. Ernst, a shy, pleasant woman with frameless glasses, now tilted sideways on her face.

The three teachers, assisted by several men now, held the attacker down until two uniformed policemen burst into the room, guns gripped in both hands, shouting, "Down. Everybody. Down on the floor." One called for backup while the other kneeled to handcuff the struggling teenager. Anthony stepped aside to let an ambulance crew into the room with a stretcher.

"Over there," the heavyset teacher who had pounced on the assailant screamed. She pointed to Ms. Ernst, whose leg was bleeding. "Nicole's hurt."

"Coming through," the paramedic called out.

"I'm OK. Really, I'm fine," Ms. Ernst murmured.

The paramedic knelt and examined the wound. "Not too deep. Bullet grazed the surface." He bandaged her leg and said, "We'll have to take you to the hospital, Ma'am. Clear the way, please, everybody."

Anthony approached the heavyset teacher who had grabbed the gunman. He helped her to her feet and got her name. Ms. Costello. "That's my best friend who got shot," she said.

"You spoke to the kid with the gun, Ms. Costello. Do you

know him?"

She was still panting. "A Northbrook senior. Willard Scherd. Quiet. Keeps to himself."

"Sure you're not hurt?"

"No, just out of breath. I think I'll—" She turned and huffed out through the door behind the platform.

Anthony stood near a policeman and copied witnesses' answers into his own notes while the cop questioned them and let them leave one by one. The woman in the hejab was taken into custody along with the attacker.

2

Office politics

The nature of bad news infects the teller.

—Shakespeare, *Antony and Cleopatra*

Before he left the room, Anthony gave his description of the attack to the police. They didn't ask him for any names, so he didn't give them any. Outside, he tapped a rough report into his phone and called the *Ledger* news editor. No answer, but Victoria picked up.

"Hey, Vicky. Would you ask Ralph to clear a spot on tomorrow morning's front page? I just emailed it in."

"Front page for a report on a Board of Education hearing? Get serious, Anthony. Anyway, he just left for the night."

"There was an attack. A teacher was shot. Would you call Ralph and get his OK to squeeze this in for the morning's paper?"

He heard clicking over the phone. "OK, I see it." Victoria was reading. "Come on, Anthony. *Two parents claiming to be armed fled while three unarmed teachers subdued the attacker*? You know Pop's not going to allow that in the story. You're in enough trouble already."

Victoria was the *Ledger* publisher's daughter. Following her, everybody called the publisher slash editor-in-chief "Pop." He was tight with Andrew Mauer, the County Executive, who liked to stir up voters by talking about gun rights—a sore spot with Anthony.

"Well, that's what happened. I recognized the man. Derek Grosbeck. And I assume the armed woman was his wife."

"Britney, you mean? Just forget it, Anthony. You know Pop plays golf with Grosbeck. I'm definitely taking it out." He heard her typing. "For your own good."

"Anyway, tell Ralph I'll have more details by tomorrow afternoon for the Saturday morning paper, would you? I have to go."

"So, I was thinking," Victoria said, "we could go to Sur le Dessus for dinner. They're not so busy on Thursday night. Can you get changed and pick me up by eight?"

"Dinner? Vicky, I'm off to the police station. I need to get more details by the next deadline." The fact that this was the most dramatic story he'd ever had the chance to cover in his three years at the paper didn't seem to impress her.

"So? No dinner together?"

"Don't see how I can do it, Victoria. Sorry."

The county police station was only a couple miles away. No reporter was there from the rival *City Paper*, Anthony was glad to see. The police spokesman, Rob, was a friend of Anthony's from high school. Rob recited what the cops were willing to make public. Two people had been taken into custody. Names being withheld for now.

"How about the age of the gunman?" Anthony asked.

"Eighteen."

An adult—Anthony could report his name. "OK, Rob. Anything else you can tell me?"

"The ballistics lab is examining the gun. Forensics will be searching the school multi-purpose room for evidence. The school will be closed tomorrow."

"Thanks, Rob." As soon as Anthony put the assailant's name into Google, the address for Willard Scherd Plumbing popped up. He pulled up to that Northbrook address in his Kia at about 9 p.m. It was a house with an enormous garage in the back yard—a home business. A woman in a loose flowered dress cracked open the door. Inside smelled faintly of propane.

"Police?" she whined. "We told you all we know."

"I'm sorry. I know it's late. I'm from the *Shady Park Ledger*. One of Willard's teachers says he never caused any trouble. I just wondered what his parents could tell me about him. I've heard this isn't like him at all." In the three years he'd reported for the *Ledger*, Anthony had perfected the I'm-on-your-side introduction.

Willard's mother softened. Her husband came and stood behind her. He opened the door wider but not enough for Anthony to come in.

Anthony slipped out his notebook as casually as possible. "Did you talk to him at the police station?"

"They called us in," the woman told him. Her husband gave her a warning jab in the back.

"Willard couldn't say much," the mother finished. But she had to add, "He's not a terrorist. You can put that in your paper."

Willard's father spoke up now. "He's always been a good boy. A true Christian."

Anthony asked if he knew where his son got the gun.

"I have a license for all my guns. I trained Willard how to use them myself."

Anthony kept eye contact with them, taking only desultory glances at his notebook as he scratched their comments down—best way to keep people talking. The father brought a framed photograph of Willard standing in a suit next to a young man in army fatigues. "That's his older brother. Serving in Afghanistan now. Willard wanted to be just like him."

"He was planning to join up as soon as he graduated." Willard's mother wrung her hands and wiped them on her dress. "He was disappointed when he didn't do well enough on the aptitude test."

From Northbrook, just south of the city line in Piskasanet County, it was a twenty-minute drive on North-South Highway to Shady Park, where Anthony lived. He picked up some fried chicken at the Grab 'n Go and sat in his apartment on the bed eating the crunchy wings from a styrofoam box.

He couldn't finish. A vision of his five-year-old brother choked him up. Years ago, Anthony had heard a shot and found Billy in his friend Roger's house next door slumped on the floor, bleeding, dying. Roger was still holding the pistol, crying. He'd only wanted to show Billy his father's gun.

Anthony scrolled through the pictures of the School Board shooting on his phone, his heart pounding when he blew up a photo of the gun in Willard's hand. The idea that we should carry guns for protection didn't make any sense to him. He wanted to be a good reporter and treat the issue even-handedly, but if there was more logic on one side, he was going to point that out. Of course, it didn't matter much. Pop's paper considered gun rights a sacred cow. He was required to leave that issue alone while he stuck to covering elementary school science fairs, fundraising runs, and "grand openings" of real estate offices.

Despite Pop's admonitions, he'd been able to expose Bea Doggit and her crony Pastor Mitchell Rainey for their Riverside Paradise scheme to defraud residents along the Piskasanet River of their property. With the help of a pretty housewife named Emma, he'd written articles that shamed them into paying for the property they took. Pop didn't want to publish the stories, but Ralph, the editor, convinced him the facts would come out anyway, probably in the *City Paper*, whose reporters now roamed out into the county if there was ever anything big going on.

When Pop had found out Anthony was about to tie Derek Grosbeck to the scheme, he blew up. "Mention his name and you're fired," he thundered. "False accusations like that are never going to appear in this paper."

In fact, Anthony was sure he would have been fired if Victoria hadn't intervened. She did so on the condition that he not even mention to Pop any evidence he'd found that the County Executive might also be in on the scheme.

Now he sat on his bed in his cramped one-room apartment wondering if he should contact Emma again. She knew Derek Grosbeck and his wife. Maybe she could confirm they really did own and carry guns.

His phone rang. He knew it would be Victoria. She just had to tell him how "scrumptious" her crab soufflé was. "Except I was the *only one* there without a date." She didn't ask what more he'd learned about the school shooting. Instead, she gave him the newest gossip about her former sorority clique and their latest boyfriend dramas. "Everybody kept asking me where you were."

Victoria was in a talkative mood. Anthony checked the time on his phone. "I can't talk much longer," he said. "I need to call the police station back to see if the night shift has any more information from ballistics yet—get as much of the story as I can for the follow-up in Saturday's paper."

"Oh, the terrorist thing? It's all over Facebook already."

"What do you mean?"

"Everybody's saying it was a Muslim terrorist and he coordinated the attack with a Muslim woman at the meeting. They were going to kill everybody."

"Facebook, right. Must be true, huh?" He reminded her the gunman's name was Willard Scherd. "Anyway, I do need to see if he has a profile on Facebook."

"Hold on." There was a pause. Anthony knew she was flipping through pages on her iPad as she did constantly at the office. "Oh, here." Another pause. "Oh, this is weird. *Death to Jihadis. Tread them under. Keep America Christian.* That's what it says on his timeline." A longer pause. "Ugh. I can't look at this any more. The guy's too creepy—tattoos all over his body, guns." There was a silence.

"You OK, Vicky?"

"It's just, I think you should keep away from this guy, Anthony. Let it go."

Anthony had been surprised when the boss's daughter took an interest in him. She was brought in as soon as she graduated, a couple of years after he was hired. On her first day in the office she gave him a red lipstick smile and chose a seat at the carrel just next to his. He watched in fascination as she immediately accessorized the area, hanging a little stuffed bear and monkey from the upper corners of the desk separators, setting up a foam smiley face and some kind of bobble head lower down. She beamed at this array of admirers facing her and brushed a few strands of blond hair aside with iridescent fingernails. She was pretty, with skin as smooth as a doll's face. Definitely out of his class, Anthony thought.

Then, to show her how to log on to the newspaper's network drive, he had to lean over her shoulder, his face almost touching hers. She giggled and amazingly seemed to like it. When the screen filled with instructions, she screwed up her mouth and looked at him, her eyes pleading for help. Anthony was unexpectedly touched.

Victoria showed up at the office every day looking like a fashion ad for young professionals—pale silk blouse, open to display a strand of pearls, loose-fitting skirt just above the knees, pumps matching her skirt, sometimes even stockings. Her blond hair, chin-length, was cut straight across with a little inward curl at the end. Bangs in front. Anthony remembered that style from the girls in his high school.

He didn't know what she saw in him and suspected she had allowed her mind to create an imaginary Anthony who met her criteria. Either that or it was a matter of convenience, his being an acceptable escort when she needed one. As for Anthony, he generally resigned himself to dating girls who took the initiative in approaching him. Victoria was one of these.

She had invited him on their first date. It was more like an announcement, really. "Anthony, would you like to take me to the Daughters ball?"

Did she mean Daughters of the American Revolution? Anthony couldn't believe he even knew somebody who was a member. His family were poor 19th-century English and Irish immigrants who struggled to survive and passed down their disdain for elitist pretensions. Did he want to go? Definitely not. And yet Victoria was asking him. She was pretty. And she did seem to like him. And she was, after all, a girl. His father had referred to his lack of a social life for most of the past year as monkish. He'd insisted he wasn't a monk. He was focused on becoming a good reporter, that was all.

"You have a tux, I guess." Her eyes had a wide-open, expectant look as if she'd just announced he'd won the Publishers Clearing House contest.

Anthony shook his head—no tux. If he had to wear one, he'd rent, not buy. He had to assume the prize she was offering was actually only a one-month trial subscription.

While he sat speechless, Victoria had squinted, examining him the way a makeup artist might check an actor before he went on set. "Hold on." She used her fingernails to tease up his hair. The gesture was intimate but done in a professional, detached manner. She stepped back and admired her work. Anthony wondered if his trial subscription was for *GQ* magazine. In any case, he couldn't refuse. He'd gone.

Awkward was how he remembered the evening. A lot of standing around as Victoria introduced him to the other Daughters, some as old as Anthony's grandmother. He felt like a mannequin, smiling stiffly, holding a glass of champagne. Victoria took much more interest in the women than the men at the ball. He danced with her three times, her corsage and stiff stays keeping him at a distance. He danced with her grandmother once. She held him closer than Victoria. When Victoria said good-night at her door—she still lived with her parents—she turned her face to let him graze her cheek with his lips.

3

Romancing Victoria

"How then, sir, can I act, but by shewing my abhorrence of every step that makes towards my undoing?"

—Samuel Richardson,
Pamela, or Virtue Rewarded

Anthony lay in bed running the details of the shooting through his mind until almost daylight. When he awoke late from a deep sleep, he picked up the Friday morning *Ledger* from the landing outside his door. The brief story he'd tapped into his phone from Northbrook High had made the deadline and was squeezed into a corner of the front page, edited, as he expected. Now to write a fuller story for Saturday's paper. He called the police station once again. No more details available, Rob told him. He called the hospital. The wounded teacher, Ms. Nicole Ernst, was in satisfactory condition and was expected to be released the next day. From the school online directory Anthony learned she was 37 years old, single, and had been teaching for 12 years. He took what information he had to the newsroom.

The *Shady Park Ledger* stood on a road just off North-South Highway. It was in an old brick building that had housed the paper since the end of the Second World War. Before that it been a fire station, and the entrance was still the huge arched opening for a fire truck, now bricked and glassed-in except for a front door. Anthony had wanted to work in that building since the fifth grade, when a reporter came to tell his class what it was like to work for a newspaper.

Before Anthony was hired, the *Ledger* had stopped printing the paper in the rear of its own first floor. Now it was printed off site by Nationwide Imaging, the same company that did the *City Paper.* The *Ledger*'s former press room was used only for inserting advertisements into the papers after they were delivered by the printer. The *Ledger* staff shrank every year as fewer people in the community went to the printed word for their information or entertainment. The budget of the *Ledger* also decreased every year, and Anthony knew Pop's threat to let him go was real.

The gray-haired woman at the Classifieds desk on the first floor sat staring into space.

"Business slow, Nora?"

"You know it. That Craiger's List and Bay-something are ruining the Classifieds."

Sharise at the Print Ads desk said, "Advertisements down, too. Except maybe for the online version."

"No help here, either," Jerry called out from behind a glass enclosure in the back of the cavernous first floor. "All we do is post the print ads."

Nora pulled a pencil from the gray bun at the back of her head. "Now, Jerry? He could get a job somewhere else if he had to. Not me. Sharise could, too. She's young enough."

"Nah," Sharise said. "I like it here. Got to hope at least some people keep reading the newspaper."

Anthony agreed. He climbed the stairs to what served as the *Ledger* newsroom. The editor was coming out of his office, his round black reading glasses pushed up over his forehead. He was a good-looking man, Victoria had once declared, "if he would lose those stupid glasses."

"Hey, Ralph. More on the school shooting. Shouldn't be any rush this time."

Ralph was a man of few words. He pointed to the keyboard on Anthony's carrel. "Oaky doaky. Put it in."

Just as he finished typing his story onto the network drive for Ralph to edit, Victoria called. "Pop wants to make sure something gets into the story. Ready?"

"Go ahead."

"County Executive Andrew Mauer said this attack calls for renewed efforts on the part of the Federal government to combat terrorism. Immigration from terrorist countries must be stopped, the executive said. Got that?"

"There's a problem, Victoria. As you know, the attacker was an American. From Piskasanet County, not from a 'terrorist country.' In fact, he was aiming at a woman who *was* from one of those 'terrorist countries' when a teacher knocked him down with a chair."

Victoria sniffed. "All right. So just put in the first sentence. OK? About *renewed efforts to combat terrorism.*"

Anthony shrugged and typed it onto the end of the story. It was a non sequitur. Maybe Ralph would cut it.

"And Pop wants to be sure the headline says, *Terrorist Attack*. Tell Ralph, would you?"

"Hmm. Everybody was terrified. That's for sure."

"You seem hesitant."

"No. Just so you know, you can see a tattoo of a cross on the attacker's arm in the picture that's going in the paper. If he's a terrorist, he's a Christian terrorist."

Victoria sighed. "Fine. I'll tell Pop we can't call him a terrorist."

They'd been going on "dates" since that first ball. Victoria related to him by flirting. She fixed his collar, fluffed his hair with the tips of her glossy fingernails, smiled at his wrinkled button-down shirts, gave him pats on the cheek, squeezed his hand. If he reacted, she giggled, "Don't look at me like that." She introduced him to her girlfriends as "my handsome beau."

Anthony was excited by her flirting and wanted to take it beyond that. But there never was a chance in the places they went—classical concerts, dinners in restaurants followed by gatherings at her parents' house, cocktail parties thrown by her sorority sisters from college. Anthony was in awe of this world, new to him, and tried to fit in, but it was a strain. He sometimes thought he would tell her he didn't want to be her "beau" any more. But then she would take his hand, kiss him on the cheek, and tell him how excited she was about their next date.

That night she'd invited her friends Chad and Jennifer to join them for dinner. "And don't come with that humongous phone hanging on your belt," she insisted.

At the restaurant, he kept running his finger under his collar to loosen it until Victoria frowned her embarrassment. He was starving and searched the Sur le Dessus menu for a hamburger. "I'll have this. *Sandwich à boeuf allemand.*" She gave him an indulgent roll of the eyes.

Jennifer dipped the very tip of a piece of bread into a saucer of seasoned olive oil. Her long nails were painted a color Anthony would call orange, although he was sure the correct word would be something like "tangerine." Jennifer put down her bread without tasting it, gave Victoria a long glance, and said, "It must be so exciting working for the paper. I'm so envious."

Victoria put on a little *moue.* "Not really. My major was broadcasting. You wouldn't believe how hard it is to get on TV."

"For you?" Jennifer simpered. "You have to be kidding. You definitely have the looks."

"She does," Chad said. His first remark of the evening.

Anthony, meanwhile, was stuffing himself with a third piece of bread drenched in oil.

"The only thing I could suggest," Jennifer went on, "you

should probably let your hair grow out." She shook her own long hair away from her face. "Like Megyn Drumpfer, you know."

"Oh, she's hot," Chad agreed. "Saw her on News at Six reporting a terrorist attack yesterday at Northbrook High School."

The waiter brought Victoria and Jennifer their salad entrees, Chad his *contrefilet*, and Anthony his hamburger.

"I tell you," Chad said. "Terrorists are ruining it for everybody."

Anthony swallowed his first bit of a sandwich so heavily seasoned he couldn't taste the meat and said, "They're not ruining it for the news media. We thrive on it. Only sex scandals improve the ratings more." He reached for another piece of bread. "I guess we all love to be scared and titillated."

Victoria's mouth dropped open as if he'd said a bad word.

Chad put his hands on his breast. "Don't know about scared, but I'm always waiting to be titillated when Megyn comes back on TV with her *big developments*."

Jennifer gave him a scolding slap on the shoulder.

Anthony had seen Megyn's report on the attack. WPSK TV, with a camera set up at the high school, filmed the heavily made-up blond woman in front of the empty building repeating for the camera nothing more than what had been in Anthony's morning newspaper story. He glanced at Victoria and couldn't resist saying, "The big developments will be in the *Ledger* tomorrow morning. You don't have to wait till tomorrow night for Megyn to repeat them."

Chad shrugged, munching his steak. "I don't mind waiting. Don't read papers. Get my news from TV. That and Facebook. Or Reddit."

Jennifer poked at her salad with a fork. She looked nervous. "It's scary to think there's a Muslim terrorist right here in Piskasanet County."

Anthony had to speak up. "The gunman's not Muslim." The term "fake news" was going around these days. It annoyed him that people were starting to use it to mean *news I don't like*. "Here are the facts," he said. "His name is Willard Scherd. He's a county resident. He's 18, the youngest child of five. Father a plumber, mother a homemaker. Into video games—*Call of Duty* his favorite. His oldest brother is in Afghanistan. Sends him texts about killing 'hajis.' Willard planned to join up but flunked the army aptitude test. Plenty of guns in his house. When he attacked the school yesterday, he was aiming his gun at a woman in a hejab. You can't help thinking he might have been going after what he considered a *local* haji." Except for the last comment, this was basically a recap of what he'd given Ralph to be put in the next morning's paper.

If Jennifer had taken this in, there was no way of telling. She put down her fork and changed the subject. "Look what Chad gave me for our two-month anniversary. She lifted up a necklace with a circle of what looked like diamonds on it. "We started dating eight weeks ago." She beamed at Chad like a bride about to slice a wedding cake.

"Awww," Victoria crooned. "That's so sweeeet." She glanced at Anthony as if he were expected to say something.

He noticed she was on her third martini. Her cheeks had become a creamy red, and she'd stopped eating. She leaned towards him and took his hand under the table.

"Don't know about anybody else," Anthony announced, "but I won't be needing dessert."

"Me either," Victoria trilled.

On the way to the car, she took his arm. Anthony hoped it wasn't just to steady herself. Before he could start the engine, she turned the rear view mirror towards her face, picked a blond hair off the strap of her violet dress, and said, "Do you find me as attractive as Megyn Drumpfer?"

"Definitely," Anthony assured her. "Sure. Even prettier."

"I hope so." Her tone was softer than usual. He leaned over to kiss her, excited by her martini breath. The flesh is weak, Anthony had heard it said, and yet Victoria was inspiring rather a stiffening of Anthony's flesh at the moment.

Victoria snickered. "Now look. You have red lipstick on your mouth." She pulled a tissue from her purse. "Here. You can wipe it off with this."

"Want to come to my apartment?"

"I do feel kind of romantic. Maybe you can tell." She cleared her throat. "But, Anthony, the way you describe your place, it would spoil the mood." She sighed. "I don't want to go home, though. How about taking a drive somewhere?"

She settled back in her seat humming Adele's "Hello" as Anthony drove to a place he knew on Piskasanet River Road. Before they got there the humming stopped. She was asleep.

It was dark along the old gravel and oyster shell road. Here and there Anthony could make out a dim yellow light in a fishing shack set back among the tall trees. His car crunched on the roadbed until he came to a very short section that was paved in front of an incongruous new villa rising on a lot recently cleared of trees. It belonged to Beatrice Doggit, the Board of Education woman who had fainted during the attack at the high school, the corrupt realtor he had exposed in his articles. He smiled to see that the place looked abandoned now.

"Victoria," he said when he parked the car on a high point overlooking the river. "Victoria, we're here." He nudged her shoulder, but she didn't wake up. Her head was resting back against the seat, turned aside towards the window, but the moon lit her face, and he sat watching her. Even asleep, she projected an elegant, refined look. He couldn't remember what color her eyes were.

A strand of hair had fallen across her cheek, and he

reached over to gently brush it aside. Her friend Jennifer had been right. The only thing Victoria might change to make herself as glamorous as the TV reporter she admired would be to let her hair grow longer. Her bangs gave her a cute look that conflicted with the sophisticated appearance she seemed trying to cultivate.

Lots of women in the prestigious Bay Hills area where Victoria lived with her parents wore their hair the same way as their daughters. That might explain Victoria's innocent-girl hairstyle. But Victoria was only twenty-two—no need to try to look younger. Studying her hair now, he wondered if there was another explanation. He imagined her clinging to the style as a charm to preserve her childlike immunity from the cares of the grownup world.

"Victoria, wake up. Look at this view." He took her hand, and she jerked out of sleep, rubbing her eyes.

"What? Where are we?" She blinked at him as if trying to recall who she was with. "Did I fall asleep? I must look a mess." She twisted the mirror to check.

"Come on, Victoria. Let's get out of the car. We can walk down to that pier and see how big the moon looks over the water."

Victoria shuddered. "Get out? It's pitch dark." She clicked the lock on the car door. "Why are we here?" She touched her forehead. "I have a headache."

"Maybe it was that third martini." Anthony smiled.

Victoria gave him a penetrating stare. "How long have we been here? She sat up straight, glanced at the hem of her dress, and gave it a reassuring tug. "Come on Anthony. Please. I'm scared. I want to go home."

4

An upbeat paper

I am not the editor of a newspaper and shall always try to do right and be good so that God will not make me one.

—Mark Twain, *The Galaxy* magazine

On Saturday morning, Anthony went to the *Ledger* newsroom to work on his story for the next issue. He had an update on Ms. Ernst. She was already released from the hospital. And there would be room for more pictures of the shooting in the Sunday paper. Victoria probably wouldn't be in. She hated coming to work on weekends and constantly begged her father to hire a part-time substitute.

His phone pinged. Text from Victoria. *Planning to get tickets for Colonial City Symphony tonight. Starts at 8. Mom and Pop going, too. OK?*

Somehow he'd been expecting some reference to the night before. That's what was on his own mind. He and Victoria had been going out together for several months. Ever since the Daughters of the American Revolution ball, whenever she wanted to go somewhere that required a date, she would take him along. He kidded himself that he was her accessory. The drive to the river last night—just the two of them, finally—seemed like it might have been the beginning of something more serious, more physical. Apparently not.

Anthony had twice been to a symphony with Victoria and her parents. Her mother kept forgetting Anthony's name. He hated classical music. He wasn't really sure Victoria and her parents liked it, either. Her father—always—and her mother—usually—fell asleep. Victoria enjoyed looking at the other women. Sometimes she drew his attention to one of them and mouthed a comment like "scary eye shadow."

Without answering her text, he called Rob at the police station. "What is Scherd being charged with?"

"Initial charge is attempted homicide. That and he's 18 and you have to be 21 to have a license to carry a gun in this state. So illegal possession. And it's illegal to take a gun onto school property in this state. So that, too." Rob said they'd released the woman in the hejab as "no longer a person of interest."

Anthony got the correct spelling of her name: Shahnaz Delpak. "Are you going to refer Scherd to the FBI for terrorism charges?"

"The FBI and U.S. Attorney's office both say there's not enough evidence yet."

"Any results from ballistics?"

"None yet." Rob added, "The police will continue searching the school for evidence over the weekend. It'll be open for classes on Monday."

After Anthony typed in this information for the next day's story, Ralph slipped out of his office holding the printout. "You're at work early today." He dropped his glasses down from his head to focus on the paper. "So. Not an Islamic terrorist attack, it seems."

"Attempted homicide. Piskasanet County boy."

Ralph sighed. "That's not what the 'social media' is saying, according to my son." He ran his hand over his head feeling for glasses that were already on his face. "It seems I'm supposed to keep track of *that* now, too."

"My information is from the police and the gunman's parents."

Ralph dropped Anthony's story onto his desk. "Better hold on to this for now. Pop's coming in. Said he wants to talk to you." He headed towards his office but turned back. "Hang in there, pal."

Anthony held his head in his hands trying to come up with an excuse to miss the concert with Victoria and her parents. He had come up with nothing when Sam Yeager arrived with the weekend's sports stories. Shady Park children's teams, high school baseball, soccer, lacrosse, and field hockey—these were his beat. He also covered the community college and state university teams.

It was the beginning of football season. Anthony was chatting with Sam about State's new quarterback when Pop arrived. Pop was a big football fan.

"Think the new guy can turn things around for State?" Pop asked Sam. He turned to Anthony, his bald forehead jutting over his deep-set eyes like a helmet. "Need to talk to you in my office, young man."

A long hallway off the newsroom led to the office of Harold Whitman, Publisher. Anthony had only been inside a few times. They weren't pleasant experiences. The last time, Pop said he would have to let Anthony go if he didn't tell who his source was for the stories exposing Bea Doggit and Pastor Mitch Rainey's Riverside Paradise scheme. Anthony refused, resigned to take the consequence. But he'd been saved when Victoria unexpectedly burst into the room and took his side. "Come on, Pop," she cajoled. "You can't fire a reporter for not disclosing his source." Anthony had realized long ago that Pop would give her anything she wanted.

The dark paneled walls of Pop's office were covered with plaques—Lions Club, Shady Park Rotary, the local Chamber of Commerce. Bookshelves displayed duck decoys and sailing trophies. On the wall behind his desk hung a double-barreled shotgun. A huge new photograph hanging above the trophies drew Anthony's attention. It was of a small island in the Piskasanet River.

"Like it?" Pop asked.

"I remember sailing there in my Peanut dinghy and exploring it when I was a kid. I still sail there in my Laser sometimes."

"Unbelievable view from the top of that little hill. Fantastic place to build a house, don't you think?"

Anthony preferred the island just the way it was and didn't answer.

"Anyway, glad for your help crewing on *Dynamo* in the PHRF-A fleet race the past few Wednesdays." He opened a wooden box on his desk and took out a cigar. "You've been here about a year, haven't you?"

"Three years."

"Right." Pop spread a copy of the *Ledger* on his desk. He pointed Anthony to a black leather chair while he picked up a brass cigarette lighter shaped like a miniature Canadian goose. "Don't know what to do with you, son." He blew out a line of gray smoke. "I warned you about those stories of yours defaming developers who only wanted to build a nice place where people could live along the river—supporters of our County Executive, I might add." Pop relit his cigar. "We can't afford to have Andrew Mauer for an enemy. I happen to know he's already planning a run for U.S. Congress."

"Well, defaming? I didn't—"

"Sure. Sure. You got the goods on that preacher and that Bea-woman. But you didn't stop there, did you? Just when Mauer was ramping up his campaign for re-election you had to question the immigration roundup he orchestrated with his Federal connections. 'False arrests,' you reported."

"Most of the people arrested were here legally."

"Yeah, lucky his voters didn't understand or care about that." Pop tapped his cigar on the edge of a brass ashtray. "What they care about is terrorism. It used to be crime they cared about, drugs—those fears sold plenty of papers. Now it's Middle Eastern terrorists. That's the fear that's going to get Mauer re-elected, and that's the fear that sells newspapers nowadays."

"I understand."

"I'm not so sure you do." Pop picked up the newspaper from his desk and tapped it. "There's something missing from your story about the shooting." He furrowed his huge brow. "The television reports are calling it an Islamic terrorist attack."

"The police haven't called it that."

"I saw the picture of that woman with the headgear. A lot of people think that looks suspicious. You can't blame them."

"The police questioned and released her." Anthony couldn't help adding, "You did see the tattoo on the gunman's arm?"

Pop waved his cigar. "Yes, yes. I'm just blowing off steam, I guess. Of course, we can't say it was a Christian terrorist attack. But now listen to this. This is important. Mauer's voters like their guns."

Anthony nodded.

"So. Guy walks right into a school and shoots a teacher. Makes you think folks are right who say teachers ought to be armed, doesn't it. There's a story there, don't you think?"

"Three unarmed teachers subdued him." Anthony was sure Pop knew this from his story, but he put it out there anyway.

"Right. Lucky break. Point is, if terrorists knew teachers and staff were armed, they wouldn't be so likely to try anything. You got to admit that."

"Maybe." He added, "Of course, with an assault rifle, a kid could still kill a lot of people before a teacher got his or her gun out. Assault rifles are legal now." Anthony saw Pop's displeasure, but he went on anyway. "Actually, two of the parents at that meeting claimed they were armed. Derek

Grosbeck and his wife—Britney, I'm told. They fled out the back door."

"Yeah, we took that out of the report. No need to stir up trouble where there is none."

Derek Grosbeck was a financier who, along with Andrew Mauer, had been involved in the Paradise scheme. Pop had kept both names out of Anthony's reports. Anthony had agreed to let it go and stop looking into their connection because the scheme had been shut down without mentioning them.

Pop flicked the long gray end of his cigar into the ashtray. "Let it go, I say. Talk like that might embarrass Andrew Mauer. We need him on our side."

"On the paper's side?"

Pop peered at Anthony from under his huge brow. "Here's the point, young man. The *Shady Park Ledger* is a community newspaper. An upbeat paper. We don't hire investigative reporters to dig up dirt on upright citizens. As long as we're the kind of paper you want to report for, fine. Otherwise, maybe you need to look somewhere else."

He picked up the phone and swiveled his chair away from Anthony. "Ralph, listen, I want you to give Mr. Mansfield here a nice quilting club story to report on, will you? Or maybe a bake sale. Something to keep him busy today." He slapped down the phone and swiveled back. "You're lucky, you know that? I'll tell you the truth. I would have fired you after your first Riverside Paradise article if it wasn't for Victoria. Especially when you refused to tell me who you were getting your information from. Victoria took your side. Likes you for some reason." He seemed to find that amusing. "So, OK. Here's what you're going to do. You're going to team up with Victoria today on whatever story Ralph comes up with."

"I don't know if she's coming in today."

"Call her. You tell her she has to." Pop seemed disinclined

to give her the order himself. He stood up. The meeting was over. He led Anthony to the door, a hand on his shoulder. Before he opened it, he lowered his voice. "Victoria doesn't actually have to write the story, you know what I'm saying? She can take the pictures."

5

Dandelions and waterfalls

As, I confess, it is my nature's plague
To spy into abuses, and oft my jealousy
Shapes faults that are not.

—Shakespeare, *Othello*

Ralph sent them to cover a painting exhibit at the Piskasanet Community College art gallery. Anthony knew it well. His mother took free art courses for seniors at the college over and over again, often exhibiting her watercolor scenes. Even after he transferred to State, he always came back to see her exhibits.

Victoria, still annoyed at having to work on Saturday, stopped inside the glass doorway, shifting the camera strap off her shoulder and scanning the long, narrow room. She tilted her head towards Anthony. "Kind of small."

Students in raggy jeans and dark T-shirts were running the show. A girl with orange hair and a face full of silver studs asked them to sign in.

"Doesn't look like there's any wine and cheese," Victoria whispered to Anthony. "Is this a real art exhibit?" It was the kind of question Anthony had learned to ignore.

The matte white walls were spread with luminous oil paintings. Anthony was immediately attracted to a series featuring short Hispanic-looking workers in the lawns and gardens of houses like those he'd seen in Nottingham Estates and Bay Hills. The emphasis on the hard-working laborers in the foreground seemed to cast an ironic light on the exaggerated splendor of the houses in the background. Anthony paused in front of one that featured a dirt-smeared man pulling up dandelions with calloused hands.

"Jeez," Victoria said. "If these were photos, it wouldn't take a minute to Photoshop those scruffy guys out of the picture." She moved on to paintings that were more to her taste, scenes of mountains and waterfalls. Since Victoria wasn't going to photograph the paintings he liked, he took pictures with his phone camera.

"Nice, aren't they?"

He turned. It was Emma Bovant.

"They're by a friend of mine," she said.

Emma's face was brighter, more radiant than it had been a month or so ago when she'd been under a lot of pressure from Bea and the pastor's schemes. She'd given Anthony crucial information for his articles exposing them. Bringing their scheme to an end had obviously improved her spirits.

"There's something about the paintings that intrigues me," he told her.

"The feeling for the laborers? That's what I like about them."

"I think that's it."

Emma's face glowed a deep pink. "Anthony, I'll always be grateful for your articles. My friend kept his house. My husband, well, he's back." Then she touched his arm. "There's something more I'd like to tell you, when you get a chance."

Anthony turned a page in his notebook.

"Not now, though." She stepped closer to him. "Maybe you can call me when you have the time."

Anthony made a quick note and started to give her his card, then sheepishly tucked it back into his pocket realizing she must have plenty of them already.

"Nice seeing you again, Anthony," Emma said hurriedly. "I have to run and pick up my son, Todd. Talk to you later."

Anthony turned back to the paintings. Victoria stood watching him. "Goodness, it looks like I have a rival. She's pretty. She didn't stay to introduce herself."

"Oh, just somebody ...." He didn't want to identify Emma as the source Pop had tried to get him to reveal.

"Somebody you made blush, I noticed." Victoria sighed. "What am I to think if you won't tell me her name? You wrote down something in your notes. Will you let me see it?"

"No. No, I was just getting some information." He waved his hand at the paintings, slipping the notebook into his hip pocket. "For the article, you know."

"You're kidding, Anthony. I can't believe you." Victoria looked through the glass door Emma had left by. "Don't think I'm not going to find out what you're up to." She clamped her camera case shut and announced, "These paintings are stupid. I'm finished here," then whisked out of the gallery.

Anthony called to her, but she didn't stop. He was left to interview the artists and snap photos of them and their paintings on his phone. Those paintings of the workers that he most admired were unsigned, and the artist wasn't there. He could call Emma to get the name of the artist, but the real point of the article was to let the artists get their pictures in the paper.

Doing the job by himself had actually been easier, he realized, as he drove back to the *Ledger* to give Ralph the story.

A column of tiny pink sticky notes from Victoria was waiting on his desk:

"Not sure I want you to come with me"
"to the concert tonight."
"Not going to let this go."
"How old is she anyway???"
"Too old for you."

"Going to find out who she is."

"Call me."

Ralph came out of his office, tapping his head to locate his glasses. "Before you start typing in the art gallery story, I need to double check some things about the shooting. You're sure of all the facts, I suppose?"

"Absolutely."

"The shooter has often received texts from his brother in Afghanistan about killing hajis?"

"According to his mother."

Ralph stroked the corners of his moustache. "What can I say? This has to go in. Maybe we'll both end up pounding the streets for a job." He walked back into his office shaking his head.

While Anthony was wondering what Pop's reaction to the story would be, the phone on his desk rang. "This is Beatrice Doggit from the Board of Education. I have information about the terrorist attack at Northbrook High School. The police haven't acted on it, so I'm calling the press. It's about what I witnessed."

"Yes? I'm recording this if you don't mind."

Bea despised Anthony because of his past reports, but she didn't ask who she was talking to or seem to recognize his voice. "There was a Muslim woman at the meeting. I saw her reaching into her baggy clothing. I'm sure she was an accomplice in the attack."

"Did you see what she was reaching for?"

"I ... it might have been a gun. Or maybe she was going to set off a bomb, Lord help us."

"You told this to the police?"

"I told them at the school, and they arrested her along with the man. Yesterday they came to my office and asked me more questions. I guess they didn't believe me, because I just called them back this morning and they said they let her go."

"All right. Did you actually see a gun or a bomb?"

"I'm pretty sure I did."

"What did the object look like?"

"Now you're sounding like the police. Will you just tell the public what I witnessed? That woman is a danger to our society."

"I'll definitely investigate it. One more question. Did anybody else see what you saw? It would be good to get another witness."

"Dear Lord Jesus, are you insulting me now? Maybe the *City Paper* will treat righteous citizens with more respect." She hung up.

Anthony had been at the Board meeting himself, of course, and hadn't noticed the hejab woman doing anything suspicious. And he had learned some time ago that Bea Doggit wasn't truthful. Apparently, the police had decided the same thing. But Anthony's eyes hadn't been on the hejab woman the whole time, he had to admit. The best way to follow up would be to talk to the woman herself. Give her a chance to deny Bea's accusation.

He checked his notes and called the police station to get Shahnaz Delpak's address, but Rob wasn't available. He Googled her but came up with nothing.

6

Weekend fill-in

Love is so very timid when 'tis new:
She blush'd, and frown'd not, but she strove to speak,
And held her tongue, her voice was grown so weak.

—Byron, *Don Juan*

He was tapping on his notebook with the eraser of his pencil when he heard a knock on the open door of the newsroom. A girl about Victoria's age stood in the doorway, amber-flecked brown eyes glistening in the fluorescent light. She seemed to be holding her breath, hesitating to come in.

"Can I help you?"

"Oh, yes. I'm Pari. I've been hired to work here on Saturdays and Sundays now. I guess Mr. Whitman told you?" She ventured a couple steps into the newsroom. "Or maybe he didn't. Sorry if I surprised you."

Her white polo shirt hung casually outside of her jeans. Her dark wavy hair was pulled back into a loose ponytail. She said, "I didn't get the message from Mr. Whitman until just a little while ago. I came right in."

Anthony stood up and shook her hand.

"I can't believe I'm actually going to work in a newspaper office." She searched Anthony's eyes as if to confirm it was true.

"I could show you around. Most of the reporters write their stories at home and load them onto the *Ledger* network drive from their computers or cell phones these days. If you want to talk to the editor while you're writing the story, that's when you have to come in to the newsroom."

"I see." Pari stopped at the carrel next to his. "This has to be Victoria's desk. I recognize the Justin Bieber bobble head." She gave Anthony a questioning look. "Victoria said I should use her desk. Is that right?"

"Sure. Definitely. So you and Victoria are friends?"

"We took some classes together at State. I mean I wasn't in her sorority. We didn't hang out socially or anything." Pari touched the back of Victoria's chair. "May I?" She eased into the chair, trailed her fingers across the keyboard, and smiled. "Mr. Whitman mentioned covering a Shady Park Barbershop Quartet Songfest?" She swiveled towards Anthony, ready for instructions.

"Oh. Right. That's been canceled."

Pari nodded, her pursed lips a deep pink. Waiting.

Ralph hadn't listed any more assignments for the day. If Victoria came in on a weekend, she mostly just sat around texting her friends. He took Pari into Ralph's office to introduce her. "Nice to meet you," Ralph said. "Anthony, anything more on the high school attack?"

"You have my profile of the attacker for the morning. Still waiting for more information from the police. If I get it by deadline, I'll make sure it gets to you in time."

"Your guy Rob will call you before he gives it to the *City Paper*, right?"

"Always does."

Pari stood with fingers over her mouth, wide eyes searching back and forth between Anthony and the editor. Ralph noticed. "A little more cutthroat than they make it seem in journalism class?"

Pari gave a single nod. "More exciting, actually."

Back in the newsroom, Anthony said, "I could show you what I'm working on."

He filled her in on the high school shooting. "Someone

who witnessed the shooting just called me. Claims she saw a woman at the meeting reaching for a weapon—the woman the police arrested and let go." He tapped his eraser on his notes. "Shahnaz Delpak."

Pari gasped. "What? I know her. There can't be two people around here with that name. She's a friend of my mother's. They're both Iranian."

"Seriously? I mean, could you get her to talk to me? To us? Do you know where she lives?"

"You sound like she's in trouble." Pari got Shahnaz's phone number from her mother and started texting furiously. "She won't be home till six."

"That's OK. I don't think she's in trouble. Maybe we can still get her on the record before tonight's deadline." Anthony pulled his phone off his belt, smiling. "So. Guess I'll just have to break an appointment I have for this evening." He typed his regrets to Victoria.

Shahnaz's apartment was in the low-priced Northbrook complex where foreigners often lived. Anthony had been there before, covering a story about some permanent U.S. residents who'd been wrongly arrested. The rooms were small, sometimes with no windows, and the floors were vinyl tile. But Shahnaz's floor was covered from wall to wall with Persian carpets in vibrant floral designs.

Shahnaz wore no hejab inside. She and Pari brushed cheeks, and she shook hands with Anthony, leading him to a sofa beneath a gilt trimmed mirror. A brass samovar sat on a glass table beside it, and she nervously offered Anthony and Pari some tea. Anthony tried to refuse, but Pari flashed No to him with her eyes and an almost imperceptible shake of the head. Shahnaz's son Jim brought three little glasses of tea and set them on a marble-topped table beside a bowl of sugar lumps.

Anthony said, "Ms. Delpak, I hope you don't mind if I write some things down? We'd like to get your description of what happened at the Board meeting."

"Good tea," Pari interrupted, clinking her glass down on the table, and Anthony realized he might be going too fast.

"Yes, thanks," he agreed. He decided to let Pari take the lead.

Shahnaz's husband worked evenings in an all-night gas station and had already left for work. Her son Jim played baseball for Northbrook High—catcher. Shahnaz had met Pari's mother, a nurse, when Jim had to go to City Hospital.

"A pitch hit me in the shoulder," Jim explained.

Anthony sipped his tea. Now and then he jotted something in his notebook—Pari left hers in her pocket—but mostly he just listened as Pari helped Shahnaz to relax, taking her time before getting back to the subject of the Board of Education hearing.

"Anthony was interested in what you were saying about the textbooks," she told Shahnaz. "He says you didn't get a chance to finish."

There was something about Pari that made you feel at ease. At least Anthony thought so. With Pari's genuine interest, Shahnaz was encouraged to give a fuller account of the changes in the new textbooks, like removing Thomas Jefferson and replacing him with John Calvin as a key figure influencing the Founding Fathers and including units on "creation science." She showed them passages she had highlighted in the books.

Anthony reached for his phone to take pictures of book titles, authors, pages, but stopped and asked Pari if she would use her phone instead. "I ... I don't want to turn my phone on right now."

Pari took the pictures. "Maybe we could do a story on the curriculum change?" she asked Anthony.

He nodded, and Shahnaz smiled for the first time, sipping some of her tea. Pari twisted her glass in her hands. When Jim went back to his room, she took a breath and said, "Shahnaz, can you tell us exactly what happened when the gunman burst into the room?"

Shahnaz shrugged. "All I know is there was a scream. I looked up and a young man was aiming a gun at me. There was a noise, a gunshot I guess. Everybody went crazy. Then some teachers jumped on him and held him down."

Pari asked the exact question Anthony would have asked. "What did you do when you were standing there?"

"I don't know. It all happened so fast."

"You see, Shahnaz, a witness told the *Ledger* office you seemed to be taking something …." She couldn't finish.

Anthony cleared his throat. "Out from your clothing," he read from his notes, leaving out the word "baggy."

Pari held a hand over her heart. "We have to ask."

Shahnaz nodded. "The police asked me the same thing." She set her tea glass on the table. "They searched me. Everywhere. No, of course, I didn't have any weapon or anything. I wasn't reaching into my clothes. I was just standing there, frightened to death. Those teachers saved us."

Anthony scribbled in his notebook, waited to see if Pari would ask the next question.

She did. "Do you have any idea why anybody might think you had a weapon? Anything at all you can remember?" Then Pari added something in a language Anthony couldn't understand.

Shahnaz's eyes teared up. "I understand, dear. No need to apologize. No. I can't imagine why anybody would think I was reaching for a weapon. I just stood there frozen." She turned to Anthony. "Scared stiff. Is that what you say?"

Anthony confirmed it with a nod.

Pari asked the next questions. Did Shahnaz know or recognize the young man with the gun? She didn't. Did her son know him?

"No. He knows the teacher who was shot, though. His homeroom teacher. Very kind. His favorite teacher."

"Do you know her?" Pari asked.

"Yes. Ms. Ernst. Dark hair, pretty smile, very polite. Such a shame."

Pari asked if Shahnaz actually saw the gunman fire his gun. She didn't.

Anthony became a scribe, writing down the answers to the exact questions he would have asked. Pari's compassionate tone made the interview bearable for her mother's friend.

"The police asked if I was a terrorist," Shahnaz told them, clicking her tongue in a *tsk*.

Pari swallowed and turned away.

Anthony closed his notebook. "Shahnaz, I was there, you realize. We'll make sure the *Ledger* readers know the police found no reason to hold you."

It was sunset when Anthony and Pari walked out of the apartment building into the clear September air. A magenta sky pierced through the tall green trees in the distance, casting a glow on the lot where the Northbrook kids had earlier been playing ball. The air itself seemed to take on a purplish hue.

"Look!" Pari gasped, and stopped short. The light was reflecting in her eyes.

"Beautiful," Anthony said, before turning towards the sun.

After a while, he turned his phone back on. Four texts from Victoria.

Pari noticed and grinned. "Victoria can be intense sometimes. I remember from college."

Then Pari's phone beeped. "A text from Mom. I'd better call."

Anthony heard Pari tell her mother not to wait on her for dinner. He scrolled through Victoria's messages. Three of them said the same thing: *where RU?* The fourth said *Call me!* followed by a frownie emoji. He turned his phone off again, and they sat on a bench watching the sunset fade away.

"It's late," Anthony said. We won't make it back to the office in time. I'll have to call in the quotes from Shahnaz before the editor finalizes the story and leaves."

"What time is that?"

"Uh, tonight? About 8:00" He checked his phone. "Yeah, I guess we could make it. I just don't feel like hurrying."

Ralph hated to take reports this way, but Anthony called it in. "And, oh," Anthony told Ralph. "For the byline would you put me and Pari ... um." He realized he didn't know her last name.

"Shandule," Pari giggled.

"Shandule. Pari Shandule." He spelled it for Ralph, then turned to Pari. "Ralph needs your phone number. Just in case."

She sat on the bench facing him, legs pulled up under her chin, her cheeks aglow in the last rays of the sun. Neither said anything. He watched as Pari rested her chin on her knees and closed her eyes. In only a few moments, it was dark.

"You asleep?"

She opened her eyes. "No. Just thinking."

"About?"

"All kinds of things." She straightened up. "But, one thing. If the gunman was aiming at Shahnaz up on the platform, how did he hit somebody who was sitting down in the front row?"

Anthony was glad she was the one to say it.

7

Ramen and other joys

He took a full spoonful from the plate. "Chrise," Nick said, "Geezus Chrise," he said happily.

—Ernest Hemingway, "Big Two-Hearted River"

The older section of Shady Park, where Anthony lived, lay on the west side of North-South Highway. The only apartments were in private houses. Anthony lived upstairs in an early-20th-century bungalow owned by a widow with a huge brown and white part-foxhound, part-something else. From the front, Mrs. O'Leary's house didn't seem to have a second floor, but the roof pitched up towards the back, leaving a small upstairs room with bath that could be reached by an outside stairway.

Thumper was waiting. Anthony stroked his head and gave him a piece of Grab 'n Go biscuit he'd saved. "How's that leg, Boy?" It seemed to be healing. "Going to leave the raccoons alone from now on?" In Thumper's world, raccoons and groundhogs received the same respect that corrupt politicians and underhanded con men did in Anthony's—with less justification, Anthony believed, but Thumper could not be convinced.

At the top of the stairway was a little landing outside Anthony's door. If you stood on a chair, you could reach up to the roof fascia. That's where Anthony had nailed his antennae, one for cellphone reception, and one for over-the-air TV. The cables led through a little hole he'd drilled below the window frame into his living/dining/bedroom. He was the only person on the street who had good cell reception indoors, and the only person who had free network TV. Mrs. O'Leary made him promise to "take that stuff off of there" if he ever moved out.

From the steel cabinet over his stove, Anthony pulled out a bag of Top Ramen noodles. While the water boiled in his single pot, he cut up some sticks of celery he found in his dorm-sized refrigerator. He sniffed the yellowed broccoli. Better not. As a flourish, he cracked an egg into the pot. He poured the noodles into a bowl on his computer desk-slash-table to let it cool, then turned off the light bulb hanging from the ceiling and sat on his bed in the light of the moon. Mrs. O'Leary paid the electric bill, and he always tried to do his part to keep it down. Leaning back against the wall, he watched shafts of moonlight streaming through the little window high up on the wall. It made him think of Pari.

He finally thought of an excuse to call her. While the phone rang, he switched hands to wipe the perspiration off his telephone hand. Caller ID would let her know it was him.

"Hi." She spoke in a low voice, and he heard a rustle that might mean she was moving to another room. "This is weird, Anthony. I was checking the pictures I took of Shahnaz's books. Remember? I took a picture of the sunset, too, when we left her apartment. I was just looking at that when you called."

"Oh."

"It was beautiful."

"Yeah. It was."

Pari was silent.

"I wanted to talk to you, Pari."

"Yes." It was a confirmation, not a question.

"I wanted to give you the contact number of somebody you could try to interview. Nicole Ernst, the teacher who was shot at the School Board hearing."

"Really? Didn't you talk to her already?"

"I did, but she's shy, scared to say much for fear of getting into trouble with her new principal. She was transferred from Shady Park to Northbrook after a parent accused her of 'unfairly' giving her daughter an F for plagiarism."

"Poor thing." Pari used the same phrase Anthony's mother often used. "If you ask me, we need more teachers to make sure students don't copy other people's work."

"I thought you might try talking to her. You were so good with Shahnaz. By the way, Ms. Ernst seems to have a strong opinion about the Board's choice of textbooks. I couldn't get her to say much. Maybe you can."

Pari trilled, "So that means—I didn't know for sure—it's OK if I work on things like this? I was hired to take over Victoria's weekend assignments."

"Don't see why not. You're a *Ledger* reporter. Ralph can decide if he wants to print your story or not."

"Anthony, I have to tell you. My father was on the Board of Education before he was replaced by Bea Doggit. He would have voted against the new curriculum. I can't say I'm unbiased about this. I promise I'll stick to the facts, though. But won't Victoria—"

"Don't worry. You won't be encroaching on her territory." He sniffed a laugh. "She's bake sales and lost dogs. Not the least bit interested in things like the high school curriculum." He waited for Pari to say something, but she was silent. He held on for an awkward moment, then said, "So I won't see you again until next weekend? Is that the plan?"

"I guess. Yeah."

"But you're starting on a school curriculum story, right? What if I dig up some material before the weekend?"

"You have my phone number."

Anthony kicked off his shoes and used chopsticks to flick the noodles up to slurping distance at the edge of his bowl.

He loved Ramen the way Nick loved beans mixed with spaghetti in Hemingway's "Big Two-Hearted River." And now his elation went beyond the Ramen. "Geez," he said. "*You have my number*. Geez," he repeated happily.

8

The Ernst file

Love enters cloaked in the guise of friendship.
—Ovid, *The Art of Love*

Victoria gave Anthony a sideways glance as she came into the newsroom. "Thanks for ducking out of the symphony. Pop and Mom both fell asleep, and I had nobody to talk to."

"Sorry. I needed to—"

"Mm. Sure." She took a mirror from her handbag and gave her pink lipstick a touch up. "So," she said. "You have a new girlfriend now."

"Girlfriend? No. Pari's—"

"Pari? As if. You know who I'm talking about. The art gallery woman." She snapped her handbag shut. "I've been thinking. She's probably the reason you stood me up the first time, too."

"The night of the shooting? Come on, Vic."

"Maybe I'm not experienced enough for you. Maybe that older mystery woman pleases you in ways I can't."

"Vicky, that's ridiculous." But he realized if she'd said instead "not warm enough," there might be some truth there.

"Tell me her name."

"I can't, Vicky." Emma was a source who had to be kept anonymous. There was no telling what revenge the Riverside Paradise people would take on her if they found out how much information she'd given him for his articles.

"Fine. I'll check at the art gallery. Maybe she signed in."

"Her identity needs to be protected, Victoria. Please

don't."

Victoria's phone chimed. She glanced at the text. "It's something important. Got to go." She put her jacket back on and left in a hurry. No explanation. She was being mysterious, but Anthony had other things on his mind.

As soon as she was gone, he texted Pari: *Any luck contacting Ms. Ernst?*

Pari called him immediately. "The TV news must have seen her name in your story. They've been badgering her for an interview, calling her a victim of terrorism."

"She's a victim of something, I'd say."

"She told me she refused to talk to the WPSK TV reporter. But she said she'll talk to me. Well, not actually talk. If I meet her in the cafeteria during her lunch duty, she has something to give me. Notes a friend of hers took at a closed session of the Board of Education."

"Good. But when you get them, I'd rather not discuss them in the newsroom. Maybe you could bring them to my apartment?"

"Um, well, sure."

Thumper wagged his tail, twisting wildly as Pari scratched him behind the ears. A guest! The happiest day of my life! He lifted a mournful face as Pari and Anthony ran up the stairs.

Pari slipped her shoes off by the door. Anthony slid the chair out from his computer desk-slash-table for her.

"All these wires," she laughed. "What's that gadget on top of your little TV?"

"Digital converter. You need one for old analog TVs to work."

"And this blinking thing, with the antennas sticking up?"

Anthony was looking in the cabinet. "What? Oh, the internet router. Tea?" He had the idea Iranians preferred tea to coffee.

Pari smiled. "Sure. Thanks. You have cardboard boxes everywhere. What's in them, files?"

"And pictures. And some interviews on USB drives."

"You don't keep this stuff at the office?"

"Most of it's there. Some things I keep here. Like second copies of things." He tapped Ms. Ernst's folder. "You probably know this, but you can never say where this information came from."

Pari blushed. "Journalism 101." She opened Ms. Ernst's file on the little desk and started looking through it. "I thought Board of Education meetings were supposed to be public. State sunshine laws, right?"

"Supposed to be." Anthony was busy figuring out how to make two mugs of tea out of his one teabag—without it being noticed, if possible.

"This is a closed session they held 'to get legal advice' before the open session where they approved of … one member in the closed session calls it 'Christianizing the curriculum.'" She flipped through several pages. "Oh, I see Ms. Ernst's point. They weren't actually getting legal advice. They were making sure everybody was on the same page before they took it to the open meeting for a vote. That's how they made sure the new curriculum passed."

Anthony used a tall mug as a tea kettle and poured some out for each of them.

Pari was still reading. "Looks like the board members talked about more than just putting 'creation science' into the curriculum. There's a lot here about making teachers carry guns."

"In the closed session? Can I make a copy of that?"

"You have a copy machine in here?" Pari laughed again.

Anthony pointed to it. "Print, copy, fax combined."

"Fax? Don't you need a landline for a fax?"

"Surprised you know that. I have one. Not from the telephone company. It works over the internet. I'll give you the number. The only person who calls me on it is my mother." He edged two mugs of tea onto the computer desk.

"Looks like I'm sitting in the only chair," Pari observed.

"I don't have a lot of guests."

"You don't?" She seemed to be thinking this over.

"We could sit on the bed, I guess."

They sat side by side, setting their tea mugs on the floor. Pari opened the folder on her lap. The bed was saggy, and Anthony felt her shoulder touching his.

Pari leafed through the pages, reading quickly. "This is insane. The vote was on the curriculum, but actually the closed discussion was just as much about teachers carrying guns."

"That's what I was afraid of. That's why I didn't want to discuss it in the newsroom."

"What do you mean?"

"I've been working on the guns-in-school thing. I don't want Victoria or her father to know."

Pari's soft brown eyes searched his. "All right. But I don't understand."

"Victoria's father is in favor of guns in schools. Or at least pretends he is."

"Why would he pretend? That doesn't make sense."

"It's part of supporting Andrew Mauer for re-election."

"But why would he support somebody if he doesn't approve of his platform?"

"Good question. Mauer himself probably doesn't care about guns one way or another. He just knows he has to tell his voters what they want to hear."

Pari closed the file. "This is too much for me."

"I guess Journalism 101 doesn't encourage keeping the lid on a story because your boss would disapprove?"

Pari put her hands on her cheeks.

"It's not only that," he said. "You saw they mentioned

Mrs. Winwright a lot at that meeting? I've been in touch with her. I want to give the gun control side of the story."

Pari chuckled. "Well, obviously you're not afraid to be fired."

"What do you mean?"

She waved her arm through the air. "You have your own private newspaper office crammed right into this little room."

Anthony forced a smile. Like Thumper, he'd been inclined to think "This is the happiest day of my life." But the thrill of sitting shoulder to shoulder with Pari on his bed was now dulled by this talk of Victoria and Pop.

Pari tapped his foot with her toe. "You seem a little down."

"Yeah?"

"Yeah." She touched his hand. "I'd like to think we're friends. I feel like we are."

"Me, too."

"So. What's your problem, Buddy?"

He managed a weak laugh. "You really want to know?"

"Sure. Tell me."

He gave her a glance, then said, "Victoria's my problem."

Pari tensed, closed her eyes.

"I know you weren't expecting to hear about personal problems."

She looked into his eyes.

"The thing is, I don't know what Victoria assumes. About me and her."

"She's your girlfriend, right?"

"Yeah. Except I never intended that. Victoria comes on kind of strong."

Pari stared down, shuffling the papers on her lap.

"Sometimes I wish I could work for a different paper." He left unstated *and get a different girlfriend.* But the flush on Pari's face might mean she understood.

After Pari left, Anthony sat in his room staring at his phone, the box of leftover fried chicken untouched on his desk. He was racking his brain for an excuse to call her. Finally, he punched the Call button anyway. She answered with a throaty "Hi."

"Didn't wake you up, did I?"

"No." She giggled. "It's only six o'clock."

"Right. I was thinking. It's a beautiful evening."

"It is. I was just looking out the window."

"I wondered ... want to look at the sunset together?"

"We could." She suggested meeting him in Parking lot B, up on the hill at the community college.

Since he'd gone to Piskasanet Community College before transferring to State, he knew exactly where she meant. Every day the parking lots emptied at about noon when the morning shift of students went to work. Most had full-time jobs and crammed a full-time study schedule into the mornings. The campus was dead between noon and 5:30 p.m., when the night students poured in. Since Anthony had taken morning classes, gone to work at Grab 'n Go, then returned for evening classes, he'd often had to park in lot B at the top of the hill.

She was there first, leaning against her car, turned towards a gigantic autumn sun sinking into the trees beyond the hill. She smiled when he shut his car door, hurried towards him. "I brought something for you." She found his hand and put a small object in it. A blue USB flash drive. "My story," she explained. "What I have so far."

"From Ms. Ernst's file?"

"Plus, I called her to get quotes. I had to write 'one teacher' said such and such. Promised I wouldn't use her name." Pari was getting excited. "She gave me the name of other teachers. Ms. Costello is one. I can't use her name either. But teachers being afraid to criticize the textbooks—that's a story in itself, don't you think?"

Her animation was catching. Anthony nodded heartily.

"And I called my brother," she went on. "He's a teacher in Syracuse. His friend helped fight a School Board in the Southwest that mandated evangelistic textbooks. He's going to get details and email me." She touched Anthony's hand holding the flash drive. "So this isn't finished. It's just a start. I wanted you to look at it."

Pari turned towards the sun. "Look. Can you believe it? I've come here so many times, alone. Our house is just beyond those trees. You can see one of the upstairs windows if you look closely."

"Then I've looked towards your house lots of times. I took classes here for a year."

Pari said, "When I was in high school, that must have been. So I was home when you were looking towards my house—but I didn't know it." The sun cast bronze highlights in her hair. "You know, my father teaches here. We used to sleigh ride down that hill in the winter when it snowed."

They stood without talking until the purple haze in the sky completely dissolved into darkness. The windows of the distant college Humanities Building cast the only light.

The first evening classes let out, sending a trickle of students onto the lot and up towards their cars. A woman smiled at Anthony and Pari as she walked by. A younger student turned away as if trying not to stare.

Pari whispered, "They think we're—"

"Yeah."

"Of course, we're not."

"No."

"Are we?"

"I guess not."

She was looking into his eyes. "I keep thinking. You said

you never meant Victoria to be your girlfriend."

Anthony had surprised himself by telling her this.

"So it made me wonder. How can a girl tell if you mean her to be your girlfriend?" The sunset lit up the amber speckles in her deep brown eyes.

Anthony held his breath. He couldn't help it. He stepped closer to her. She closed her eyes. He took her hand, and she closed it on his. He put his arm around her, pulling her close, then held her in both his arms. Her arms were around him. "Pari," he said.

The phone on his belt sounded off—Victoria's ring. He reached down and silenced it.

"Oh. But it could be something important."

"It's Victoria. She'll text."

Pari slipped out of his arms.

Ping. He read the message. *Any more info from police about the school attack?*

It wasn't like Victoria to take an interest in one of Anthony's stories. He stared away towards the darkened trees, wondering what this meant, why this change.

Pari must have noticed his concern. "I'd better go," she said. "It's getting late."

9

Scoop

How dreadful knowledge of the truth can be
when there's no help in truth!

—Sophocles, *Oedipus Rex*

Anthony sat twirling Pari's flash drive in his hand. She'd told him it contained just a start, but what Anthony read—and loaded onto the network drive for Ralph to read—was the beginning of a polished story about conservative efforts to control what is taught in schools. It was headed "Part 1: Mandating Textbooks." Notes that followed her story indicated what she was still working on could be "Part 2: Truth or Propaganda?"

"Anthony." Ralph called him into his office. "What the hell is this?"

"Pari, the new girl, wrote it."

"Amazing. She can spell." He tapped his screen. "Can she tie this in to the school attack?"

"Pretty sure she's going to."

"I want to see it all. I'll wait." He smoothed his mustache and narrowed his eyes. "But as long as Pop doesn't kill it, this is going in. I don't want my son being taught that Old Testament stories are the literal truth."

Pari bounded into the newsroom. "It's me. Not the weekend, I know. I just wanted to give you some more of the story." She opened her hand to show Anthony a red flash drive. Her hair was flowing free—no ponytail. She saw Anthony noticed and brushed some strands aside with her fingers.

He took the flash drive, keeping hold of her hand to put the blue one in her palm. "Trade you."

Pari noticed Victoria's empty carrel. "You got a message last night. Is Victoria sick?"

"No. Lately she's been taking off to 'take care of some things.' Acting a little mysterious, actually."

"OK if I sit a minute?" Pari took off a thin black jacket and hung it over the back of Victoria's chair. As soon as she sat down, they heard a sound in the newsroom doorway.

"Ah-ha," Victoria teased. "Taking over my desk, I see."

Pari stood and picked up her jacket.

"Nice," Victoria remarked, eyeing Pari's white pleated blouse. "A little summery." She checked her *Ledger* voicemail, jotting something down. "Well, it looks like I can't stay today." She turned to Pari. "What brings you in today, anyway?"

"I'm working on something about school books in the county."

"My goodness," Victoria exclaimed. "Bake sales, Pari. That's what you need to write about. Church pancake breakfasts. Watercolor exhibitions. That's what the *Shady Park Ledger* reports on."

"Well, sure," Anthony put in. "But we cover the Board of Education, too. The public might like to hear about curriculum changes. I'm sure Ralph will back me up. In fact, I was hoping Pari could talk to some teachers today. Get their point of view."

Victoria tightened the bow on the front of her blouse. "Pari, I need you to cover the Nottingham Estates ladies' golf tournament for me. Something important's come up and I can't do it."

Anthony tried to control his frustration. "You can't? You know all the Nottingham ladies already, Victoria. Your mother's one of them."

"I just got a message I have to meet somebody. Before that, I need to get my nails done. Gel coats look good and they last three weeks, but when your nails grow and leave bare spots, you have to go back and get the coating professionally patched or taken off."

Anthony and Pari eyed her nails. The polish had a lustrous white glow.

Victoria slipped her purse strap over her shoulder. "Show Pari where to check out a camera. And, Pari, make sure you get the ladies' names. All they want is to see their picture in the paper. Some of those golf ladies are wives of our major advertisers. Come on. I'll fill you in as we walk out."

Anthony waited in the office for a call back from the county police about the ballistics report. It was taking too much time. Something seemed odd. All he could do was leave another request for Rob to call him back. He knocked on Ralph's door and asked if he wanted him to go get some lunch.

"Thanks. I like that chicken at the Grab 'n Go."

Anthony did, too. And Victoria wouldn't be there to tease them for eating it.

The Sikh clerk at the Grab 'n Go was more quiet than usual.

"Anything wrong, Kaila?"

"Well, as you know there has been a shooting at the Northbrook High School and, you see, the Grab 'n Go customers are assuming that it was a Muslim terrorist attack and unfortunately they seem to believe that I am a Muslim and they make remarks questioning my loyalty to the United States, of which I am a naturalized citizen, and some have commented to the effect that I am perhaps a jihadi killer and should be sent back to where I came from, even though I have lived in this country longer than most of them."

Anthony sympathized, but all he could do was suggest

Kaila report this to the police. "And maybe write a letter to the editor of the *Shady Park Ledger*," he added. The clerk gave a curt nod and handed him a large box of fried chicken.

They ate it in Ralph's spartan office, its bare walls the same beige color as the tile floor. A huge beige CRT monitor took up most of the space on Ralph's desk—he refused to let them upgrade it to "one of those skinny DCL or whatever jobbies."

Ralph's worn gray chair squeaked as he maneuvered it over to the table without getting up. Anthony used the only other chair in the room. Ralph spread a paper napkin in front of him, and Anthony ate from the box.

"I was talking to Kaila," Anthony told him. "Since the school shooting, some customers have been telling him, 'Go back where you came from.' They're afraid he might be a Muslim terrorist."

"Sheesh." Ralph held a napkin over his mouth to keep chicken from flying out. He swallowed. "Ignorami." It was one of his favorite words—the plural, he insisted, of "ignoramus."

"Yeah, so, I was thinking of doing a story on the reaction of county residents to the gun attack. Get some good quotes. Then bring in Kaila's experience, if he agrees. Show the harm that xenophobic panic can cause."

Ralph wiped his mouth, lifted his glasses up onto his head, and fixed Anthony in a steady stare.

"What? Not a good idea?"

"Are you actually trying to get fired?"

Pari came back, her face ruddy from standing out in the sun at the golf course. "Hey," she beamed. "Still here, huh? What a day I had with the ladies."

Anthony knew what she meant. "Lots of talk about their children and husbands and friends and nothing at all about golf?"

"And lots of posing. Every one of them had to approve each picture and I had to delete any they didn't like."

Anthony showed her how to load the pictures onto the network drive. "So who won the tournament?" he teased.

"Not sure they were keeping score. Victoria's mother, Michelle, told me to say everybody improved a little."

"What did you think of her?"

Pari turned a deeper red and didn't answer.

"A bit assertive, some people say."

Pari pursed her lips.

"So you met the County Exec's wife, too?"

"And a state senator's wife, and the wife of the zoning commissioner, and the wife of a BMW dealer. There was a lot of talk about the upcoming election. Victoria's mother told the County Exec's wife the paper would endorse him for re-election."

"No surprise there. The *Shady Park Ledger* is one of his main supporters."

Pari frowned. "The ladies said some pretty catty things about Mrs. Winwright. That's the woman mentioned in Ms. Ernst's Board of Education file. She used to be chair of the state Republican Central Committee, they said."

"Until she came out pro gun-control. Then she suddenly became the enemy."

Ralph emerged from his office. "Got your pictures, young lady." An ironic smile spread below his thin mustache. "Looks like once more the tournament result is 'everybody improved a little.' Nice report."

Before Pari could thank him, Victoria dashed in with a Macy's shopping bag. "Nice report? My story on the American University Women's used book sale, I assume?"

Ralph gave an exaggerated bow. "That, too."

Victoria dropped the bag on her desk, held her fingers up

to Anthony. "What do you think? I went for a complete removal and re-do." She raised her eyebrows. "The technician agreed it gave me a more 'mature' look. I thought that might please you."

Another reference to Emma? Anthony tried to shrug it off with a weak smile. He noticed Pari peeping at her own nails, then slipping her hands into her pockets.

His cell phone rang and he flinched. It was Rob, with the ballistics report, talking fast.

"Hold on, Ralph," Anthony said. "Let me get this down." He couldn't believe what Rob was telling him.

Ralph, Victoria, and Pari stared at him when he hung up.

"Willard Scherd's gun was never fired," he told them.

"You're kidding?" Ralph pushed his glasses up on his head.

"All the bullets were still in the magazine. The gun was clean."

Ralph hurried into his office to change the lede to Anthony's story. "All righty, then," he said. "A scoop for the *Ledger*."

Victoria repeated the word "scoop." She glanced at the clock on the office wall and picked up her shopping bag. "Well, I have to meet somebody, and I can't be late for dinner. Esmeralda promised to cook something special since Mom would be starving after the tournament. Ciao." She blew Anthony a kiss and rushed out.

10

The local shootings

"They flee from me that sometime did me seek."
—Sir Thomas Wyatt, "They Flee from Me"

He was tired as he climbed the stairs to his apartment. It wasn't physical exhaustion. It was from the tension Victoria caused in his chest, especially when Pari was with him. He turned on his TV and sprawled on his bed to watch the news.

"The Local Shootings"—that's what Anthony's mother called the evening TV newscasts. If the shooting or drug arrest or traffic accident or fire occurred in Piskasanet County, Anthony already knew about it and had probably written about it because the morning reports in the *Ledger* were generally the source of these evening "breaking news" reports on television.

Megyn Drumpfer came on the screen with "breaking news about the terror attack at Northbrook High School." She stood in front of the closed school, whisking her hair out of her eyes, while she recited, "WPSK News has learned a police ballistics report shows the suspected terrorist's gun was not fired in the attack."

"Well, Megyn, this is surprising news," the TV anchor said on cue. "Witnesses reported a shot was fired. Do the police have any theories about who fired that shot?"

"John," Megyn said, holding a finger to one ear, "the only INFORMATION we have is that the assailant's gun was not fired. We will continue to COVER the story and keep you informed of the latest developments."

"Thank you so much, Megyn, for this exclusive report,"

John intoned, an air of deep concern in his voice.

Rob had assured Anthony tomorrow morning's *Ledger* report would be the first public announcement that the gun was not fired. He tossed in bed for hours that night, wondering how Megyn Drumpfer had been able to report the news first.

The morning *City Paper* didn't have the story either that the assailant's gun wasn't fired. WPSK TV had been the first news outfit to report it. Had Rob given it to them, after all? Anthony called him from the newsroom.

"You're the only one I told, Anthony. The *City Paper* didn't ask. Neither did the TV news. Don't know how it got out to them. I'm the official spokesman, but I guess it's possible somebody else here leaked the information."

"All right, thanks, Rob." He tapped on his notebook. "By the way, anything yet on who might have fired the shot?"

"Sorry, no. We're still looking into it."

Anthony's hands were trembling. He called Victoria. "Vic, did you see the WPSK TV report this evening? I can't believe they knew about it."

"I thought Megyn looked great. You know, beautiful but concerned."

"Rob says I'm the only one he gave that report to. Nobody else knew but Ralph, Pari, and—"

"Maybe Pari told them."

Anthony felt a painful tightening in his rib cage. "It's you, Victoria, isn't it? You're the one who gave WPSK the story. Why?"

"Let's not talk about that now. This is important. You need to be ready to come to my house tomorrow night by eight o'clock. I might have something to celebrate."

The second he pressed End Call, his phone rang. "I've been trying to get you." Pari's voice was pitched higher than usual. "I saw the TV news report. Sorry you didn't get the scoop. How did that happen? I guess the police gave the story to WPSK, too?"

"No."

"Then how—"

"I'm pretty sure Victoria gave it to them."

"You're kidding. Why would she do that?"

Anthony had an idea but didn't want to say.

"I'm so sorry, Anthony."

Victoria didn't come in until late the next afternoon. She was carrying a slim black leather portfolio he'd never seen before, softly singing under her breath one of her favorite popular songs. "I can't love you in the dark. It feels like we're oceans apart."

"You OK?" Anthony asked.

"Sure. What do you mean?" There was a faint smell of alcohol on her breath. She checked her reflection on the computer screen and brushed some fingers through her hair.

"Just, you didn't come in this morning. Thought you might be sick."

"No. I'm feeling great, in fact. You know John Rowland? The WPSK TV anchor? He wanted to have lunch with me." She seemed too excited to sit down. "I couldn't believe how the waitress and women customers kept ogling him." Her eyebrows lifted thoughtfully. "Well, he is about the handsomest person on television."

"Maybe he thought you were the most glamorous person *not* on television."

She smiled, running her fingers over her new portfolio. "Maybe he did."

Victoria's phone chimed. She walked towards the door to talk, but he could still hear her. "Oh," she trilled. "What a surprise. Really? Oh, don't flatter me." Her voice trailed off as she left the newsroom. When she came back in, her face was flushed. "I have to go in to talk to Pop." She avoided looking at Anthony.

It wasn't long before she came out of Pop's office. She said, "Um, Anthony, I have to go home now. Pop has something he wants to tell you."

Every time he was called into the publisher's office, Anthony worried about keeping his job. He could smell Pop's cigar from under the door.

"Close it behind you, if you don't mind, young man." Pop pointed to the leather chair. "I'm afraid this is going to be awkward." He re-lit his cigar, obscuring his face behind a pale gray cloud of smoke. "Here's what I understand from Victoria. Seems she invited you to our house tonight. A celebration?"

Anthony coughed away some smoke. "She mentioned she might have something to celebrate. She didn't say what."

Pop tapped a red-tipped ash from his cigar. "Well, I can tell you. This took me by surprise, I have to say. She's taken a job with WPSK TV. Sort of a reporter-trainee thing."

Anthony was putting some things together in his mind.

"I feel let down, to tell the truth. I've run this paper almost as long as she's been alive." He sent another blast of smoke into the air. "But anyway, she's my daughter, and this is what she wants."

"Sure," Anthony said.

"Now here's the rest. You know John Rowland?"

"The TV anchor? I've never met him."

"Apparently he's the one who got her the job. He accepted her invitation to come to our house to celebrate tonight." Pop eyed Anthony, twisting his cigar between thumb and forefinger. When Anthony had no reaction, he continued. "Victoria says it would be awkward for you and Rowland both to be there."

"Oh."

Pop sighed. "Women. You can't figure them out, can you? Here I thought Victoria was onto you like a retriever on a mallard." He chuckled. "But now—guess I'm the one designated to tell you—she's picked up another scent. This Rowland guy is all we hear about these days."

Anthony began a series of slow nods meant to show his submission to the inevitable. He tightened his lips, trying not to show his relief.

"You're actually a good reporter, son. "That *Eat to Be Slim* story? Doubled our restaurant ads. I wouldn't want to lose you over a thing like this this."

When Pop stood up to indicate the meeting was over, Anthony had to ask, "To be clear. Victoria won't be working here any more?"

"That's right. We'll have to look around for somebody to cover her beat. How about that new girl? Polly, or whatever. She any good? The women's golf tournament thing was right on."

"Pari. Yes. She's perfect."

Pop turned towards the picture of the island on the wall, hands behind his back, lost, it seemed, in other thoughts. "Tell Ralph to contact her." It was just a murmur.

The pathetic fallacy consists of ascribing one's own human feelings and thoughts to inanimate objects. Anthony remembered this from his Romantic literature class. It wasn't something he tended to be guilty of. Yet as he passed Victoria's desk, he could have sworn the Justin Bieber bobble-head was staring at him with a satisfied grin. And a string of glittery plastic beads hanging beside Victoria's monitor, a souvenir from a Mardi Gras trip to New Orleans with her sorority friends, seemed to be winking at him.

Pari would take over Victoria's carrel now. It was like a sudden gift from above. Yet Anthony was surprised by a feeling of melancholy, as well, as he stared at Victoria's empty chair. He found her approach to the world superficial, yes, but also soothing. With his own thoughts occupied by corrupt politicians, sleazy businessmen, hypocritical preachers, and the like, it had been pleasant at times to put all that aside and bask in the carefree comfort of Victoria's world.

He sat at his desk and called her. Victoria answered but didn't speak right away. He thought he heard a sigh.

"It's OK, Vicky. Your dad told me everything."

"I'm sorry, Anthony." Her voice was thick.

"No, it's all right. Congratulations. You finally got into TV broadcasting. Just what you've always wanted."

He could hear her breathing, but she said nothing.

"You OK, Vic?"

"Anthony, see, John got me the job. He's important at the station. That's why—"

"Sure. I get it. I'm happy for you, Vicky. Seriously."

"You are? I knew it." Her voice brightened. "John's older than me, I know, but handsome. Charming." There was a shallow giggle. "He likes me."

Is it possible to feel protective of a girl dumping you for somebody else? For Anthony it was. He had heard Nora and Sharise downstairs gossiping. John Rowland was supposedly a ladies' man. He ventured, "You trust him, Vic?"

"What a funny thing to say."

"No. I just—"

"I'm trying to tell you. He's so .... He's just so .... I'm in love, Anthony."

11

Changing partners

If ever any beauty I did see,
Which I desired, and got, 'twas but a dream of thee.
—John Donne, "The Good-Morrow"

He called Pari as soon as he got home. "Did Ralph contact you yet?"

"He did. I can hardly believe it. Full time. What changed their minds? I'm sure it was you."

"Pop and Ralph both liked your golf tournament story."

She chuckled. "Maybe, but—"

"Also, Victoria quit."

Pari gasped. "Anthony, are you upset?"

"Surprised. That's all. She'll be working for TV now. What she always wanted."

"Oh. Well, I guess that's good."

"I want to see you, Pari."

"Yes." There was a silence. "What do you mean?"

"Can you come to my place?"

"You mean now?"

He heard her running up the creaky stairs. As soon as he opened the door, she gave him a sympathetic hug. They sat on the bed, her thick pony tail coming loose, covering his arm. Then her eyes darkened. "Are you sad about Victoria leaving, Anthony? Tell me."

His throat felt tight. "The truth is ... sitting here with you ... I've never been happier."

"Honest? Because me, too. Ever since ...." She closed her

eyes and let him kiss her. The thrill of her soft lips was so powerful he wondered if he was hallucinating.

"I'm crazy about you, Anthony," she breathed.

He answered with a long kiss.

They fell to the bed, his hands trembling at the tender responses of her body. Her skin was so soft he wondered how it could be real. She held his face to her breast, gasping at his kisses. It seemed like a dream, and if Anthony had died at that moment, he wouldn't have cared.

It was night when he awoke, the room lit only by the moon shining through the window. Pari lay naked beside him, asleep, dark hair covering her face, motionless, beautiful. He kept still, watching her sleep, unwilling to touch her as if that might break the spell he was under.

Finally, she stirred, turned to face him, smiled through the dark strands of her hair, and lay her head on his chest. Still half asleep, she whispered something in words he didn't understand but which her soft caress seemed to explain. He stroked her hair, her cheek, her shoulder, as if to convince himself this was truly happening.

Awake now, she sat up, eyes wide in the moonlight, a puckish smile on her face. "What time is it?" She leaned across him and reached down for her phone on the floor. "Oh, no. 10 o'clock. I have to call my mom."

He kissed her on the shoulder while she dialed. He had no idea what she said to her mother in Farsi, but she looked pleased when the call ended. "I'll tell her the full story when I get home. For now, I just said I was at a friend's." Then she held her face, speaking through her fingers. "She asked if I was going to stay over."

Anthony drew her hands away and held them to his lips. "What did you say?"

"I said 'Yes.'" She buried her face in his chest. "I know. I should have asked first."

He lowered his head, kissed her hair. "Pari."

She looked up at him, eyes sparkling in the moonlight. "Know what it means? My name? It means *fairy*."

An involuntary shock coursed along his spine. "Fairy? No. Please, Pari, tell me you're real."

Pari called him. "Can you come over to my house? Please."

It would be the first time he went to her house. She talked about her parents, but he hadn't met them yet. A recollection of the first time he'd met Victoria's mother hit him like a migraine. There was only one way to describe the look on her face. *Not him—you're kidding?*

The Shandules lived near Piskasanet Community College in what Anthony assumed was the original stone house on a farm that had been subdivided into acres of lots covered by vinyl-clad houses. Pari was alone. He noticed some shoes near the doorway and took off his. She threw her arms around him, then stepped back. Her eyes were clouded. Something wasn't right. The look of uncertainty on her face was new.

"I told my parents." A shadow fell across her face. "About us." Her pained look must mean her parents didn't approve. Before they'd even met him. He probably wasn't the person they'd imagined for their daughter. Local news reporter living in a one-room apartment over a widow's house. Working-class family. Wrong religion, maybe.

Pari pursed her lips. "They know you and Victoria were together. They say I shouldn't take you away from her. It's not right." She wrung her hands.

"Is that all? Not that they think you should aim higher than a local—?"

"Anthony, what are you talking about?" She took him into the living room. He guessed it was the living room. The only piece of furniture was a low table with some cushions around it. He followed her lead and sat on one across from her.

"Pari, I didn't mention this before, but when Victoria quit, she told me she's in love with John Rowland. She's moved on from me."

"What? You didn't tell me a thing like that? You didn't think I would want to know that?"

He hadn't told her probably because he assumed Victoria's infatuation wouldn't last. Besides, he thought it made her look foolish. It would be like revealing an embarrassing intimate secret she'd confided to him.

Pari was tracing her fingernail on the table.

Anthony knew this would be a time to "clear the air," as his father would say. But it was hard for him to talk about personal feelings. He'd assumed Pari knew how he felt about Victoria. It seemed simple enough to him. He wished her well. That was all. He'd never actually "desired" Victoria, although she was a pretty girl and, if she'd been willing, he certainly would have .... As for Pari, he'd been entranced by her from the moment he met her. She was the only girl he'd ever been in love with.

"What are you thinking?"

"Nothing."

There was a sound at the door. A woman wearing a thin sweater over a white nurse's uniform came in. She shook Anthony's hand. "You must be Anthony. I'm glad to finally meet you. I'm Mastaneh, Pari's mother."

Anthony was struck by the resemblance. She looked just like Pari but older with graying hair. He liked her at once.

Pari said, "Excuse me. I have something to tell my mother." She took her into another room.

Anthony looked around the room he was in, noticing for the first time the paintings and sketches on the walls. He went up to a charcoal sketch of a man hunched over in a field, cutting wheat with a sickle. He had on a curious tan felt hat with two sides turned up, baggy pajama-like trousers, and a worn suit jacket. It seemed to be a scene from a different country, Iran, he presumed, but something about the focus on the worker reminded him of the paintings he'd admired at the college art gallery.

Daughter and mother were all smiles when they came back into the room. Anthony asked about the sketches. "They remind me of some unsigned paintings I saw at the college art gallery, the ones with the landscape workers in the front yard."

"My mom did them, too. Isn't she great?"

"I didn't mention them in my article—"

"I noticed." Pari made a pouty face.

"Because they weren't signed. Do you mind?" He unclipped his phone and took pictures of the sketches. "I'll do a separate story now. Just on Mrs. Shandule's work."

"Sufi," Mastaneh said. "I kept my own family name."

"Maybe some day I'll tell you why," Pari grinned.

Mastaneh's cheeks reddened. "Let's change the subject. You have to stay for dinner, Anthony. Pari's dad will be home any minute."

Mr. Shandule had white hair and a big smile. "Mark," he introduced himself. "Pari can't stop talking about you, Anthony." He seemed uncertain what else to say. "Hope she hasn't uprooted your whole life."

"Dad, will you come into the kitchen with me?" Pari asked. "I want you to check the khoresh."

Mastaneh cleared her throat. "You see, Anthony. Mark and I have been worried. We didn't think it was right for Pari to, well, step between you and her friend."

Anthony shook his head. "No, it's not like that at all. Pari is a wonderful—"

"Cook," her father cried out happily, returning from the kitchen.

Khoresh was a kind of stew they ate with rice. Anthony didn't like the taste at all, but he said it was delicious.

"Better than Ramen?" Pari teased. "It's a traditional Iranian dish. Glad you like it."

12

Cat rescues plus

News is what a chap who doesn't care much about anything wants to read.

—Evelyn Waugh, *Scoop*

The newsroom seemed like a different place the next day. At Victoria's request, Ralph had taken down all her decorative paraphernalia. And there was Pari, sitting at Victoria's carrel. It was as if a magic wand had made the transformation. She mouthed "I love you" to Anthony while Ralph was pointing to a sentence on her screen.

Ralph seemed unusually chipper. He was going over details of the *Ledger* style sheet conventions that Victoria had never taken an interest in. "Like the *City Paper*, we call everybody Mr. or Ms. or Mrs.," he told her. "Now let's take a look at your report on the new school curriculum."

"It's not finished yet," Pari cautioned. "I wrote that Ms. Beatrice Doggit's support was instrumental in getting the new books adopted. Then I described some new things in the books. I mentioned objections in other states and counties to what they call Christianizing the curriculum. I've been, you know, trying to give both sides of the debate."

Ralph gave her an approving nod.

"But before it's printed, I'd like to get some information about the textbook publisher."

The smell of cigar smoke announced Pop making his way through the newsroom towards his office. He stopped behind Ralph and Pari with folded arms, looking at the carrel. His eyes, Anthony thought, betrayed a sadness that his forceful pose might be trying to hide. "Going to miss all those thingamajiggies Victoria had hanging everywhere." He shrugged. "Guess she's happier now."

Pari politely stood up. Pop shook her hand. "Welcome aboard, young lady. My wife enjoyed that story you wrote about the golf tournament." He lifted his chin towards the monitor. "And Ralph says you can spell. Kind of rare to find that in someone your age nowadays."

Pop bent to look at the screen. "Bea Doggit? You're working on a story about her? Ralph, print out a copy of this article and bring it to me will you?" He turned to Anthony. "I don't want you encouraging our new girl to stir up trouble of any kind. Understand? She's hired to cover Victoria's beat."

A rare squawk burst out from the police and emergency scanner on the table near Ralph's office. *Truck number 749, call from homeowner at 108 Shady Park Lane. Cat in tree.*

"There you go," Pop said. "Take our new girl and show her how to cover the kind of story we need her for."

Anthony handed the camera to Pari. They sped down Shady Park neighborhood streets, ran a few stop signs, and screeched to a halt at 108—just in time for a picture of the fireman reaching for the cat at the top of the ladder. Anthony wrote down the cat owner's name. Fireman's name and rank. Cat's name. Pari wrote down a distraught comment by the cat woman. Done. The WPSK TV news truck pulled up just as the fire engine was roaring away. There would be a feel-good clip on TV tonight featuring the cat lady holding Tiger—and sobbing if Megyn Drumpfer could succeed in making her cry on camera. Anthony knew what Megyn's question to the woman would be: "How happy were you to get Tiger back?"

On the way back to the newsroom, Pari said, "That was fun."

"Uh-huh. That's what Pop thinks staff reporters are for. Rushing out to cover car crashes, fires, fallen trees. That and sports. The *Ledger* has freelance reporters for stuff that isn't time-sensitive."

"I'd like to do cat rescues *plus* researched articles."

"I've managed so far. With censorship."

Ralph was waiting for them, stroking the ends of his moustache. "Pop wants to see you. He said both of you."

Pari sat in the leather chair. Anthony stood beside her. Pop waved a printout at them. "This won't do."

Pari looked hurt. "The curriculum story? It's meant to be a follow-up to the Board of Education hearing you sent Anthony to cover."

"I don't see a story here. The books have already been approved. All right, some teachers object. A few parents. That Muslim woman." Pop's eyes searched Pari's face from under the ridge of his brow. "I don't know which one of you is actually behind this story—hard to believe somebody who just came on board had time to dig all this up—but whichever of you it was, it has to stop."

Pari frowned. "I'm sorry, Mr. Whitman."

"Pop."

"I just thought the public should know what's in the books. Because most people in America would consider certain of their claims controversial. Or actually untrue."

Pop paced around his desk and towered over Pari, dropping the article in her lap. "Maybe. But this isn't going in the paper. I need time to look into it myself. Understand?"

Pari nodded.

Anthony stepped in. "Pop, it's just books. I don't understand. You let me print articles exposing the Riverside Paradise scheme."

"And that's coming back to bite me in the butt now, I can assure you. I guess you haven't noticed real estate advertising is down. But more important, this new school curriculum isn't a 'scheme,' as far as I know."

Anthony wondered how Pop could be so sure of that. Anyway, since Pop was already irritated, this might be as good a time as any to let him know he was starting on a gun-control story. "You know," he told Pop. "Opinions pro and con."

A single thick wrinkle spread across Pop's brow. "One word on either school books or gun control and you're fired."

"You mean, not even—"

"You heard me."

13

Staying here

The fair breeze blew, the white foam flew,
The furrow followed free;
We were the first that ever burst
Into that silent sea.

—Samuel Taylor Coleridge,
The Rime of the Ancient Mariner

Pari took his hand as they walked to their cars. Neither spoke. It was a Shady Park autumn, clear blue sky with cool air warmed by the sun when the puffs of wind subsided. They stopped beside Anthony's gray Kia hatchback, still holding hands. "If you're fired, I'm quitting, too," she assured him.

He grinned. "You can't. Who will rush out and do the cat rescue stories?"

She ignored that. "What's that thing on your car roof?"

"A rack. For my Laser. A little sailboat I keep in Mrs. O'Leary's back yard."

"Anthony! Take me on it. Please."

The next morning the air was light, but Anthony knew it would build up by early afternoon. Pari helped him lift the bow of the boat up and slide it onto the rack. They drove down a narrow dirt road and launched at a public ramp in a creek on the Piskasanet. They took off their shoes, rolled up their jeans, and Pari stood up to her knees in muddy water holding the boat while he put up the mast. It was great to have some help. The Laser was a single-handed boat, and this was the first time he'd taken somebody with him.

"How come you're tying everything down?"

"You know. Just in case."

A slight offshore tide helped them drift away from the tree lined bank. Leaves of red, yellow, green, and silver flashed in the sunlight along both sides of the river. Soon a light breeze filled in from the starboard quarter. Anthony eased the sail, raised the dagger board slightly, and ran before the wind, he and Pari on opposite sides of the boat. She stroked his toes with hers.

The water turned greener as they slipped away from the shore. Lines of ripples rolled in from the windward side of the boat. "Hold on to the rail," he cautioned as he dropped the daggerboard, trimmed the sail, and crossed over to sit next to her. "Put your feet under that strap." The light boat heeled and shot forward instantly. Pari gripped the strap on the back of his life jacket.

A white wake streamed out behind them as the hull rose up on a plane. "This is great," Anthony cried. "With twice the weight on the rail, the speed is fantastic."

"With—? Hey, not *twice* the weight." Her pony tail was flying back. "We're not going to flip, are we?"

"No. But if we do, hold on to the boat and try to grab the painter—that rope on the bow."

As the breeze got heavier, it backed until they were on a close-hauled course straight for the island. The wind, blowing against the current, whipped up little waves that splashed across the deck and over their legs. They heard the whoosh as the water rushed across their feet and was sucked out through the bailer. His hat blew off and dangled from its cord.

"See that beach between the stump and the rock? That's where we'll land." They had made it in a single tack. He looked at Pari and laughed.

"What?"

"Nothing. Just you're wet up to the waist."

"You, too."

The island was Anthony's favorite place to sail to. In middle school, he'd sailed here in a gaff rigged Peanut dinghy, and since high school in the Laser. He knew every foot of the terrain. They sat on a white rock still warm from the sun, watching curious mallards paddle in circles near the boat. A box turtle with a yellow and brown shell crawled towards the rock they were on, then stopped motionless when it saw them.

Out in the river, an osprey dove down, plucked a fish from the water, and soared towards the island. They watched him land in a huge nest at the top of a tall, bare tree on the highest point of the island. "They usually make their nests on pilings or day markers in the middle of the water," Anthony mused. "I guess he considers this little island isolated enough for safety."

He pointed over to a marshy area of the shoreline. "Look. A blue heron. His nest must be … there it is, up there in that huge oak tree." Pari had pulled her phone from a zip lock bag and was taking pictures. "Who owns this island, anyway?"

"Nobody. Or I should say Piskasanet County. It's a county nature preserve."

Before long, the sun and the warm rock had nearly dried their clothes. Anthony took out the tuna fish sandwiches he'd made and opened a bottle of limeade. A hummingbird with a red throat hovered briefly near the bottle. "That's OK," Pari trilled. "You can have some." But he helicoptered away

After eating, they climbed to the highest point on the island. Birds fluttered up as they trod through the underbrush towards a forested plateau. Through the trees they could see in the distance where the river met the bay. On the south bank, they could make out the steeples of the historic churches of Colonial City.

"Let's stay here forever," Pari said. She held her cheek to

his, gazing down the river.

High in the trees, the wind was picking up. Thin lines of whitecaps appeared on the water. Anthony didn't want to leave, either, but it might be best to get on their way.

The wind was directly behind them, the mainsail eased beyond square. They sat on opposite sides of the boat, sailing by the lee. He lowered the daggerboard part way to help counter the rolling from side to side. The high-pitched vibration as the blade tore through the water made his heart pound with delight. "Woo-ha," he yelled. Then, "If the boom starts to move, duck. OK?"

They were heeled to windward, Anthony using his weight to steer. Except for a few fishing boats some distance away, the river seemed to be theirs alone. Then they heard the distant diesel throb of a boat grow louder and louder as it approached from behind. Anthony looked back. The boat seemed immense. Its huge wake fanned out on each side as it plowed ahead, straight for them. At the last minute, it swerved away sharply, exposing its name in white letters on a red hull. *Shoreline Construction.* The quick turn sent a huge wave rolling towards them, capsizing their boat.

The boat floated on its side, its sail flat on the water, Anthony standing on the daggerboard. He didn't see Pari. He yelled, listened. Then he saw her brown hair and yellow life-jacket come out from under the sail. "Grab onto anything," he shouted. She was gasping for breath, confused. Then she lifted her head and saw Anthony. She started swimming towards the bow of the boat. Anthony couldn't believe it. She was holding the painter.

"Got the rope thingy like you told me. What now?" she yelled.

A fisherman was rowing his dinghy towards her. "Hold on," the man called. He brought his boat beside her and took hold of her life jacket. With his other hand he seized the painter and fastened it to his boat. "You should be able to right it now," he called to Anthony.

Anthony crouched on the daggerboard, held onto the rail, and leaned back. Slowly, the sail lifted out of the water. Ducking under the swinging boom, Anthony leapt aboard as the boat quickly flipped upright. He pulled on the painter to bring the boat head to wind beside the fisherman's boat.

"You OK, Pari?"

"I can take her to shore in my boat," the fisherman called out. Anthony had a feeling he'd seen him somewhere before.

"I'd rather go back with Anthony."

"OK, Pari. Just hold onto the rail, throw one leg over, and pull yourself back into the boat." When she stared at him, he said, "Like climbing out of a swimming pool."

She did it with surprising grace. He held her close to warm her. Her hands were icy.

"Thanks," Anthony called to the man in the dinghy. Then it came to him. He was a friend of one of his sources, Emma Bovant. He hadn't met him, but he'd see him on a daycare center video tape. "Are you Andre Smyth?" he shouted.

Andre grinned. "At your service. I'll wait here till you get going again."

Anthony pulled in the sail. "Plenty of wind," he said. "We'll be back in no time." They took off again on a plane, the water draining out of the shallow cockpit through the bailer with a sucking sound. He waved good-bye to Andre.

"Does this happen a lot?" Pari was smiling, he was happy to see.

"Not that often."

Steam filled his cramped shower. They could feel but couldn't see each other. They didn't come out until they'd used up all the hot water. Then they dove under the covers of his saggy bed. Pari whispered, "I'm staying here tonight."

14

Smyth with a y

In a word, my work is digressive, and it is progressive too,—and at the same time.

—Laurence Sterne,
The Life and Opinions of Tristram Shandy, Gentleman

There was a bruise on Pari's arm.

"Looks like you got banged up a little yesterday when we capsized."

She rubbed her arm. "Actually, I think this happened last night when you rolled onto me in your sleep. The bed kind of sinks down in the middle."

It had always seemed a perfect setup to Anthony. The narrow bed, the mini refrigerator, the little table for both eating and writing—all crammed into a single all-purpose room. Now, for the first time he began to wish he had a nicer place. If there were even a place for Pari to keep some of her clothes, she might start staying over more often. He could probably afford to move, as long as he kept his job. But that was the point. Giving up his spartan life would mean giving up the security of knowing he could live on the cheap if Pop ever fired him.

"Hey. Cheer up, Buddy. I'm not complaining about the bed. Let's eat some of your famous Ramen."

"We could go out and get something else."

"You mean fried chicken? That's OK. Ramen's fine."

Maybe it was hubris, wanting to tell the public what he thought they should know. If he resigned himself to writing about pancake breakfasts, he could stop worrying about his job and maybe become an editor some day. He wondered how much Ralph made.

"Your Ramen's getting cold." She lifted her bowl and slurped down the last of hers. "Are Ralph and Pop going to be mad that we didn't go in yesterday?"

"Some days I don't go in. Victoria was always taking off. Nobody says anything. If there's an actual deadline, Ralph will give us a call. Otherwise, he fills the paper up with health articles written by doctors or chiropractors looking for business, advertisements disguised as articles by home improvement contractors, and—the latest rage—'parenting' advice from somebody with a degree in psychology or sometimes just by anybody with an opinion."

"Parenting's a thing? Too late to tell my mom."

"She would've laughed anyway. It's a first-world thing."

He opened the apartment door. The *Shady Park Chronicle* was on the landing. Thumper always found it and brought it up, no matter where it dropped when the delivery kid's mom threw it out her car window.

Anthony opened the paper on his kitchen table-slash-desk. "See, Pari. Ralph filled up an extra half page yesterday with more national and world news from the Associated Press. Hmm. *President Tweets He's Not a Racist.* Well, that's nice to know."

"Maybe we should Tweet stuff. Or, actually, I could add a section on 'The Textbook Controversy' to my blog."

"You have a blog? I want to see it."

Anthony's phone rang. Ralph. "There's a man here to see you. Brought in a letter to the editor, or maybe it's an editorial, but he wants to give it to you personally. Andre Smyth, with a *y*."

They heard Andre's deep voice resounding from Ralph's

office. Anthony picked up the phrase "bourgeois urge to acquire."

"Here you are!" Ralph sounded like he was thanking somebody for pulling him out of quicksand. He took Andre's arm to usher him out the door. "Mr. Mansfield here and Ms., uh, Ms. Pari will talk to you out in the newsroom."

Pari held out her hand to thank Andre for helping them on the river. When he smiled, she ventured a hug. Andre was older than Pari and Anthony. He had pale blue eyes, a deep tan, and sun-bleached hair. Anthony stepped up and thanked him, too.

Andre began, "The nautical rules for a vessel overtaking a right-of-way vessel require two short blasts of a horn to request permission to pass, and, of course, a vessel under sail power alone is always the right-of-way vessel."

Anthony smiled. "Yes, but in my experience, if the overtaking vessel intends to capsize the right-of-way vessel for the fun of it, the horn regulation isn't generally observed."

Andre grinned. "Right. *Shoreline Construction* tries to capsize me all the time. I saw them heading towards you and rowed over as fast as I could."

"Coffee?" Anthony offered.

"No thanks. But could I have a cup of tea? With a spoon of honey in it?" Andre resumed his explanation of maritime law.

Pari and Anthony both jumped up. "I'll get the tea," Anthony said. "No, I'll get it," Pari insisted. "We don't have any honey, though."

Anthony pointed to the thick sheaf of papers Andre was holding. "Our editor says you brought in something for the paper?"

"Yes. The concept of separating news from opinion in a journal originated when Horace Greeley—"

Pari said, "Sorry to interrupt. Your tea, Mr. Smyth. We

don't have honey. I don't know if you heard me."

Andre set the mug on her carrel.

"May I?" Anthony took the papers from Andre's hand. He lifted the stack up and down as if weighing it. "This is longer than the typical piece that the *Ledger* prints, you realize." He began to read as Andre watched him expectantly.

The document began with an explanation of the ancient Roman stone-covered drainage ditches that were used to flush sewage into the Tiber River. "This is interesting," Anthony said. "I don't know if—"

"It was Emma Bovant who suggested I contact you," Andre remarked. "She said you helped get the Riverside Paradise project to repay my neighbors for the houses they took. She thought you might be interested in the new sewer line the county's putting in."

"Ah," Anthony said. "So is this related to the Riverside Paradise project?"

Andre nodded. "Yes. It's complicated. I think you'll need some time to read my explanation."

He stood up, smiled at Pari, and gave a little bow.

"Thanks again for rescuing me, Mr. Smyth."

"Not at all," Andre said. "It was like helping Venus in blue jeans rise from the sea." He turned to shake Anthony's hand and left without touching his tea.

"Crazy guy," Anthony said.

"Yeah? I kind of liked him."

"Uh-huh."

Ralph's door cracked open and he peeped out.

"It's safe, Ralph." Anthony winked.

Ralph reached to push up his glasses, which were already up on his head. "Something that might please you. I told Pop any paper worth its salt would try to talk to the school gunman, see what his story is. He reluctantly agreed."

Pari picked up her notebook.

Ralph said, "Only one person at a time can talk to a prisoner. Sorry. Pop wants Anthony to go."

Pari's pursed lips showed her disappointment. "Any story for me to work on, Ralph?"

He twisted one tip of his moustache, then the other. "We'll listen to the police and fire scanner."

Anthony dropped Andre's wad of papers on her carrel. "Here, Venus. Maybe you can go through this while I'm gone."

15

An upright citizen

O judgement! thou art fled to brutish beasts,
And men have lost their reason.

—Shakespeare, *Julius Caesar*

The Northbrook Detention Center sat on a dead-end road not far from the county police station. A tall pole flying an American flag marked the front of the wide brick building. Anthony found a place to park in the back of its fenced-in lot.

Visiting hours for relatives and friends were from 2:00 to 3:30 for Willard Scherd's detention block. Anthony was early. Every sound in the building echoed. He waited in front of the high, paneled visitor intake desk, sitting on a round white stool. Like every item in the area, it was fastened to the floor by a black rod.

At 2:00, he stood and approached the uniformed woman behind the desk, trying to get her attention away from a computer screen her eyes were glued to. A Tastee Donut box, lid open, sat next to the screen. He coughed. Cleared his throat. Said, "Excuse me." No response. "*Excuse* me." The response was an annoyed look down from the desk.

"I'd like to visit—" From the corner of his eye, he saw Willard Scherd himself flanked by his parents and a tall man in an exquisitely tailored suit. They were echoing down the long hallway in Anthony's direction towards a glass-enclosed booth opposite where he stood. Willard wasn't in prison clothes. He seemed to be wearing the same camouflage T-shirt he'd had on during the attack. It didn't look like he'd shaved. Sparse black hairs sprouted from his chin.

They stopped at the booth. Willard glared at the uniformed guard standing there, then across the hallway at Anthony. It was hard to interpret the meaning of his stare. His expression was totally blank. Anthony noticed Willard had a slight tic causing his head to twitch just a little to one side every now and then.

The man in the suit signed something on a clipboard that the guard handed him, and the group passed by Anthony on their way out. Anthony caught up with them outside the building. "Mr. Scherd," he called to Willard. "Mr. Scherd, I wonder if I could speak to you. I'm a reporter for the *Shady Park Ledger*."

At the word "reporter," the man in the suit stopped. Willard fixed Anthony in his blank stare.

"I represent Mr. Scherd," the man in the suit said.

Anthony said, "Since no one under 21 can obtain a gun permit in this state, and it's illegal for anyone to bring a gun onto school property, and he aimed the gun at someone, I assume those are the charges?"

The lawyer said, "The major charges have been dropped, and Mr. Scherd has been released on probation before judgment."

"My boy did nothing wrong," his mother yelled hoarsely.

Willard's head twitched. He stared at his mother, lips slightly parted.

The lawyer said, "We would appreciate it if the press would cease its fake news and stop slandering this upright citizen whose only concern was and will continue to be the safety of our community."

Anthony bristled. "Are you denying he aimed a gun at somebody during a Board of Education hearing?"

The lawyer turned away.

Anthony followed them until they stopped beside a black Suburban. "Mr. Scherd, Willard, if I could speak to you. Can you tell me what you were doing when you seemed to aim a gun at a speaker on the platform?"

Willard's eyes widened, not from hate or fear or surprise or any recognizable emotion. It seemed to be some kind of reflex.

Willard's father grabbed Anthony by the front of his shirt. His hands were huge, covered with yellow hair. He shook Anthony. "I've had enough of you snowflake libtard pussies. We're Americans. We have the right to carry guns. It's in the damn Constitution. If it hadn't of been for Willard, there would've been a major slaughter that night."

Anthony started writing in his notepad, and the man slapped it out of his hand. When he pulled his phone from his belt, the man knocked it to the ground and pushed him back against the SUV. "I hope somebody comes at you with a gun some day. You'll be wishing you had one to defend yourself."

Anthony persisted. "I'd just like to hear from Willard what he told the police about having the gun at the Board of Education hearing."

The lawyer stepped in, pushing them away from each other like a referee. He cleared his throat and told Anthony, "Mr. Scherd has no comment."

16

Guns for Jesus

"I come to bury Caesar, not to praise him."
—Shakespeare, *Julius Caesar*

Pari was in the newsroom so engrossed in poring over Andre's tome she didn't notice Anthony come in.

"Getting all the details about how the Romans drained sewage into the Tiber River?"

"Oh, hi. What happened to you?"

He didn't understand.

"Your shirt is torn. You have red marks on your neck."

He felt his neck. It did hurt when he touched it. "There was a little scuffle."

She gaped when he told her about it. "It sounds like the father is more violent than his son. I think you should stay away from them."

"The father's just a crass bully. If you could see the spaced-out look on Willard's face, you'd realize he's the one to be more afraid of."

Ralph slipped out of his office, the trace of a smirk forming below his moustache. "Bea Doggit called. Insists the *Ledger* cover some shindig at a Northbrook church tomorrow." He grinned at Anthony. "Thought you might want to take that yourself. You and Ms. Doggit being such good friends and all."

The Church of the Invokers of Jesus was on North-South Highway just on the county side of the railroad tracks marking the city line. A cross rose above the building, which had been a small hardware store until it was run out of business by a Home Depot put up a few miles away. Anthony parked in back next to a faded red pickup truck with a *Guns for Jesus* bumper sticker. A black Suburban slid in on the other side, nearly hitting his door. The vehicle's license plate read *NRA 2 AMD*. Anthony recognized the man who got out as the lawyer who'd managed to get Willard Scherd released from jail, almost certainly a lawyer from the National Rifle Association.

Two groups of sign bearers marched towards the church. The smaller group held placards saying things like "Stop the Carnage" and "Guns Are Killing Us." The signs of the larger group had messages like "The Right to Bear Arms" and "Good Guys With Guns." This group also carried signs supporting Andrew Mauer for re-election.

There was little to identify the room inside the building as a church except that a man with a black suit and a forced smile stood behind a lectern painted with a white cross. It was Pastor Mitchell Rainey, one of the major players in the Riverside Paradise scheme that Anthony had helped to expose.

On a slightly raised stage, seated in front of a huge *Elect Andrew Mauer* sign, Anthony recognized Beatrice Doggit along with the NRA lawyer and Willard Scherd. Two men in suits who had come in with the lawyer were quickly folding up all the metal chairs in the room, stacking them against the walls to clear space for the crowd pushing in to stand shoulder to shoulder. A gravely voice rang out, "Take my gun at your own risk. No liberal wimp can't stop me protecting my family." A woman next to Anthony cupped her hands to her mouth. "This is America, crybabies. Keep your hands off our guns." There were a few boos and cries of "Stop the killing" from another side of the room.

Anthony was squeezed in so tightly it was an effort to pull his phone off his belt. The crowd gradually hushed when Pastor Mitch, as he asked to be called, raised his hands. "Brothers and sisters in Jesus," he intoned. "Brothers and sisters in the Lord, will you pray with me? You who walk with Jesus, will you pray with me?" He opened a black bible on his lectern. "In the Gospel of John we read of the righteous anger of Jesus: 'And when he had made a scourge of small cords, he drove them all out of the temple.'" The pastor raised his eyes to the ceiling, then dropped them down, scanning the crowd. "With a scourge, my brothers and sisters, with a whip made of painful cords. This is how Jesus drove the sinners from the temple."

"Drive them out! Drive them out!" The crowd was excited.

The pastor's mouth seemed to flap like a puppet's when he raised his voice. "With a scourge we will drive the sinners out." He let the crowd roar a minute or so before he stretched out an arm to Bea with a toothy smile. She bent forward, a thick gold cross dangling from her neck into the cleavage framed by her red satin dress. Bea took the center of the stage.

"Jesus, hear our prayers." Bea held out her arms until the room was completely quiet. "We're here today to honor one among us who lives by the word of the Lord. To show our support for a young man who stands ready to drive sinners from our midst."

Anthony noticed a black woman squeezing through the doorway. It was Amanda Winwright. Bea paused, watching as Ms. Winwright edged along the wall towards the stage and stopped.

The lawyer sprang from his chair. "I think we'd all agree that acting to prevent a terrorist attack is no crime." He extended his hand to Willard, signaling him to stand. "Mr. Scherd has come here to speak out for our God-given right to carry firearms to defend ourselves and our loved ones. Stand and come forward, Mr. Scherd. Tell us what you saw, what you did to protect the people at that school meeting."

Willard's hands trembled as he stood, and the twitch of his head was noticeable. Looking at the floor, he let the lawyer and Bea maneuver him to the front of the stage.

"They want to hear from you," Bea urged. "These are supporters of your godly cause."

Willard stared blankly into the crowd.

"Tell them," Bea encouraged. "Tell them what Jesus says about sinners who deny him."

The young man opened his mouth and managed to bawl out, "Crusade for Jesus!" then "Army strong!" He then stood motionless, eyes wide but focused on nothing.

The lawyer prompted, "And, Mr. Scherd, as the pastor tells us, does Jesus require us to drive sinners from our temple?"

"Kill the enemy. Hooah!" Willard became more animated. "Hooah!" he repeated, and some in the crowd echoed him. But then he seemed to be drawing a blank and fell silent again.

The lawyer put his arm around him. "What Mr. Scherd is saying, I believe, is that our freedom is being threatened by forces determined to take it away. He was arrested, wrongly we believe, for what was an act of self-defense." The lawyer glanced at Pastor Mitch and the crowd, then added, "I'm sure you all agree. Jesus wants us to fight for our right to defend ourselves."

A voice thundered out, "Jesus would want our streets safe." It was Amanda Winwright. "Gun violence is the danger we're facing." The portly woman made her way towards the stage. She was the only black person in the room, and the crowd gave way.

The pastor's huge jaw dropped. It was clear she was going to take the stage. "An unexpected pleasure," he said. "The chair of the City Central Committee of the Republican party."

He shook her hand. "Paying a visit to our county, it seems."

Amanda was slightly taller than the pastor. She presented an imposing figure in a black pants suit set off by a triple strand of pearls around her neck and a diamond broach on her bosom. She began, "Like most of you, ladies and gentlemen, I come to show my support for Andrew Mauer. Like you, I support the party of Abraham Lincoln. I am not here to praise the opposing candidate."

There were a few cries of "Mauer. Mauer."

"Yes," Amanda said. "Mauer says his opponent is for big government."

"Booooo."

"His opponent wants the government to regulate every aspect of our lives." She paused to let the crowd murmur their displeasure. "We must fight against excessive and unwarranted regulations."

"Fight. Fight."

"But just yesterday a child playing on Cathedral Street in the City was hit by a stray bullet, a bullet fired by a shop owner at a robber. The robber got away, but the little girl died." Amanda paused to take a deep breath. "Andrew Mauer says proposed new gun regulations are excessive. Do you want to know what's excessive? We have over 300 people a year shot to death in the City, many from stray gunfire. That's what I call excessive."

The crowd got quiet, although one woman called out, "Guns for protection."

Amanda went on. "Excessive regulations stifle our freedom. Andrew Mauer says this, and I agree with him. But excessive gun violence is killing our city. I would not like to see this plague spread to Piskasanet County. Common-sense regulations to prevent gun deaths are not excessive."

There were a few shouts of support. The pastor moved towards Amanda, but she went on. "Andrew Mauer's party says preventing mentally ill people from buying guns is excessive regulation. I don't think so. They say requiring background checks for gun show and online gun purchases is excessive. I don't think so. They say it is our second amendment right to own assault rifles made to kill masses of military enemies. I don't think so. For personal protection, I think that kind of gun is excessive."

"Thank you, Ms. Winwright." The pastor held out his hand.

But Amanda wasn't quite finished. "I'm not here to criticize Andrew Mauer," she said. "I'm here to support him. But I'm also here to beg you—to beg you to ask his party to drop their objections to sensible gun control."

Anthony's phone was cracked since Willard's father knocked it onto the parking lot, but it still worked. He was holding it up to record all this. Amanda nodded to him as she made her way out of the church. He'd interviewed her before but hadn't written anything yet. Now he was determined to print an article about this meeting. Or rally. Whatever it was. Whether Pop liked it or not.

"So. Those are my notes on the gun rally."

Pari dropped his pad onto his little table. "Sounds like a scary crowd."

"Now look at Ralph's edited version that's going in tomorrow's paper—the version Pop insisted on." He pulled it up on his screen. It was a single page. The headline: *Gun Drawn to Defend against Terrorist, Lawyer Says*. "It doesn't mention Amanda Winwright at all. It's half of my story."

Pari's voice was breaking. "*To Defend against Terrorist.* So everybody will think my friend Shahnaz is a terrorist?"

She looked back through his notes with unsteady hands. "And now the man who aimed a gun at her is on the loose. I guess he still has his gun?"

"The police kept that one, but there are others. His father referred to 'all our guns.'"

II

17

Take 'em all out!

It was, in the night, as though I had been faced by my own reflection in the depth of a somber and immense mirror.

—Edgar Allan Poe, *William Wilson*

Pari sprinkled some of her special seasoning into the tomato sauce and ground beef Anthony was stirring in his only frying pan. She "practically lived there nowadays," her mother had teased. Mrs. O'Leary said it was nice that Anthony had found "a companion." It was rare, though, that Pari stayed the whole night. She said it was because her parents would worry, but Anthony knew his accommodations weren't really adequate for Pari to think of moving in.

Mrs. O'Leary had given him a second chair. The worn upholstered seat smelled like Thumper, but it was a welcome addition. They ate spaghetti at the table and turned on the early evening TV news.

"Here! Now! The latest news, up-to-date reports, weather, and sports! This is WPSK News with John Rowland and Megyn Drumpfer."

John Rowland came on. "Megyn is on assignment today. For our breaking story, we go to Victoria Whitman at the Church of the Invokers of Jesus in Northbrook. Victoria, what do you have for us?"

"John, I'm standing in front of the Northbrook church. It's closed now, but this is the place where the disturbing revelation came YESTERDAY that the young man previously arrested at the Board of Education HEARING was in fact responding to a terrorist attack. The young MAN'S actions were what prevented the ATTACK."

John Rowland said, "Victoria, have you found out any more about the aborted attack?"

"John, we only know that an attack was planned. No further details have been made public."

"Thank you so much, Victoria, for this shocking report. I know you'll keep us up to date as the story develops."

Pari raked her fork through her noodles. "That was disgusting. A rehash—a misconstruction, really—of Ralph's highly censored version of your story in this morning's *Ledger*."

"Yeah. I need to set her straight. I will."

"Good. She's standing truth on its head."

It was crazy, but despite the harm Victoria had done, Anthony was impressed by how quickly she'd achieved her dream. "Do you think she looked the part?"

"What?" Pari slammed down her fork.

"No, just, her girlfriend said her hair was too short for TV."

"Anthony. I can't believe you. People are thinking Willard is some kind of hero. And they know who he was aiming the gun at." Her eyes were teary. "I'm in a panic thinking he'll be coming after Shahnaz and her family, and you're wondering if Victoria's hair looked good on TV."

"No, I—"

"I have to go home. My mother needs to warn Shahnaz."

Pari was right. He had to stop Victoria's dangerous broadcasts. But Victoria didn't answer his calls or texts that night or the next morning. He knocked on Pop's door and found him brushing cigar ashes from blueprints spread across his desk. "Little busy right now. Not bringing me another crypto leftist anti-gun defamation of one of our distinguished county residents, I hope."

"It's about Victoria."

"Well, go ahead, sit down."

"I guess you've seen her TV report. In his edit of my *Ledger* story, Ralph made sure to say it was the gunman's lawyer who claimed he was trying to prevent a terrorist attack. Victoria left that part out and stated the claim as a fact."

Pop jammed out his cigar, slowly nodding his head. "I saw it. I told her not everything somebody says is a fact. She just asked me how she looked. Not sure she got my point. Might as well try to talk sense into a cat."

"Pop, I hope she becomes a popular TV news personality and all. But a report like that can ruin the reputation of an innocent person. Shahnaz Delpak isn't a terrorist."

"No proof yet, but how can you be so sure? Have another look at those pictures you took during the attack. The hejab woman is directly facing the teacher in the first row who got shot. The Scherd guy's gun wasn't fired."

"The hejab woman, as you call her, opposes the new school textbooks that Beatrice Doggit introduced. Is it a coincidence that it was Bea who arranged the Invokers church rally where they implied Shahnaz was a terrorist?"

"You're saying Ms. Doggit has a bone to pick?" He chuckled at his own joke. "I thought you were showing Vicky the ropes while you two sat together in the newsroom all that time. She says you were." His heavy brow furrowed. "Don't know who she's taking the lead from nowadays. That Rowland fellow, I guess." He leaned towards Anthony. "Listen. I'm not sure he can be trusted. Our girl Esmeralda told my wife something. She said Rowland tried to hit on her. Wife says Esmeralda's just fantasizing. I didn't mention it to Victoria. I don't know."

Anthony decided it was probably even more stressful to be Victoria's parent than her boyfriend. "Anyway, Pop, this

Willard guy is dangerous."

Pop narrowed his eyes. "Probably right. And Victoria says Rowland wants her to interview him. I want you to feel him out first. You've got 24 hours. Come back to me with what you find."

Mrs. Scherd peeped one blue eye out through the open crack of her door, blinking at the bright sunlight. Anthony tried to force a jovial voice. "Congratulations are in order, Mrs. Scherd. It's Anthony Mansfield again. I hope you've read the *Ledger* article saying the lawyer describes your son as a defender of our citizens." She opened the door wider, still with a suspicious glower. "The social media are calling Willard a hero," Anthony said. She let him in.

"I'd like to finally get his side of the story. Do you think that would be possible?"

"He's in the back. In his room. I don't know." She led Anthony outside past two vehicles sitting on the grass, a rusted pickup truck raised on cement blocks with its wheels off and a small gray car with one red fender. They entered a huge garage with *Willard Scherd Plumbing* over the entrance, and she knocked on a smaller door inside. No answer. "Willard, somebody here to see you." No answer. She opened the door. "Guess it's OK to go on in." The sound of an explosion boomed from a speaker, followed by an artificial, synthesized voice saying, "Got 'im." Willard's mother turned back to the house.

The darkened room had a strong smell of gun oil. At first, Anthony didn't see Willard. Instead, he was struck by an array of copper pipes covering the walls, soldered together to form sturdy brackets and shelves that allowed a free flow of air to the masses of electronic equipment they held.

Anthony was impressed with the pipe shelving idea and with the equipment. A network router with at least four antennae sprouted yellow ethernet cables feeding into a hard-drive enclosure with a massive tower of bays, into a disk duplicator, into an uninterruptible power supply block, and into three laptops. Blue USB cables connected the laptops to each other and to three different printers and the hard drive tower.

Anthony was embarrassed to realize he'd like to have a setup like this himself.

Except for the guns, that is. Copper pipe brackets also held military rifles and pistols of all types on three of the four walls. Under each gun hung a color printout of a picture showing, Anthony presumed, a scene in which this kind of weapon was used in a battle or skirmish or by a sniper on a rooftop. He recognized one picture as an Associated Press photo from the third battle of Fallujah which he'd seen in the *New York Times*.

As his eyes adjusted better to the dark, he made out Willard sitting at a game console in front of a screen that flashed with soldiers in army fatigues shooting balls of fire at ragged men in turbans whenever they stepped into a long dusty alley between shattered adobe walls. "Take 'em all out!" a shooter cried out. "Aargh," a turbaned man shouted out in pain, blood squirting from his head as he fell to the dirt.

"Mr. Scherd? Willard?" Anthony raised his voice. "Mr. Scherd!"

Willard jerked and turned.

"They're calling you a hero, Willard. I was hoping you'd tell me your story."

Willard switched off the video game. He sat stiff and silent.

"Nice setup you have here."

Willard grinned but didn't speak. He turned back to the laptop, hit a few keys, and brought up something on his screen. It was a video of an ISIS beheading. He studied Anthony, who watched for a moment before having to turn away.

"Huh huh," Willard said. Anthony took it to mean "How about that?"

"That's hard to watch, but I think I know what you mean, Willard. There's some terrible cruelty going on in the world." He added, "In the name of religion."

Willard stopped the video. "Huh?"

"I guess beheadings like that make you want to fight back," Anthony ventured.

Willard shrugged and for the first time actually spoke. He said, "How about you? That don't make you want to fight against evil?" He turned back to the screen and after a few clicks was immediately absorbed in a search for "weapons" on eBay. Apparently, the interview was over.

Anthony stood there for a minute. On the floor beside Willard's computer desk was an open camouflage backpack. It held a thin blue loose leaf binder, a Star Wars lunchbox, and something wrapped in a dirty hand towel. Sticking out from the towel was the tip of a thick gray gun barrel.

Anthony waited at his desk while Pop took the report into his office. Willard was crazy and dangerous. That was the only conclusion. In a few minutes, he heard a booming "No" in Pop's office. Pop came out and dropped the story on Anthony's desk. "I cannot let Victoria interview this man."

"No. But it's OK to print the article?"

Pop shook his head. "Too dangerous. You realize what will happen. Victoria will rehash the article on TV, probably standing in front of Willard's garage. We're not going to let that happen."

When he was back in his apartment, the recollection of Willard's room in the garage haunted Anthony. He cast his eyes around his own room—at the computer, the boxes of files, the copy machine, the router, his note pad—and shuddered as if he had peered into a mirror and discovered a frightful reflection of himself. He and Willard were both driven, both confident in their view of the world. They were both determined to make their mark. He wondered if they were both crazy.

18

Breaking news

Falsehood flies, and truth comes limping after it.
—Jonathan Swift, *The Examiner*, XIV

A call from Pari helped him shake the idea.

"Sorry I left in a huff last night, Anthony. Forgive me?"

"I talked to Pop about Victoria. He doesn't like her reports, either, but he doesn't seem to have much influence over her."

"Let's forget it for now. How about coming over for dinner? Mom made khoresh. You said you like it."

"Sounds great," he lied. He was more a fried chicken and Ramen guy.

Her mother, Mastaneh, gave him a warm hug. Her father put his hand on his shoulder. They acted as if they'd known him for years.

He could develop a taste for khoresh, he figured. The flan Mastaneh made for dessert was great. After dinner, her father said, "The faculty at the college is up in arms over the new conservative school curriculum in the county. A lot of them have kids in the schools."

Instinctively, Anthony took out his notebook.

"Going to interview my dad?" Pari laughed.

Anthony felt a blush but said, "Why not? He was on the Board of Education before they made the change."

"There's supposed to be a program on Public Broadcasting tonight about the curriculum controversy in several states," Pari's father said.

Mastaneh turned on the TV.

"—breaking news. We go to Victoria Whitman, who is standing with Beatrice Doggit at the school where the recent gun attack took place. Victoria, what do you have for us?"

"John, I'm TALKING to Beatrice Doggit of the Piskasanet Board of Education. She is upset that the police do not have the SHOOTER in custody. Members of the Board and parents of the students HERE are demanding that they MAKE an arrest."

"Victoria, I understand Ms. Doggit was at the hearing when the attack occurred. What does she tell us?"

Victoria held the microphone for Bea to talk.

"We want results," Bea said. "That's what I can tell you. We don't know why the woman they originally arrested was released. The parents who fear for their children's lives want an explanation."

Victoria took the mic back and said, "John."

"Victoria, thank you so much. We'll have continuing coverage of this story as it develops. Keep tuned to WPSK TV."

Mastaneh wrung her hands. "Shahnaz. That's Shahnaz they're talking about. As if she's some kind of terrorist."

Pari's father shut off the TV. "And now the whole county probably thinks it's true."

Pari nudged Anthony's arm. You have to write about Scherd so the public knows he's the one who's dangerous."

"I did. Ralph liked it, but Pop was afraid Victoria would get hold of it and ... anyway, he wouldn't print it." Anthony gripped his fists. He was sure Victoria's head was full of scatterbrained ambition rather than malice. It didn't matter. She had to be stopped.

Controlling Victoria wasn't going to be easy. The *Ledger* TV downstairs in the online office was tuned to the afternoon news. Anthony and Pari sat watching.

"—we take you to Victoria Whitman at the Shady Park

Elementary/Middle School."

The school behind her was closed and dark. "John," Victoria said, "I'm standing where a demonstration was held earlier today by MOTHERS demanding protection for their children."

"Victoria, thank you. I understand you spoke to one of the mothers who is concerned about the children's safety."

"Yes, John. We have a clip." The video had been made hours ago. Victoria must have returned with a cameraman long after everyone was gone to present her "Live News" broadcast. "John," she said in the video clip, "I have Britney Grosbeck with me, who says she fears a repeat here of the INCIDENT at Northbrook High."

In the video, Britney was holding a sign. *Protect our children. Arm our teachers.* A few other mothers, attracted by the TV camera crew, were standing near her, most of them talking or texting on their cell phones. One held the sign for Britney while she took the microphone.

Eyes wide and glassy in the sunlight, Britney barked out, "This has to stop. Teachers must be armed to protect our kids. Terrorists are right here in our county. Look at Facebook, and you'll see. The Northbrook terrorist was sent here by ISIS, the Islamic State. It's been proven. If this woman stays on the loose, there's nothing we can do but arm ourselves. I have assurance from the County Executive that he'll help us get signatures to support the bill that a House of Delegates candidate promises to introduce requiring teachers to carry guns."

The TV news went live again. "That was Britney Grosbeck, John, demanding more protection for SCHOOL children. John."

"Victoria, thank you. Rescinding the law against firearms in schools would require statewide support. Is the candidate for House of Delegates confident he can bring this off?"

"John, according to Britney Grosbeck, in her words, 'all Frank Fortunato needs is enough signatures.' John."

"Thank you, Victoria. There seemed to be a lot of cars blocking the street in the clip of the demonstration. What can you tell us about that?"

"John, I'm told it's like that every day when school lets out. The mothers say they can't wait for the bus to bring their CHILDREN home. They'll be late for ballet lessons, soccer practice, other after-SCHOOL activities. But there's no room for all their cars on the school parking lot, so they simply stop their cars in the road waiting to PICK their children up. John."

"Thank you, Victoria." The handsome face of John Rowland returned to the screen. "We'll be sure to keep you up to date on efforts to make our schools safe."

Anthony turned to Pari. Tears were rolling down her cheeks. He couldn't think of anything to comfort her.

"We can't let this go, Anthony. People have to be told the truth. ISIS? Shahnaz is Iranian. Iran is the staunchest enemy of ISIS."

"I know. It seems you can say anything you want on Facebook or Instagram or Twitter. And if people *want* to believe it, they will."

19

Shh!

"It's really dreadful," she muttered to herself, "the way all the creatures argue. It's enough to drive one crazy!"

—Lewis Carroll,
Alice's Adventures in Wonderland

Lincoln Navigators, Toyota Highlanders, Suburbans, and at least two Range Rovers jammed the parking lot at the Shady Park Library, where the County Executive and Frank Fortunato, a candidate for the State House of Delegates, were holding a discussion and signing of the Arm Our Teachers petition. Clearly most people attending were coming from the east parts of Shady Park, from Nottingham Estates and Bay Hills. Anthony had to park his west-side Kia a block away on the street.

Women with the blond bangs and hairbands that Victoria favored, or at least had favored, walked towards the library holding signs over their heads as protection from the light drizzle. *Protect Our Children. Make America Safe Again.* A young policeman stood just inside the doorway to the meeting room, looking bored. Anthony came in and paused to take out his notepad.

The wide, tightly skirted hip of a woman brushed against his leg. The woman turned, indignant, alcohol breath wafting through purple lips. "Hands off, if you don't mind," she squawked, loud enough to make people turn and gape at Anthony. It was Britney Grosbeck, the woman who'd claimed to be "armed for protection" at the Board of Education hearing in Northbrook. "Ah, a reporter," she said, noticing his *Shady*

Park Ledger nametag. "I wish the TV news was here. Then we'd get the publicity we deserve." Her full hips grazed one person after another as she forced her way to the front of the room.

County Executive Mauer rose from behind a table where he sat with Fortunato, Bea, and the chair of the Board of Education. He scanned the crowd with a frozen smile. "Derek," he nodded to Britney's husband. "Good to see you here. Your wife has been very helpful in getting this petition started. Pastor Mitch, glad you could make it. I hope everyone concerned for our children's safety will know that I hear you, and I'm with you."

"Mauer, Mauer," someone shouted as if trying to start a chant.

Mauer grinned. "We're here to ask you to sign a child safety petition that my voters are calling for and that my friend Frank Fortunato has promised to introduce as a bill in the Legislature if he's elected." He pointed to pads of paper on the table. "Now we can take any questions you might have."

"Guns for teachers!" a woman shouted.

Fortunato rose to a formidable height behind the table. His black bushy hair and deep tan gave him an athletic look. "Yes," he boomed, "this will happen if you give me your vote. I can promise you that."

The blond women stood and waved their signs. "Guns for the good guys," a man shouted. The Board of Education chairman sipped some water from a plastic bottle and tapped diffidently on the table with a gavel. His widened eyes projected a look of bewilderment bordering on fear. Word was he'd been elected chair of the Board because he was a "nice guy," with no particular opinions, who would go with the flow. Anthony still couldn't remember his name.

Ignoring the chairman, Britney bumped against the table, turned, and cried out, "Just come up and sign the petition.

How could there be any questions? I see parents who fear for the lives of their children, who want our teachers to protect them in our schools."

"It's their job!" a woman agreed.

"Give them guns!" someone else shouted.

A rumble of voices joined in. A man in a dark suit boomed out, "The terrorists are armed. So arm our teachers." Anthony saw it was the National Rifle Association lawyer who had defended Willard Scherd. He looked around to see if he could identify anybody else. Amanda Winwright, standing in a corner, was easy to recognize.

"I have a question," a woman in a State University sweatshirt shouted out from the back of the room. "Teachers, do you really want to be armed?"

Anthony was surprised to see Ms. Ernst raise her hand. In a trembling alto, she answered, "No." She took a breath as if to go on, but that was all she managed to get out. A heavyset teacher next to her raised her hand. It was Ms. Costello, the teacher who had grabbed Willard Scherd by the neck at the School Board hearing. "No," Ms. Costello echoed. Then another teacher raised her hand. "No." Then another.

Britney aimed a long, glossy fingernail at Ms. Ernst. "This woman who's afraid to carry a gun was wounded by a terrorist at Northbrook High School, if you remember. If she had been armed, that wouldn't have happened."

Anthony was videoing everything. He waited for somebody to point out that Britney, by her own account, *had* been carrying a gun when that shooting occurred. No one did.

The chairman stood, eyes shifting from one person to another in the room. He banged his gavel harder than before. "Order," he muttered. Then louder, "Order." A white haired librarian slipped in through the doorway. Anthony wondered if she was going to say "Shh," but she simply rolled her eyes, then left, shutting the door behind her.

Britney placed herself in front of the chairman, blocking him from view. "Well, Ms. Ernst, what do you say to that? Are you going to tell us you don't wish you'd had a gun to defend yourself?"

"Guns have no place in school," Ms. Ernst said. "I urge you not to sign this petition."

"Listen to your teachers." Amanda Winwright's sonorous voice brought a hush to the room. Up in Northbrook, closer to the City, the residents knew who she was, but here in Shady Park she was less known. Amanda was a large dark woman, and the gaping mouths and wide eyes around the room reflected an instinctive fear. Anthony heard whispering. "Watch out." "What's she up to?" One woman ran to the door, alarming the cop standing there.

"If you want your children to be safe, keep them as far as possible from guns," Amanda said. "Bringing guns around children is asking for trouble. I know. In the City, scores of children are wounded or killed by guns every year, and not by terrorists but by crossfire, by accident, by family members with bad aim."

Frank Fortunato stood again and crossed his arms above his head. "Time out, everybody. We're not here for another debate on guns. The parents of our county know what they want. This is the time to show your support for an Executive and for a Delegate who will turn your wish into law."

County Executive Mauer snatched the gavel from the Board chairman and gave a single cracking rap on the table that made Bea jump. "Yes, the time for discussion is over," he squeaked. "Whoever is in favor of this referendum, you may come up to the table to sign."

"But first," Bea called out, rising beside Mauer, "let us pray for inspiration. Pastor Mitch, would you come up to the table?"

The pastor sidled forward, smoothing his black hair with

his fingers. Anthony wondered if he would repeat what he'd said in the Church of the Invokers of Jesus. He did. Apparently, when Jesus drove the money changers from the temple, he was signaling that teachers should be armed.

Ms. Ernst limped to the table and stood with her arms outstretched as if to block the petition from being signed. "Please," she said. "This whole idea is absurd."

Britney yanked her arm. "Move aside, bitch. You give teachers a bad name." Holding Ms. Ernst by the wrist, Britney hissed, "If you can even call yourself a teacher. Everybody, this is the most unfair teacher you'll ever come across, just ask my daughter. Just ask the principal who kicked her out of his school." She tugged at Ms. Ernst's wrist and wrenched her to the floor. Anthony saw it was going to be hard for Ms. Ernst to get up with her wounded leg and forced his way to the front to give her a hand.

As Ms. Ernst struggled to get up, Ms. Costello came and put Britney into a choke hold from behind.

"Cat fight!" a man's voice called out.

The young policeman, mouth gaping open, approached the grappling women. Ms. Costello seemed old enough to be his mother. "Ma'am," he said. "Ma'am, step back." Then to Britney, "Ma'am, you too."

Britney said, "No way," and when Ms. Costello let go, gave her a punch in the stomach.

"That does it," the cop said. "Ma'am, I'm going to have to arrest you for assault." He reached for his handcuffs.

The County Executive stepped around the table motioning for the cop to back off. "I'll take care of this, Officer. No need for alarm. Mrs. Grosbeck here is a respected member of the community. I can vouch for her."

Anthony helped Ms. Ernst limp towards the door as the Exec was calling everyone to come and sign the petition. It looked like about two-thirds of those attending went up to stand in line.

Ms. Ernst was trembling when he held her car door. She said, "You're not going to mention—"

"I won't put your name in the news report," he assured her. "You're very brave, Ms. Ernst. And everybody I talk to tells me you're an excellent teacher."

"Do you think this petition will ever become a law?"

"My publisher says no. He says it will get support from our conservative county, but there's no way enough people throughout the state will back it. And this is confidential. He says Andrew Mauer knows that, too. He's just posing to get the votes of the security moms."

Anthony typed up a full report on the meeting and emailed it to Ralph from his apartment. Then he called Pari. She chuckled at his description of the "cat fight," but her mind was somewhere else. "Anthony, it's so unfair that people think Shahnaz is some kind of terrorist."

20

Making America great

If a lie be believed only for an hour, it hath done its work.
—Jonathan Swift, *The Art of Political Lying*

The next morning, Anthony's miniature fridge held nothing but half a head of lettuce, blackening at the edges, and creamer for coffee. He made a cup, then picked up the paper on his landing to see what version of his gun petition story Pop had allowed in the paper.

Mauer, Fortunato Support Voter Mandate to Arm Teachers

Oh, well. He stopped at the Grab 'n Go on the way to the newsroom. Instead of Kaila, Tran was there, the Vietnamese night manager whose whole family had been falsely arrested in a political "crackdown" on illegal immigrants staged by the County Executive using his influence with some Federal ICE officials. Anthony's reporting had made it known that Tran and his wife were actually permanent residents, and their children were U.S. citizens.

"Mr. Anthony, welcome. I am happy to see you."

"You, too, Tran. Kaila on vacation?"

"No, it is so sad." Tran said two customers attacked Kaila in the store early that morning. His nose was broken, and his face was cut. "He call police and wait for me to come. Then he go to hospital."

"You have a security camera in the store?"

"Yes. Video in crowd. Police get piswar to see."

"Crowd?"

Tran circled his finger up into the air.

"Ah, cloud. Password. Can I look at it?"

"Sorry. Not know how."

Anthony crammed down an egg muffin as he sped past auto body shops, liquor stores, and motorhome displays towards the police department in Northbrook. His friend Rob was behind the intake counter and let him go back to his office to watch the video.

The video of the incident turned his stomach. A bulky man in his fifties, white shirt with "Free Paint Estimates" above its pocket turned to Kaila while pouring himself a cup of coffee and said, "What're you looking at, raghead? Go back where you came from. That's how we start making America great again."

"Careful. Hot," Kaila called to him. The coffee spilled over onto the customer's hand. He threw the cup onto the floor, then crashed the whole decanter onto the floor. A curly haired man with "AC Tune Ups" on the back of a blue shirt came up to look.

"Son of a bitch made me burn myself," the painting estimator said. Kaila brought a mop. "Careful of the glass. Step back please." The estimator slapped him. When Kaila held up his hand to defend himself, the AC tune up guy punched him in the face and threw him down on the floor. Both customers left before Kaila could get up. The video didn't show what vehicles they were driving.

"Any idea who these guys were?" Anthony asked Rob.

"No company names on their clothing. Lots of contractors stop in early in the morning for coffee on their way to jobs. The victim says he didn't recognize them. We'll put out pictures, but it's not likely we'll find them."

Rob let Anthony copy pictures of the men to take back to the newsroom. Pari was busy, so he didn't show them to her before turning them in to Ralph. Anyway, he didn't want to get her even more upset about the anti-foreign rage that had swelled up recently. Ralph accepted the story without edits.

Store Clerk Victim of Hate Attack

After the story and indistinct pictures came out the next morning, the *Ledger* received a press release from the County Executive's office declaring the incident a simple argument and saying it couldn't be determined who started it. WPSK TV had obviously received the same release:

"John, I'm here at the Grab 'n Go where YESTERDAY an argument at first suspected to be a hate crime TOOK PLACE. We are told by the office of the County Executive that it is impossible to determine WHETHER the clerk or the customers initiated the argument. The injuries to the clerk, not a U.S. native, are said to be minor. There is no indication yet that his fight with the customers was an ACT of terrorism. But the County Executive says we must be on the alert. John."

"Thank you so much, Victoria. These are dangerous times we live in. Take care."

Anthony texted Victoria: *You have to stop these deceitful reports.* No response. He called Pari. She was crying when she answered. "Shahnaz is getting threats, Anthony. She's scared. I don't know what to do. Mom wants me to go talk to her."

"I'll go with you."

The hallway in the Northbrook Apartments was dark. The bulbs in the ceiling fixtures had probably burned out long ago. There were little metal frames on the doors for the residents to insert their names, but none of them did. Most of them were immigrants supplying cheap labor for wealthy families in Shady Park, Nottingham Estates, and Bay Hills. Many were here illegally, which made them even cheaper to hire.

Black graffiti were spray painted on Shahnaz's door. One said, "Take 'em all out." It smelled fresh. Anthony snapped a photo.

"Who is it?" They heard a lock turn and a chain lock rattle before Shahnaz opened the door. Her son stood close beside her. "Jim," she said. "Make some tea, would you?"

"No tea," Pari insisted. She didn't even sit down. "Jim, my mom says you've had some trouble at school?"

"Some kids are saying my mother wants to blow things up. They say she hates America."

Shahnaz added that Jim's girlfriend wouldn't talk to him any more.

"This weird guy was talking to her," Jim explained with a catch in his throat. "Now she's afraid of me."

"What did he look like, the weird guy?" Anthony unclipped his phone.

"Just, I don't know. He has tattoos. Real short hair, like short but sticking up. He stares at people. He started shoving me around, then other guys did, too."

Shahnaz gasped, obviously hearing this description for the first time.

Anthony scrolled through the pictures on his phone and held one up for Jim.

"That's him."

Shahnaz took the phone for a closer look. "Oh, no. Oh, no."

Jim said, "What's wrong, Mom?" Then it hit him. "Is that the guy with the gun?"

"Yes, I hope you told Ms. Ernst about him?"

"I told her a little. She told the class not to believe everything they see on Facebook. She said there's no way our family are terrorists."

"Any other problems?" Anthony tapped his pencil on his pad.

Shahnaz swallowed. "We've been getting threatening phone calls on our landline."

Pari was shaking and had to sit down. Anthony stood writing in his notebook. "What did they say?"

"Terrorist. Get out of our country. America first. I stopped answering, and they left messages."

Anthony listened to the messages. One sounded like Bea Doggit. "This is a Christian country. Stop trying to destroy the curriculum we voted on or we will silence you." Another was a long, breathy pause followed by "Hooah! Shoot to kill."

"Have you notified the police?"

"I'm afraid to. It was terrifying when they took me in and questioned me."

Anthony called Rob.

"The police say not to answer the phone unless you know the caller. And don't answer the door unless you know who it is."

"This can't be happening," Pari muttered through her fingers.

"Rob said calls like this usually stop after a while." Anthony knew this wouldn't be much comfort.

Shahnaz's cell phone rang. Anthony couldn't understand the Farsi except that he thought he heard the word "pistol."

"This is bad," Shahnaz told them. "My husband's thinking of bringing home the pistol the owner keeps at the gas station. To protect us, he says."

"No, Shahnaz." Pari wrung her hands.

"Call him back," Anthony begged. "It's even more dangerous if there's a gun in the house." He glanced at Jim. "Anybody could be curious, pick it up, and by accident—" He choked up and couldn't finish.

21

Fear

"How vain and vile a passion is this fear,
What base uncomely things it makes men do!"
—Ben Jonson, *Sejanus His Fall*

The old part of Shady Park, where Anthony lived, was originally a station on a railroad line that ran from the City, through Piskasanet County, and across the river to Colonial Town, the state's capital. Anthony's grandparents remembered the passenger trains from their childhood, but the railroad, which traced its beginnings to the late 19th century, was finally put out of business by the construction of North-South Highway. Before Anthony was born, the railroad had been torn up and made into a bike trail. Ms. Ernst lived in one of the old cottages that backed up to the trail.

Worried about repercussions if the school knew she was talking to the press, she had agreed, after some coaxing, to meet Anthony not at school but at her home. He could walk there from where he lived. The bike trail was used less for bikes than for mommy weight control—Anthony's term. In the mornings, after Shady Park mothers had walked their children to school, they could be found in pairs or threes fast-walking along the trail, swinging their arms and chattering to each other. Most held cell phones and wore earbuds, presumably for fear of missing an important call.

Ms. Ernst's little wooden cottage was painted a cream color, at least originally. Light green mold tinted the walls. It sat under huge oak trees, and the north side of the roof was covered with moss. An arched trellis with late blooming pink roses led to the door.

"I have to apologize for how my house looks." Ms. Ernst fluttered her fingers across the room timidly. It was spotless but looked like an office supply store. Translucent blue plastic bins in the rear of the room held manila folders. Translucent red bins along the inner wall were filled with felt tip pens, colored pencils, tubes of glitter, rolls of star stickers, construction paper, scotch tape, scissors of various sizes. More stacks of smaller plastic boxes with lids stood on each side of the window. A gray cat sat on one of these.

A thick pink rug covered most of the floor, and on it was what looked like a work in progress, a sheet of poster board labeled *TODAY'S PROJECTS* in gold ink. There was no desk in the room. It seemed that Ms. Ernst worked on the floor. She brought two chairs from the kitchen for them to sit on. She sat holding one leg stretched out a little, and Anthony noticed her calf was still bandaged.

"How is your leg, Ms. Ernst?"

"Better. Thanks." She smoothed her long pleated skirt down over her legs the best she could. "It doesn't hurt much now."

Anthony scratched his head with his pencil. "I keep turning that night over in my mind. Some things just don't make sense."

Ms. Ernst pushed her frameless glasses higher on her nose with one finger. "I'm trying to put it all behind me."

He pulled out his notebook. "That's best, I guess." He bit his lip, hesitating to go on. "I wanted to ask if you know Shahnaz Delpak's son?"

"Jim. Yes."

"Can you confirm something he told me? He said he's going to quit the school baseball team because some students are harassing him. Have you noticed that?"

"Yes, I have. They're really cruel. They say his family are

all terrorists. They tell him to go back to his own country."

"Any physical abuse?"

"Just, you know, pushing him out of the line for the cafeteria. Smacking him on the back of his head. It was one boy who started doing that."

"Willard Scherd?"

Ms. Ernst nodded.

"And Jim says you told the class .... What did you tell the class?"

"That Jim's not a terrorist. That America is his country as much as it is theirs. He was born here."

"Where do you think the students get the idea Jim is a threat to them?"

"Obviously, from their parents. Plus, they see it on Facebook, so I'm told. Apparently, Facebook lets us create a bubble of like-minded people to live in." Ms. Ernst looked around the room as if to examine her own bubble. The cat let out a low meow.

Anthony noticed a shelf full of photos, ceramic trinkets, knitted bags, drawings. "Gifts from your students?"

She nodded again, lips pursed. Anthony realized they were probably from her Shady Park students before she'd been unwillingly transferred to Northbrook High. At one end of the shelf he noticed a framed newspaper clipping. "Mind if I have a look?" It was his own article about the Bay Foundation adopting an idea from a science project by Emma Bovant's son Todd.

"You know Todd Bovant, it seems."

"A delightful boy. And thank you for your article."

Anthony closed his notebook. "I have a request, Ms. Ernst. If you hear what the other teachers are saying about being armed, would you give me a call? Strictly in confidence, of course."

Ms. Ernst managed a weak smile. "In confidence? That's

good. I don't know where they'd transfer me next."

Ralph was divorced, raising a 10-year-old son on his own, with the help of a sister. He would stay late in the newsroom if necessary to get an important story in by the deadline, but he always tried to get home in time to eat a late dinner with his son. Anthony was determined to get this story on students bullying Shahnaz's son Jim into the next morning's paper. The terrorist paranoia had to stop, and Willard Scherd had to be revealed as a danger to society.

He went straight from Ms. Ernst's house to his carrel in the newsroom, found the home number of the Northbrook High principal using the *Ledger*'s subscription to Lookitup, and got him on the phone. Principal Matthew Higgenbottom confirmed there had been "hazing incidents" at the school as a result of the shooting and said he had instructed all teachers to speak to the students about treating each other with courtesy.

Terrorist Paranoia Threatens Parents, Students. This is the headline Anthony would suggest to Ralph—if he could get him to print the story. He had big hopes because Pop was on a duck hunting trip.

Ralph had him sit in his office while he read it. The frown on his face was unusual. "I know," he said, looking up. "Bobby told me this is happening here in Shady Park, too. Bobby got into a fight with a kid who called his best friend a terrorist because of his dark skin. The guy's one-fourth Puerto Rican."

"Ralph, I've got claims of harassment by Shahnaz and her son Jim, the principal's confirmation that there was 'hazing' at the school, and instances of this hazing testified to by 'a teacher'—without naming anybody. And I've already reported this to the police."

"You're right," Ralph agreed. "It's all there. As I see it, you're just telling our readers what's going on." Ralph flipped his glasses up onto his head. "It's going in."

"And the headline?"

"*Conflicts Erupt after Shooting.*"

"Whatever. Hope it calms things down."

The article appeared the next morning exactly as he had written it, but his hopes were dashed when he watched that evening's TV news.

"John, I'm standing in front of Northbrook HIGH School, where principal Higgenbottom earlier referred to 'hazing' of students, presumably by RADICAL Islamic terrorists IN the school. One teacher concerned about the hazing reminded her students that America is THEIR country. John."

"Thank you so much, Victoria. Is there any idea yet who these terrorists might be?"

"John, there is no word on this from the principal, but news on the social media has BEGUN to appear. A Twitter account"—Victoria looked at a paper she held—"@RighteousWarrior has been showing pictures of a type of bomb it claims could easily be MADE by the son of Shahnaz Delpak, the woman originally arrested by the police AFTER the recent shooting. The picture has been shared thousands of times. And a Facebook page, 'God's Country,' displays a hand-drawn sketch of the LAYOUT of Northbrook High, indicating key places WHERE a bomb could be placed. This has been retweeted"—she looked at her paper—"7,589 times so far. John."

"Victoria, thank you for this troubling report. And please stay safe."

Anthony was at the breaking point. He called Victoria, his hand trembling. When she didn't answer, he texted: *Stupid stupid do you know what UR doing?*

Pari called. "I can't come over. My mom saw Victoria's report. She's so tense. I told her I'd stay here tonight."

"I wrote that story thinking it would help. Victoria distorted it, knowing TV viewers love to be told what they need to fear. I'm sorry, Pari."

"It's not your fault. No matter what you write, it always gets twisted. But ...."

"I know. We have to worry that Willard could end up killing Shahnaz."

He heard Farsi in the background. Then Pari said, "Sorry, Anthony. I wasn't listening. Mom just told me Shahnaz's husband brought home the gun from the gas station." Pari seemed to be crying. "Oh, Anthony, what can we do?"

His heart was racing. "I'll think of something."

22

Flat tires

The native hue of resolution
Is sicklied o'er with the pale cast of thought;
And enterprises of great pitch and moment,
... lose the name of action.

—Shakespeare, *Hamlet*

He gulped down his bowl of instant oatmeal and thought of Thumper. When he was a kid and worried about one thing or another, he would call his dog to sit on his lap and instantly felt better.

Thumper was on the bottom step when Anthony came down. "Hey, boy. How you doing this morning? Looks like your leg's all better." He scratched the big dog under the chin. In no time, his mind cleared and he knew what he had to do.

He called Rob. It was illegal to take a gun onto school property. He told Rob what he'd seen in Willard's backpack.

"So he might have a gun or might not have a gun? That's what you're reporting? You know the department's not going to want to investigate something like that."

"Couldn't they go in and conduct a general search of everybody? You know, following up on the shooting?"

"I guess we could send in some guys with metal scanners and check them as they come out. The principal would have to agree, and there's paperwork involved. Bottom line, Anthony, the guy's gun wasn't fired." Rob seemed less interested in Willard than he was before, but he volunteered, "I will report you saw a gun in his backpack in the garage. Put that on record."

High school seniors in the county were allowed to drive their cars to school instead of taking the bus. Anthony cruised through the parking lot looking for a gray car with a red fender. It was there. He drove off the lot, parked on the street.

He thought of Shahnaz sitting in her apartment afraid for her life. And of Pari and her mother worried to death. It didn't seem like it was going to be possible to use the press to bring Willard under control. It seemed like a time for action, not newspaper writing. But he couldn't think of what to do. He sat rapping his hands on the steering wheel. Well, maybe he did have at least a short-term idea.

He opened his glove compartment. It was there—his combination tire gauge/valve stem tool. He walked back onto the parking lot, made sure the security guard was asleep in his car, and unscrewed the valve stems from all four of Willard's tires. They were still hissing as he hurried away.

He watched from his car. Students started pouring out the doors of the high school, some heading for the parking lot. Cars started driving off the school lot. When the lot was almost empty, he noticed some kind of disturbance. Students were gathered around the gray car with a red fender. Some were laughing. A fight broke out, and the security guard car drove up. A guard in a white shirt and blue trousers got out. "Call the police," Anthony said aloud, banging on the steering wheel of his car. "Call the police." The guard said something into a radio he wore on his lapel. "Yes!"

Anthony called Rob, just to be sure. "There's a fight in the school parking lot here. Good reason to search Scherd's bag right now. Because, you know, you had my report on what I saw in it."

Police cars, sirens blaring, screeched onto the school parking lot, one after another. Anthony saw two cops thrust Willard up against his car, hands up and legs spread as they patted him down. Another cop led a dog to sniff his backpack, then searched inside. With blue gloves on, she pulled out a pistol and put it into a plastic bag. Within seconds, Willard was handcuffed and driven away.

Anthony followed along to the station. He went in and saw Willard being led off to an interrogation room. "Lucky we were called to stop a fight at the school." Rob winked at Anthony. "Violation of probation. Illegal possession of a firearm, second offense. Possession of a firearm on school property. Second offense. He's looking at three years, minimum. His NRA lawyer will be lucky to get him out on bail.

By the time Anthony got back to Shady Park, he knew Pari would already have left the newsroom and gone home. He picked up some Grab 'n Go chicken and called her from his apartment. "I don't think you have to worry about Willard Scherd for a while."

"What do you mean?"

"I let the air out of his tires."

"Is that some kind of guy metaphor?"

"No. Long story. Tell you later. But he's back in police custody. Rob's pretty sure he'll be locked up this time. I'm hoping maybe now he'll get the psych evaluation he needs."

Pari called out to her mother while she was still on the phone. "Willard Scherd's been arrested again, Mom. Shahnaz is safe. At least for now." She lowered her voice and told Anthony, "I want to stay here with Mom tonight. She's really upset."

"Sure."

"By the way, you didn't go in to the newsroom today, did you? There's an assignment on your desk that made Ralph grin and twirl his moustache."

23

Motion transfer

Now off with those shooes, and then safely tread
In this love's hallow'd temple, this soft bed.

—John Donne, "To His Mistress Going to Bed"

In the course of his life so far, a branch of knowledge that might have interested Anthony less than most was the inner construction of mattresses. Apparently, the number and shape of coils, the use of either pocketed coils or free-end offset coils, the addition of comfort padding and/or edge support, and many other factors must be considered. Oddly enough, Anthony listened to Mad Mack McGregor, as he called himself, with interest. If he were to buy one—and he thought of it—size would be the easy decision. Nothing larger than a "full" would fit into his bedroom. Even that would be a stretch.

Mad Mack was an encyclopedia of mattress lore. He spoke fast, with a New York accent, and Anthony furiously wrote down everything he could. He asked questions, and Mad Mack was delighted to answer them, including questions about pricing. "Every mattress in every store is always 50% off," Mack admitted. "Reason? Nationwide studies show that people who come looking for a mattress, if they buy at all, are going to buy one that day or the next. They're going to buy from your store or somebody else's. And they could come in any day of the year, so it better be 50% off that day."

Anthony pointed out that 50% off every day was not a discount at all, and Mad Mack just laughed. He also admitted that it was impossible to comparison shop because manufacturers gave different names to the same mattress for each store. Before long, Anthony had enough information to write a full exposé of questionable mattress merchandising practices. It was tempting, and he smiled to picture Pop's face when he saw the article.

Then he sat on a mid-range, pocketed coil, edge supported mattress. No sagging at all. He lay down. Amazing. Mad Mack had already told him how he usually closes the deal. "I'll take it," Anthony beamed, "if you'll deliver it today and haul away the old one." Before he left, he took a picture of Mad Mack McGregor standing out front under the sign. "The story will be in the *Ledger* the day after tomorrow."

When he brought the story in to Ralph, Pari was sitting at her carrel, head drooping over a thick pile of papers.

"What's wrong, Buddy?" he asked her.

She giggled. "Ugh. Ralph asked for a summary of this tome by Andre Smyth. I still haven't gotten past his detailing of the Roman sewer system." She set her tea mug on top of the apparently pointless dissertation.

"Anyway," Anthony said, "get your mind out of the sewer for a minute, would you? You have to stay at my place tonight. I have something to show you."

She slipped off her shoes by the door as usual, without noticing it at first. Then she moved to put her little backpack by the table and had to squeeze between the Thumper chair and the bed. "This looks—"

"Pocket coils, edge support, foam infused, top choice for value and comfort."

"You bought this?"

"50% off."

Her mouth wouldn't seem to close.

"Go ahead. Try it out."

She crawled onto the bed, flipped onto her back. "It's wonderful." She spread out her arms and legs. "So big. Get on with me."

"See? Pocket coils to reduce motion transfer."

She giggled. "Really? I don't know about that. I mean, motion transfer could be a good thing, don't you think?"

"If transferred properly, of course."

They tried it out before eating dinner. When the experiment was over, he put on a frown. "What do you think? Mad Mack said if we don't like it, we can return it for credit any time the first week."

"I'm thinking it's a keeper."

"Yeah, we can test it again later, just to be sure. But now I have another surprise. He opened his mini fridge. "Vietnamese spring rolls."

"You're kidding? There's no Vietnamese restaurant in Shady Park."

"Guy I know made them for me. Tran, the night manager at the Grab 'n Go."

While Anthony warmed them in the microwave, Pari stood staring at the rising moon through his little window. Her eyes looked glassy.

"What's wrong, Pari?"

She kept her focus on the moon. "I wish everything could stay just as it is now, forever."

"It's seven a.m." He gently pushed her hair back from her face, but she didn't wake up. He kissed her cheek, and she turned sleepily away from him. A shaft of sunlight from the high window played across her back. He snuggled next to her and let the feel of her body lull him back to sleep.

When he awoke, she was dressed, looking down at him. "It's eight o'clock. Can you believe it?"

He pulled her towards the bed. She giggled and knelt astride him on the (firm-edged) bed. "Get up, lazy. Those cat stories aren't going to write themselves."

"Ugh." He stared over at his notebook on the table.

She touched his cheek. "Now what are you thinking?"

"I'm thinking maybe I should stop trying to use the *Ledger* to right wrongs. You know, mellow out."

"Fat chance of that."

"Seriously. What if we stopped wasting our time doing research for articles that aren't going to be printed anyway? Just write mattress and cat stories. I could get a second job. Maybe in advertising. Or at the Grab 'n Go. Save some money. Get an apartment with two rooms."

Pari's mocking smile disappeared. "And sleep together every day?"

"Yeah."

Her eyes sparkled. "And maybe get a cat?"

"OK." He couldn't believe he said that, but he meant it.

She bounced up and down. "Or, better yet, a dog."

"Ow. Sit still. But yeah."

She slid off. "What's for breakfast?"

Luckily, he had two eggs. Unfortunately, that was all. No bacon. No bread. No orange juice. "I have tea, though."

When they finished eating, she flipped through the pages of her notepad on the table, her eyes clouding over.

"What's wrong?"

"Nothing. It's just, most of the teachers I've talked to want to vote out the new curriculum now that they've seen what's in it. If I could put out the facts, maybe they could get enough support to get rid of it."

"Ah. Still thinking about that?"

"Yeah. Some day we might be the ones worrying about what the schools teach the kids."

"Some day? What do you mean?"

A blush spread over her face. She sat astride him on the chair, arms around his neck. "What are we going to do, Anthony? Maybe, just this last time we could try to get the *Ledger* to print the truth about something important."

"Sure. I'll help, if I can."

"I'm stuck on something. One of the teachers says Bea Doggit stands to profit from switching to the new books. I haven't been able to verify that."

Anthony thought back to Emma Bovant telling him at the art show she had some information to give him. "I know somebody who might be able to help."

Pari perked up.

"I'll call her." He dialed Emma, raising his eyebrows at Pari while the phone rang. "A confidential source, you understand."

It rang quite a few times before Emma answered. "Hello, Anthony. I'm surprised you called me."

"Well, at the gallery, you said there was something you wanted to tell me."

"No. Sorry. It's better if I don't talk to you." Her voice was loud enough for Pari to hear, too.

"Are you angry with me about something?"

"No. Not that at all. It's just—I think I'd better hang up."

"Wait. Please—"

When Anthony put down his phone, Pari giggled, teasing him. "A confidential source. Uh-huh. With such a sweet voice. And you: *Oh, please don't be angry. Please don't hang up.*"

"Mischievous fairy," he cried out.

She picked up a pencil from the table and touched him on the head. "*Jing o jing o setaré.* I'll put a spell on you to keep you for myself."

"No need, Pari. You did that a long time ago."

24

Tree house

How pleasant to sit on the beach,
On the beach, on the sand, in the sun,
With ocean galore within reach,
And nothing at all to be done!
No letters to answer,
No bills to be burned,
No work to be shirked,
No cash to be earned,
It is pleasant to sit on the beach
With nothing at all to be done!

—Ogden Nash, *Pretty Halcyon Days*

Before she did any more research on the curriculum project, Pari bit the bullet and continued to wade through Andre's document so she could give Ralph a summary. Anthony observed her, arms on her carrel, yawning, sipping tea, taking notes, Googling words she'd underlined.

"Did you know that septic systems return wastewater to the aquifer without the need for electricity or for adding chemicals to the water?"

Anthony didn't feel the need to answer this.

"Did you know that sewage treatment plants, on the other hand, can overflow when it rains too hard and consequently dump polluted water directly into the river?"

A shrug.

"Whereas septic tanks distribute the wastewater evenly under ground, where it is purified naturally, with no single point of entry into rivers, lakes, or streams?"

Anthony scratched his head with his pencil.

"Or that the digging and runoff from construction can harm a river because the silt blocks the sunlight, allowing algae to grow?"

"That part I knew."

Ralph came out of his office, glasses up on his head, eyebrows raised. "Sort of an environmental tract, isn't it? Didn't read it, but that's what I got from Mr. Smyth's monologue." He dropped his glasses down to see how far Pari had read. "Maybe we can turn a short excerpt from it into a letter to the editor. That would be good. We used to get letters. Not many these days. As soon as anybody has a thought about anything now, they send it out in a Twitter, or whatever."

"I'd need to talk to him first," Pari said. "I don't see a phone number or address."

"Anthony knows where he lives. Nothing going on here this afternoon. He could take you there."

The catalpa trees along River Road had already shed most of their giant stringbean-like pods, and their elephant-ear leaves were yellowing. The leaves of the crape myrtle trees were shiny and dark now, sprinkled with deep red berries. The green switchgrass on the river side of the road sprouted pale, wispy fronds bent over from the weight of their seeds. "Look." Pari pointed. Patches of black-eyed Susans and red and pink wild roses shot up here and there through the honeysuckle underbrush.

Anthony's Kia crunched to a stop in the turnaround at the end of the road. Blue jays screeched as he and Pari ducked under the sassafras trees shading Andre's house. The warped, paintless door hung slightly open. Pari knocked.

They heard crickets chirping inside. That was the only sound. Then giggles, from somewhere outside. It sounded like children, but the sound came from high up in the air. Anthony stepped back and looked up, feeling silly.

"Hee-hee. We see you."

Pari slipped around to the side of the house. It wasn't a sound to be afraid of except that it seemed to be coming from nowhere. "Who's there?" she called.

More giggles.

They both spotted it at the same time. Partially hidden high up in the glossy green leaves of a spreading sassafras was a lopsided tree house, bare legs of children dangling from its platform. A deep voice said, "Come on up." A girl's voice echoed, "Yeah."

Cross boards were nailed like a ladder to the trunk. Anthony went first. The kids reached out to help him onto the landing, then Pari. Against the back wall of the hut, sat Andre, cross legged, grinning, flickers of light animating his blue eyes. He nodded as if he'd been expecting them.

"I'm Beth," one of the girls said. "That's my brother Bill. I'm eight. Bill's a year older than me. Mr. Andre helped us make this house. That's Alan. He's seven." She examined Pari. "You're really pretty."

"My sister talks a lot." Bill's face reddened.

Alan clarified, "I'm almost eight, actually."

Andre sat silent as if content that the introductions were being made. A worn book lay spread open beside him on the plank. *Poems of Ogden Nash.* At his back, through cracks between the boards, the wide vista of the river ranged all the way to where it flowed into the bay. The island Anthony and Pari had sailed to was visible from here as a glowing mass of red, yellow, and green leaves.

"We built this," Bill said. "Got the boards from the dumpsters where they tore down our neighbors' houses."

"It's nice," Pari said.

"That's our house back there. And that's Alan's." Bill pointed to two weather beaten bungalows behind Andre's.

"And back there is where Fran used to live. She moved to Shady Park."

"To be with her 'boyfriend' Todd." Beth rolled her eyes.

Anthony figured that might be the Todd he'd written an article about. "Emma Bovant's son Todd?"

Beth nodded. "You know him?"

Before Anthony could answer, the crunch of a car coming down the gravel and oyster shell road made everybody turn. "Here he comes," Alan called out. It was a little white car with a red, white, and blue plastic sign on its roof. *Torino's Pizza.*

Andre, in tight corduroy pants, leaned sideways to extract a wallet from a hip pocket. Anthony saw it was made of waterproof nylon like his own, but not a color he would have chosen, baby blue. It matched the color of the little car in Andre's driveway.

A dark haired teenager carried a large white box to Andre's door.

"Over here. Up here."

The teenager jumped, almost dropped the pizza. Giggles rang out from the tree house as the delivery boy looked up to spot them.

"Basket," Andre said. He dropped some bills into a wide basket tied to a rope. Bill lowered it down along the tree trunk to the pizza man. "Keep the change," Andre called down. "That's right," he said. "Just put the pizza in the basket." Bill hauled it up by the rope.

"Beth, would you serve our guests?" Andre's smile reflected what seemed a Buddha-like inner contentment. The talking stopped while they all munched on the slices. Anthony relaxed, lost track of why he'd come.

Pari licked her fingers. "I've never eaten pizza in a tree before."

"We have." Beth chuckled. "Mr. Andre reads us poems

while we wait for the delivery."

Shouts sounded out from River Road down near Bea's villa. From the tree house, they made out two men in neon orange jackets standing beside a yellow tripod. "Surveyors," Andre said. "They've been here off and on for a week. Looks like the county's really going to put in a sewer line."

Remembering why they'd come, Anthony dropped a crust into the pizza box and raised his eyebrows at Pari. She swallowed, took out her notepad.

"Mr. Andre says we don't need a sewer line," Bill spoke up. "They dump chemicals into the river."

This seemed a cue for Andre to launch into an extended explanation. Anthony left Pari to listen to it and climbed down the tree to talk to the surveyors. He wanted to verify what Andre said. It seemed absurd to build a capital project like an underground sewer line for the few houses left along River Road. Even if houses were eventually built on the lots where Riverside Paradise had torn down the old fishing cottages, the number of people living here wouldn't justify the expense. The county was always claiming it didn't even have enough money to fill the potholes in the roads from the previous winter.

Neither surveyor acknowledged him as he approached. "Nice day to be outside," Anthony ventured. The man adjusting a device on top of the tripod was concentrating and didn't look up. All Anthony got from the other was a glance and a nod.

"What're you working on?"

The tripod man gave him a look like it was none of his business. "Marking the county property line." He waved for his partner to take some paces down the road.

"For an underground sewer?"

The tripod man spat on the ground. "We just do the surveys, but that's what I hear."

"You mean you heard it from the Public Works office?"

"We're kind of busy here."

Anthony returned to the tree house. Andre was still talking and Pari was taking notes. Bill swung from the rope while the other kids pelted him with sassafras seeds. Pari gave a relieved sigh when Anthony heaved himself up onto the platform. "It seems Mr. Smyth hopes his letter to the editor will stir up opposition to the sewer project."

"Because of the expense to the residents for the frontage assessment?" Anthony asked.

"Yes." Andre frowned. "But mainly because of the harm to the river. It's all there in my letter. The chemicals they put into piped sewage eventually seep—"

"Right," Pari interrupted. She eyed Anthony. "I'm sure we can print the letter, the key parts of it, I mean." One hand on Anthony's shoulder, she got to her feet. "And thanks for all the information, Mr. Smyth." She shook his hand. "And for the pizza."

Andre said, "We could take a walk down to my pier."

The kids followed along. In the crisp, dry air they all stood looking out across the river. The sun was high and white in the sky, and the gulls were chattering, swooping down to pluck fish from the water. Pari put her arm through Anthony's.

"You think the water's cold?" she asked.

"Naw," Bill said. He kicked off his flip-flops and ran down to the beach, the other kids close behind him.

"Let's walk in the water with them." Pari left her sneakers on the pier. The bottoms of her jeans were getting wet. "Come on in, Anthony. It's not that cold."

Andre nudged him, the Buddha grin creeping onto his face.

"It *is* cold." Anthony pulled his jeans up over his knees.

"Anyway, we're not going back to the newsroom today, are we?" Pari scooped a handful of water and splashed him.

"Not now, I guess." He reached down.

"Oh, no. You better not."

He did.

Before long they were both soaked.

"Thanks, Andre. Bye, kids." They ran off.

In the car, Pari pulled her polo shirt away from her body. "I can't go home like this."

"No problem. We'll warm up under the covers of my pocketed coil mattress."

25

The new quill

To have a pen is to be at war.

—Voltaire, *Letter to Jeanne-Grâce Bosc du Bouchet*

In the morning, he sat up on the (firmly supported) edge of the bed, tapping his fingers on his knees.

"What are you thinking? Don't say 'nothing.'"

He said, "It was fun at Andre's, wasn't it? Maybe we should take some time off every day to just go sit up in a tree."

"With our notepads?"

"No. You know that saying 'To have a pen is to be at war'? Voltaire, I think. I used to believe that. Maybe it used to be true. Nowadays, it seems a pen isn't good enough. *Plume*, that's what he called it. A quill to write with. How old fashioned. *Passé*. It's probably a waste of time writing for the newspaper these days." Anthony snorted a little laugh. "Maybe I should quit and just start writing for our advertisers."

She threw one leg over his. "You keep thinking of leaving the paper when I finally get a reporting job? You can't leave me there alone." She wiggled her leg. "Because I'm determined to report on this absurd school curriculum."

"You'd better make your report in GIFs and memes."

She smiled. "Maybe I will. I have a blog, you know."

The idea took hold of him. Maybe keyboards were the new quills, and blogs were the new newspapers. After all, the *Huffington Post* started as a blog. "Let me see it."

She went to his computer, then stopped. She was naked. "Hold on." She pulled on panties and sat in his chair. Anthony felt a new, unexpected thrill watching her naked while she was unaware, absorbed in something else.

"Here it is."

"Huh? Oh, right." He stood behind her, cupping her breasts with his hands. "*Searchlight.* That's what you call it?" He couldn't resist moving his fingers.

"Hey! What are you—? OK, if you don't want to see my blog."

"I do." He folded his arms.

Searchlight, she explained, was a new section of her blog. The original page was called *Happy Thoughts*. And that's pretty much what the earlier posts seemed to be. There were poems she'd written. Random observations. Pictures she'd taken—he thought he recognized a shot of the sunset they'd watched together on the Northbrook Apartments bench. "What's this?" Anthony teased. 'My New Friend.' Not me, by any chance?"

"Go ahead. Click it."

He did.

"Ha-ha. Surprised?" It was a picture of Thumper.

"OK, what's this? 'I Met Someone.'"

Pari's face turned red. "Just a corny poem. Skip over that. Hey!"

The purple sky above smiled on someone today.
Dark birds sailed down from clouds to greet someone today.
I closed my eyes and let the sunset fill my heart
With rays of love because I met someone today.

Pari held her hands over her face.

"Thumper must be thrilled. A poem just for him."

She rapped him on the arm.

"Only thing, I don't remember you being with Thumper in the sunset. Must be some other dog."

"OK, that's enough."

"I don't really read much poetry. At least, this one I can understand."

"It's a ghazal."

"Yeah, sure, of course, that's what I thought."

"Smarty."

Searchlight had a recently added category, "Weighing In." On this page Pari announced a plan to host discussions of controversial topics. To start, she'd introduced the topic of textbooks mandated for public schools. "When are updates required? Who should choose? Qualifications for making the choice. Avoiding books with a cultural bias. Who should profit?"

Anthony clicked on each category. They contained facts Pari had discovered about the Piskasanet County process for choosing textbooks. Under 'Who should profit?' she'd listed the titles of each of the county's newly-approved books, their cost, and the corporate owner of the company publishing them, RES-RECT. The price list showed the titles of the previous books, the number of pages, and the cost compared to the new books. The RES-RECT books had far fewer pages and cost considerably more than the old ones.

So far, there were no comments on her blog. "I might get some, though. I put a link on lots of my replies to Facebook posts and Tweets, the ones I found that seemed interested in the topic."

"You think Ralph or Pop will see your blog?"

Pari grinned. "What do you think? Pop doesn't have a computer on his desk. He only reads printouts. And Ralph talks about 'Those UBS thingies.'"

"So who will read it?"

"What I hope is educators, historians, sociologists."

"Not left wingers, right wingers, Bible freaks, Islam haters, radical terrorists of all sorts?"

"I know. It's a little scary. I just wanted to put the facts out there. Since it doesn't look like the *Ledger*'s going to."

The atmosphere at the *Ledger* was more relaxed with Pop away in a duck blind on the eastern shore of the bay, sipping bourbon and firing birdshot into the air. Nora looked up when Anthony passed by the advertising department on the first floor. "Sharise," she called, "here's your guy."

Sharise gave a loud chuckle. "Yes, indeed. Mr. Save Your Cat. Heh-heh. Come take a look at this. Cat food ad, another cat food ad, ad from a vet. That picture of Tiger the cat in the paper, I mean to say, cat food companies trying to cash in on the likes of that."

"No kidding? Pari took that picture. Should we do a dog story next? See what happens?"

"Heh-heh, you do that, Mr. Anthony. We see, then. Ads keep coming in, maybe Pop stop worrying about the paper going under."

Even Ralph was more cheerful—at least what passed as cheerful for Ralph. When Anthony and Pari came in together after skipping a day in the newsroom, he dared a bit of sarcasm. "You two look familiar. Will you remind me of your names?" That, and he hummed ever so softly when he filled his coffee cup.

"High school car wash to offset senior prom expenses, ham radio club meeting." Anthony turned to the carrel next to him. "What do you have, Pari?"

"Shady Park neighborhood yard sale, Halloween costume making at the Y."

"Trade you?"

"No way. I'm into Halloween. Last year I was a—"

"Fairy?"

"Very funny. I was a—"

"Reporter?"

"Ha-ha. That's what I'm pretending to be now."

The phone on her desk rang. The line was still labeled "Victoria." Calls to Victoria's line usually meant somebody looking to publicize their hair salon or yoga lessons or mindfulness training or spa beauty treatments. Pari turned to Anthony. "Victoria. I guess that's me now?"

"Right. We'll have to change the name on the *Ledger* staff listing, too."

He heard Pari say, "No. Victoria no longer works here ... Pari Shandule. I'm taking her assignments now ... Blog? Yes." She listened for some time. "Oh, well I'm sorry." She held her hand over the receiver. "It's Beatrice Doggit."

Anthony punched the button for Victoria's line on his phone and listened in. Bea had read Pari's blog and was furious. "I thank Jesus that my friend Britney's daughter found it. You've circulated a mass of unholy lies. Does your publisher Harold Whitman know about this? I'm going to make sure he does. If that 'blog' as you call it isn't taken off the internet by the end of the day, I have ways to deal with you."

Pari's hands were shaking, but she replied, "There's a place on the blog to enter any comment you have, Ms. Doggit. You're welcome to do so. It's meant to stimulate a discussion, get various viewpoints."

"With Jesus as my witness, I'll make a call to the County Executive and you'll not only lose your job at the *Ledger* but be blacklisted from any other news job you apply for."

"The County Executive? Yes, I've seen releases from his office saying he supports the new curriculum. All I can say is the County Executive is also welcome to explain his rationale by adding his comments to the blog."

"Insolent bitch." Bea hung up.

Anthony gave Pari a high-five. "*Searchlight* shines on, exposing machinations that lurk in the dark."

"Uh-huh. You think the last news story I ever write will be on a yard sale?"

Pop always returned from duck hunting in raucous good humor, treating his reporters like hounds eager for the chase. "What ad-bait stories have we fetched the past few days, my puppies? Anthony, that store opening article was pure gold, they tell me downstairs. Ads from mattress stores all over the county. Same for that cat story, Miss, uh—"

"Pari."

The hunt euphoria didn't last long. Pop burst out of his office, training his deep-set eyes on Pari. "What's this I hear on my voicemail? I don't understand it, but somehow you've angered Bea Doggit, our prime real estate advertiser. And business associate of the County Executive, I might add. And it's all about a book publisher?"

"I thought the public has a right to know who publishes the county's textbooks," Pari said.

"I'm not saying the public doesn't have a right to know. Nobody would accuse me of that. Look at my record as publisher of this paper." Pop shook his head. "But this about the textbook publisher. How did you find this out? What makes you so sure? I attended the proposal for using the new books myself, and this RES-RECT was never mentioned as the publisher."

"It's on the title pages of the books."

Pop stood up, his hands gripped into fists, his brow nearly obscuring his eyes. "Damn it," he thundered. "Damn those idiots." He charged back into his office.

Pari wrung her hands. "Should I take down my blog, Anthony?"

"No, you can't. You suspect Bea Doggit is using her Board position to make a lot of money, right?"

Pari wiped her hands across her jeans. "Uh-huh, the total budget for textbooks and materials in the county is over $380 million. Even if we're only talking about science and social science, there's a huge profit to be made by whoever gets to sell the county those books."

"And?"

"And, yeah, it's also a matter of whether the books contain truth or falsehood."

Anthony tapped his pencil on his desk. "I have an idea. If it doesn't work, I'll be back at the Grab 'n Go."

"Then I guess I'll be back tutoring part time at the college."

26

House tour

"My cloak has only to fall in order that thou mayest discover a succession of mysteries."

—Gustave Flaubert, *The Temptation of St. Anthony*

It was Anthony's previous articles about Bea's Riverside Paradise project that had brought it to a halt. He knew he was the last person she'd want to see. But when he told her Pop wanted him to meet with her, she agreed.

Driving down River Road, he brooded about what he'd say to her. The surveyors were finished, and now blue and white county utility trucks and a backhoe were parked along the road. It looked like the sewer line was about to be put in.

The crunchy gravel became a smooth paved surface just as it neared Bea's villa. He pulled his car past the lighthouse mailbox that marked her driveway and walked along the flagstone path that led to the enormous double front door of her ostentatious house—something he'd never imagined himself doing.

She stood in the doorway draped in a satin red robe with yellow Chinese embroidery swirling over it. He couldn't make out whether it was dragons or peacocks. "Are you going to be good? Then you can come in."

The long central hall echoed the clack of her sandals on the black and white marble tile floor. Statues on plinths stood along the walls—reproductions of famous Renaissance religious sculptures. Anthony couldn't help giving a bronze toned figure of the archangel Michael brandishing his sword a flick with his fingernail as they passed it. Plastic.

He followed her into a sitting room with gold fleur-de-lis as big as stop signs imprinted on the white walls. She took his arm, led him to an indigo couch with an arched back, and sat close beside him, her knees pulled up onto the seat. "Your publisher Harold says we can work things out. I pray to Jesus he's right." She held her hair from her face, resting an elbow on his shoulder.

"I don't know what Pop told you exactly," he started, "but we're going to need access to a computer for me to show you—"

"Computer? Can't we just talk first? I look into your pale green eyes and I know that Jesus means us to be friends, not enemies." She studied him a minute. "Something is different about you. Your hair. It used to be teased up, I remember. I'm curious why you changed it."

Anthony found himself explaining his hair style. "I had a friend who liked it pulled up like that. I don't see her any more, so I don't bother."

Bea grinned. "I like it this way. More mature. More distinguished."

Anthony coughed, clearing his throat. "So, the way blogs work," he went on, "they're public. People write their reaction to what others say. I can show you how to do that. You know, defend your own opinion?"

"Defend my—? I hoped you'd come here to tell me that nasty reporter shut down her blog."

"No. But I can tell you how to put your own comments on it. She'd welcome the discussion."

"There is no discussion about the word of the Lord." She closed her eyes. "Jesus give me the strength to rise above any anger I might feel. Help me to see that you have sent this young man to me as an instrument of your will."

Anthony tried to shift aside but was already pressed against the edge of the couch. His instinct was to run. This might be the perfect moment. After all, he'd thought of quitting his job, anyway. But a knot of guilt tightened in his chest when he thought of Pari losing her job, the reporting job she'd aimed at since high school. It wasn't fair.

Bea opened her eyes. "Let Jesus guide you." She laid a hand on his leg. "Give in to the power of his love."

Anthony stood up. "If we're not going to look at your computer, then—"

She stood and took his hand. "Of course, we can look at my computer. Come into the library, and—she squeezed his hand—we'll do whatever you want." She led him down the hallway, through a door beside a half-sized statue of Michelangelo's Moses (also plastic) and into a walnut paneled room with floor to ceiling bookshelves built into three of the walls (empty). A wide mahogany desk near a window at the far end of the room was covered with colorful brochures. Anthony went over and picked one up. A banner on the front read "Riverside Paradise—the Dream Endures."

"So Riverside Paradise is back in business?" he asked.

"We can't question the ways of the Lord Jesus," Bea said. "I admit I was furious when your articles took the side of those fishermen. But I see now that Jesus wanted us to pay them for the loss of their houses. And He has rewarded us with public approval and even more investors."

Anthony opened the brochure to look at it more closely, but she took it from his hand. "The Paradise homes are a bit out of your range, I'm afraid." She tossed the brochure back on the desk, then touched his cheek. "At least for now. Who knows about the future? As you can imagine, good publicity is very valuable to us."

For Pari's sake, he still wanted to get her to tell Pop she was reconciled to the *Searchlight* blog. Or that she saw it as an opportunity to promote her Christianized curriculum. He eyed a laptop on a high backed red velvet chair.

"What a one track mind you have. I'll humor you. Here, I'll turn it on." She put the laptop on the desk. "The darn thing takes forever to start up. Come on. I'll show you around the rest of the house."

They went through a kitchen big enough to cook a meal for 50 people but with no sign that anything had ever been cooked in it. A rear stairway led to the top floor of the villa. "I just have to show you this first. You'll love it." She opened a heavy door that smelled like cedar, and little wisps of steam drifted out. "My Jacuzzi. Would you close the door behind you, please?" She walked around to the other side of the sunken wooden pool that seemed big enough to swim in and stood gazing out the window. "Look," she said. "You can see the river."

Anthony was struck by the beauty of the scene. The window was the same height as Andre's tree house, but with no leaves blocking the view. Memories of his boyhood days launching a little dinghy from a public ramp on the Piskasanet held him mesmerized. Those days on the river were some of the happiest in his life. He looked at the island he'd sailed to with Pari.

Bea turned back to face him. "You seem impressed. The water is warm. Come in with me." She loosened her robe and let it drop to the floor. She was completely naked.

Ralph had access to syndicated articles online—Dear Abby, Healthy Eating, De-cluttering Your House—to use as fillers when he had to, like now when Anthony had skipped covering the high school car wash and whatever that other thing was.

"Where's Pari?" Anthony looked at Pop's closed door, hoping she wasn't in there.

Ralph said, "Halloween costume making. You look like you've seen a ghost yourself. Was Ms. Doggit that scary?"

"I managed to escape. Put it that way." Anthony decided Ralph didn't need to know all the details. "Bottom line," he said, "I told her the blog's not coming down, and she said she's going to make Pop fire me."

"Make?"

"I left in kind of a hurry, but I took this off her desk." He showed Ralph the Paradise brochure. "See this? 'Riverside Paradise, a RES-RECT, LLC, corporation.'"

Ralph fingered one tip of his moustache. "Hmm. Pari says the publisher of the new Christian texts is RES-RECT." He eyed Anthony over the top of his glasses. "So you're saying Riverside Paradise and the Christian publisher are owned by the same corporation?"

"Looks like it." Anthony decided it was time to tell Ralph something he'd kept to himself so far. "And remember when I did those articles on Riverside Paradise before? I found out Bea and the pastor are big campaign contributors to Andrew Mauer, the County Exec."

"Pop's pal."

"Correct. So, yes, through the Exec, Bea has some influence over Pop. She can probably 'make' him fire me. And Pari."

Pari bounced in at that moment. She had a man's fedora pushed back on her head, hiding her hair, with a "PRESS" card sticking out of the band. She wore a tie with a man's vest, and on her face were fake round black glasses and a pointy moustache exactly like Ralph's. An unlit cigarette dangling from her mouth, she growled, "Got the scoop on the car wash and the ham radio club, Chief. Costume making, too. Yard sale got postponed. You bet I'll be looking into why." She narrowed her eyes. "Blaming it on a forecast for rain sounds a little suspicious in my book, see?"

Ralph touched his own moustache, felt for his own glasses, grinning and blinking.

"Ralph, we can't let our star reporter get canned, can we?"

Thumper gave a single deep bark when Pari parked behind his car and emerged from hers still in costume. But he wagged his tail tentatively when she said, "It's only me, Boy." They carried a cooler up the stairs filled with Tupperware bowls Mastaneh had packed with rice, salty pickles, and khoresh. Why had Anthony ever said he liked khoresh?

Before they left the newsroom, Anthony had told Pari the same thing about his meeting with Bea that he told Ralph, no more. Yet the sight of Bea standing there naked in front of him lingered. He'd done nothing except maybe stand there gawking for who knows how long before he turned and ran out of the house.

He remembered that at the Board of Education hearing, the crowd had hushed when Bea stepped forward on the platform in her low-cut dress. He hadn't shared their fascination. She was older and a little too ample. But it was amazing how a little fullness could actually enhance the figure of a naked—

"You're so quiet. Something bothering you?"

"Huh?" He gave her a brief version of the whole story, including how he'd run back into the library and picked up a brochure before speeding off in his car.

"Wow. My interview at the retired guys' ham radio club was less interesting."

"I mean, there she was, standing stark naked in front of me."

"Yeah, you said."

He felt his cheeks warm.

Pari said, "The golf tournament ladies gossiped a lot about her. They called her voluptuous. So now you've had a good look at her voluptuousness. Maybe you won't find me attractive any more."

"That's crazy."

She stood peering at him as if trying to read what might be going on in his mind.

He raised his eyebrows. "Let's put it to a test, then."

Pari gave him a puzzled frown.

"Take off your clothes," he said. "I'll let you know."

He couldn't believe it. Without a word, she slowly began to unbutton her clothes and drop them on the floor piece by piece. Anthony stared, transfixed.

"Am I attractive?"

"More than you can imagine." He knew he should have stopped there, but he couldn't resist. "See for yourself. There's a mirror behind you."

She turned and saw the reflection of herself totally naked except for the hat, black glasses, and moustache.

27

Required by law

Laws grind the poor, and rich men rule the law.
—Oliver Goldsmith, "The Traveller"

The county Public Works Department had a consumer affairs number. Anthony called and asked about the blue and white trucks he'd seen on Riverside Road. Consumer affairs knew nothing about that. He settled down and resolved to put up with several hours of waiting on hold, being referred from one department to another, and leaving messages. But then he reached a gruff-voiced man willing to give him some information. He suspected it was a disgruntled employee who wanted to stick it to his boss.

The new sewer line wasn't in the capital budget for the year. No study had been done to determine if it was needed. Instead, it was being funded by money from a Federal environmental subsidy. When Anthony asked who approved it, the employee said, "I have no idea."

Something told him Emma knew more about this. In the art gallery, she'd said she had something she wanted to tell him. He couldn't understand why she'd hung up when he'd called. He decided to try talking to her in person. He'd go on Saturday when she wouldn't be home alone—the Bea episode lingering in his mind.

Emma's house on Shady Park Lane, like his, was in the old section of the neighborhood. Tall loblolly, maple, and sweetgum trees shaded the yards, and mature hedges of boxwood, juniper, or forsythia lined the sidewalks and driveways. He picked up that morning's copy of the *Ledger* from the top of a hydrangea bush in her front yard and took it up to her door.

He had been going over in his mind what he would say. He didn't want to seem unprofessional in contacting her after she'd asked him not to. On top of that, he wondered if it would be considered harassment. But some of the assurances he thought it might be wise to offer sounded like lawyer-speak. Besides, if he started giving a detailed explanation for dropping in, he feared it might sound too, well, too pushy. She opened the door, and all he said was, "Hi. Your paper."

Emma laughed. "Thanks. You guys are delivering right to the door now?"

She was still Emma, after all—a smart, sincere wife and mother who had an instinct to defend people who were being wronged. Anthony relaxed, and she invited him in.

He asked if the Riverside Paradise developers, Pastor Mitch or Bea, had threatened her in any way. That might have been why she'd stopped talking to him.

"No, that's not it." She seemed embarrassed to go on, slipping her fingers up through her bobbed hair. Anthony remembered her doing that when she was worried or scared. Then she lowered her eyes and told him, "I got a call from a reporter at the *Ledger*. A woman. She said she found our call record on your phone. She told me she was your girlfriend and warned me to stay away from you."

Victoria. Anthony swallowed his anger to say, "Emma, it's outrageous that you got a call like that. I can promise you it won't happen again. The woman who called you is no longer at the newspaper. She used to be my girlfriend, but she's moved on to somebody else. I apologize."

Emma led him into the kitchen, where she checked something in the oven. Her son Todd was playing in the back yard with another boy. Papers that looked like student essays covered the kitchen table—she was tutoring international students at the community college, he remembered. He refused an offer of coffee, then of beer, although he felt flattered that she offered him beer. He was 24, but a lot of people thought he looked younger. Emma smiled at him, and he self-consciously lifted his hand to smooth down his hair.

"Here's what I've learned," Emma told him. "Remember the corporation that Pastor Mitch and Bea formed to get those people's houses from them, INVOKIM? We forced them to shut it down. But now they're using a new shell corporation to do the same dirty work—"

"RES-RECT, I'm guessing."

She nodded. "So you already know about it?"

"I saw the name on a pamphlet. It's also the publisher of the new county textbooks."

Emma told him, "The Riverside Paradise gang has now got the county to start laying down a totally unnecessary sewer line, knowing the owners of the fishing cottages won't be able to pay the new 'frontage assessment' required by law and they'll be forced to sell and move out."

Anthony was scribbling this down in his notebook. "Can you tell me how you know this?"

"I have a friend, Esmeralda. That's her son Juan playing outside with Todd. She works for your paper's publisher over in Bay Hills now. She was serving at a meeting they had there."

"A meeting with our publisher?"

Emma nodded slowly. "And Mr. Mauer, the County Executive, and Bea and the pastor, and Derek Grosbeck."

Anthony felt an indignant rush of heat swelling in his throat. The whole Riverside Paradise scheme was rising again from its ashes. This time they were using the sewer line, a county construction project, to get their way. That meant the County Executive was almost certainly a key player in the scheme. And it looked like Pop was in on it.

Emma said, "Esmeralda heard Mr. Whitman shouting at

Bea. Something about school books, she said."

"I'd like to talk to Esmeralda."

"She gets off at 7:00 tonight. I could call and say you'll meet her at the bus stop."

The sidewalk was bathed in a bluish white glow spilling over from the little parking lot. A woman stood waiting, her long black hair gleaming in the light of a buzzing lamp. Even in the artificial light she was beautiful.

Anthony turned into the parking lot and just then saw a man in a dark suit slip out of a silver Porsche and hurry towards the woman. The light revealed the man's thick wavy hair and dark eyebrows. It was John Rowland, the TV news anchor. As Anthony stepped out of his car, he saw Rowland reach for the woman, who backed away, clutching a cloth bag to her chest. "Please, no, Mr. John," she shouted. "Is not right. I am marry."

A screech of brakes announced the bus pulling to a stop. John Rowland had his hands around the woman's waist. "Come with me, Esmeralda," he coaxed. "Dinner and a drink. That's all."

She pushed him back and jumped into the bus as soon as its door hissed open. The TV anchor stood watching it drive away. Head down, he slogged back to his car without noticing Anthony and sped away in the opposite direction, tires squealing.

Anthony's head was spinning when he got back to his apartment. Pari was asleep in the bed, a book on her stomach. He gently put it on the table, then sat in the Thumper chair, tapping his eraser on his phone. He didn't have Esmeralda's number and called Emma instead.

"Esmeralda called me to apologize," she told him. "For not waiting for you at the bus stop. It seems John Rowland has been harassing her lately."

"I saw that for myself."

"Also, I have more details about the sewer line scam that I got from Britney Grosbeck. She doesn't understand it's a scam. She thinks everything her husband Derek does is 'fantastic' and can't stop bragging. I can't explain it all right now."

"Can we meet again?"

"That's what I was thinking. Maybe you and I can go talk to Andre. I'll let you know."

"Great. Glad we're back in touch."

He ended the call and looked over towards the bed. Pari was lying there awake, a worried frown on her face. He went to kiss her, but his phone rang. They both saw *VICTORIA* on the screen.

"WPSK TV calling again," Pari trilled. "I guess Victoria needs even more ammunition for her battle to the top of the news ratings."

Anthony hit Reject Call. This was the most negative comment Pari had ever made about Victoria.

"You're still in contact with her, Anthony. That scares me. It's like Victoria's a loaded gun waiting to go off with one of her 'newscasts' that cause everybody to panic."

"I know." He took Pari's hand. "I'm not in contact with her, though."

"Weren't you just talking to her?"

"No." He trusted Pari to keep his source secret. "That was Emma Bovant."

"The name sounds familiar. But if you're not in contact with Victoria, where does she get her information?"

"From the previous day's *Ledger*, of course. She picks the low-hanging fruit."

"And makes a poison pie out of it." She sat up. "Willard's in police custody. OK. But Shahnaz and her family are still going through hell. Anthony, a lot more people get their news from Victoria's TV reports than from the newspaper. I'm constantly afraid of what she's going to come up with next." She pulled her hand from his. "Tell her what harm she's doing."

"I've tried, left messages. She doesn't answer."

"That's funny."

"What do you mean?"

"She called me when you were out. She talks like it's possible you two will get back together again."

"What? That's crazy. What did she say?"

"She seems to think it's possible. That's all. She didn't say why. She said to keep it a secret." Pari stood, picked up her jacket, gave him a kiss on the cheek.

"You're leaving?"

"I'm giving you a chance to talk to her in private. I want you to tell her she has to stop her vicious, false reports." She slipped on her shoes. "And tell her ...." She couldn't finish.

28

Trouble in the blogosphere

> *Through Thee will we push down our enemies:*
> *through thy name will we tread them under*
> *that rise up against us.*
>
> —Psalm 44.5

Anthony sat running his finger over the blank screen of his phone. He dialed Pari. She didn't answer. Probably still in her car. He texted: *I love you, Pari.* No response.

He was furious with Victoria for giving Pari the idea they might get back together. He dialed Victoria. No answer. He texted her: *Now I'm really angry.* No response.

He dialed Pari again. He phone went to an automatic recording. The temptation to give up all investigative reporting hit him again with force. No confidential sources. No secrets. No scoops. Just cats in trees. Just Anthony and Pari.

Anthony didn't get much sleep that night.

In the morning, he picked up the phone as soon as he woke up. A message on the screen said *Searchlight has been updated*—an automatic notice he'd set for Pari's blog.

> *Searchlight* has received a threat in response to its recent report that the newly approved school curriculum was backed by a corporation called RES-RECT that stands to profit from the sale of the new textbooks. The threat came after *Search-*

> *light* named real estate developer Beatrice Doggit, Pastor Mitchell Rainey, and investor Derrek Grosbeck as the RES-RECT owners.

Pari answered on the first ring. "I don't want to talk about Victoria."

"OK."

"If you look at the blog, you'll see what I've been up to. I need to work from home for a while on this right-wing curriculum thing. Comments are pouring in now, and I'm replying to them. If I get fired, so be it."

"Who threatened you?"

"Your friend Bea, of course. And her friend the pastor. They say I can't prove they own RES-RECT. If I don't retract the claim, they'll sue me for slander and ruin my reputation as a journalist."

"Pari, I've looked into this. It's a limited liability corporation set up in Delaware. The names of the owners are secret. So they're right. I don't see how you can prove it."

"I have a witness who heard them say they own it."

"You do? Who?"

"Ahem. Can't say, Anthony. You have your confidential sources. I have mine."

He sat staring at a white silk scarf Pari had left on the back of a chair. When he took it in his hands, a faint whiff of lavender rose like fairy dust from the absent Pari. He wanted to be with her, work together with her, not separately. A lot of their stress could be eliminated if they just settled down and stuck to the stories Pop wanted them to write. Or if Anthony quit the newspaper and they worked side by side on the blog—

His phone rang.

"Anthony, it's Emma. There's something I thought you should know. Pastor Mitch went to Esmeralda's apartment this morning before she left for work. Her husband and son had already left, and she says the pastor pushed the door open and walked in. He's blaming her for something. Something about books and *resurrección*. That's what she said."

Anthony was writing this down. It looked like the pastor was accusing Esmeralda of giving Pari's *Searchlight* blog information about what she'd overheard at the RES-RECT meeting.

"The pastor told her a maid's duty is to serve the family and keep quiet about what goes on in the house: it's in the Bible."

"Uh-huh."

"He reminded her of the ICE raid that got her sent back to Guatemala. Said that could happen again."

The point of Anthony's pencil broke on his notepad.

"Esmeralda was crying. I picked her up and drove her to the Whitman house so she wouldn't be late."

The problem with limiting himself to stress-free reporting on nothing but bake sales and spaghetti dinners was people like Emma. She expected the press to help keep politicians, investors, and preachers honest. In her mind, that was his job. Unfortunately, he had to agree. He got in his car and drove up North-South Highway to the Church of the Invokers of Jesus. Emma had told him the pastor drove a black Mercedes. There it was in the parking lot.

The back part of the building housed the Church of the Invokers of Jesus Youth Development Center. Anthony walked around to the front and through the Worship Room up to a door that read *Outreach Office. Private.*

Standing there, he heard Pastor Mitch say, "I'm sending you another check, Andrew. You can thank my Bay Hills congregation for their campaign support. Not that they know where their money's going."

Anthony knocked.

"Busy. Who is it?" The pastor's sing-song voice conveyed annoyance. Anthony heard him say in a lower voice, "Call you back later, Andrew."

"Well, Mr. Mansfield. Has our community watchdog decided to join the congregation of the righteous Invokers of Jesus?"

As Anthony sat in a chair opposite his desk, the pastor quickly closed a check register he'd been writing in.

"I wanted to ask if you know Esmeralda Moreno."

The pastor displayed something between a grin and a grimace, his white teeth flashing in the dim little office. "Well, now, we have many members among our Northbrook Invokers with Spanish names. It can be confusing. I really can't say one way or another. Why do you ask?"

"I understand you paid a visit to Mrs. Moreno this morning."

Pastor Mitch rubbed his substantial chin. "I make quite a few pastoral calls in my profession. That may have been one of them." He squinted. "What do you want, Mr. Mansfield?"

"I thought you would remember her. She was one of a group of people rounded up some months ago in an Immigration and Customs Enforcement raid." Anthony noted a red, white, and blue poster on the wall behind the pastor featuring a picture of Andrew Mauer. "The raid the County Executive requested his friends in the Federal Government to carry out."

"Ah, yes, the Grosbecks' Esmeralda, now working for your publisher." He waved a finger at Anthony. "You surprise me, young man. She's a striking beauty, no doubt, but isn't she a little old for you?"

Anthony just glared at him.

The pastor continued, "I'm aware that you lost Harold Whitman's daughter to a handsome TV personality. Now, I'm always willing to help the press out. If you're looking for a replacement, there are any number of fine young Latina women in our congregation that I could introduce you to."

Anthony wondered if pimps smirked like that.

"Hold on," the pastor said. He picked up the phone. "Natalie, is Maria working in the Center today? Good. Would you send her in to the office, please."

Anthony had had enough. "Pastor Rainey, Esmeralda told a friend you threatened her. She didn't understand why, but she said you mentioned something about the new school books."

The pastor's eyes narrowed to slits. "As a Christian church, we obviously support the new Christian curriculum and the corresponding school texts. I'm sure you can understand that."

"Do you have any financial stake in the textbooks? Because the editor of the *Searchlight* blog says you do. And she reported that you and Bea Doggit threatened her, too."

The pastor picked up his phone. "Natalie, call Maria back. She's not to come in." His face flushed. "Young man, we want the press on our side. You must understand that. I'm thankful the *Ledger*, at least, hasn't written anything opposing the curriculum yet, and I'm determined they won't."

Anthony repeated his question.

The pastor narrowed his eyes. "Be careful, sir. Remember, Jesus said, 'Let he who is without guilt cast the first stone.'"

It wasn't clear to Anthony where the pastor was going with this until he said, "I'm starting to think you do have a thing, as they say, for older women."

Anthony felt his throat swell with rage. "We're not talking about me. I asked you a question. Do you have a financial stake in the new textbooks?"

"But now we *are* talking about you. You see, Beatrice Doggit tells me you attempted to ravish her in her Jacuzzi spa. I must say I was shocked. I think your readers might be shocked, too, if they heard about it." The pastor leaned forward. "But I'm sure that won't happen. I'm sure you'll make it clear to everybody that I pay visits to my parishioners only to give them counsel. I'm sure you'll recognize the Christian curriculum as something to be promoted in your news stories. And I'm sure you'll see to it that the slanderous blog managed by your colleague is taken down."

Anthony tried to swallow his anger. He was about to leave when there was a loud knock on the door. It opened, and Andre stepped in wearing a long sleeved T-shirt with white and baby blue stripes.

"We're busy here," the pastor grumbled.

But Andre stood as if at attention—there was no other chair—and began: "Our last confrontation, Pastor Rainey, ended poorly for you and the Riverside Paradise venture. But it seems you haven't learned from that. Your threats against a woman and her family that I am sponsoring have gone too far. Although my sponsorship of the Moreno family is primarily a financial obligation, it is common practice to provide other kinds of support as well. Care of immigrants throughout the centuries in Europe, Asia, Africa, and the Far East has always—"

The pastor stood up. "Enough. Is this gobbledygook your way of accusing me of something?"

But Andre never stopped. "... in English common law as well as in the Napoleonic Code. Your threat to have Esmeralda deported demonstrates an intent to harm and therefore is a criminal act punishable by—"

"Out, you fool." The pastor pushed against Andre's chest, with no effect.

Anthony snapped a picture, then switched his camera to

video. Andre gripped the pastor's wrists and kept on talking.

"Do something," the pastor pleaded to Anthony.

"Should I call the police?" Anthony offered.

"Oww. Oww," the pastor screamed. "No. No police."

Andre let go. "I think we *should* call the police. I want to report that you broke into a woman's apartment and threatened her."

The pastor held down the phone receiver.

The door opened again, and Natalie, the woman in charge of the Youth Development Center, came in. "I hear shout and I come to see what is wrong." She noticed Andre. "Mr. Andre! I no see you since you quit working at the Center. You coming back, I hope."

The pastor said, "You can go, Natalie."

She took Andre's arm. "Maybe you come to Center now, see the children. They still talking about when you read them *Winnie the Pooh*."

Andre relaxed immediately into a broad smile. He nodded to Anthony and followed Natalie out of the office without another word.

The pastor leaned back against his desk, speechless.

Anthony said, "I'll take my leave, too." He hooked his phone back onto his belt. "I guess I can accurately say you didn't deny having a financial interest in the new required books? Would that be correct?"

"Get out."

29

Head clouds

I will not leave this house which is filled with light.
I will not journey from this village which is blessed by the One.

—Rumi, *Divān-e-Shams-e-Tabrizi*

Anthony picked Emma up and drove her to Andre's house. Andre was a friend of her family. He'd gone missing a while back, and Emma had teared up when she told Anthony about it. He'd never seen her and Andre together, but it was clear from how she talked about him they were close. It was a puzzling relationship, Anthony thought. Not romantic in any ordinary sense. She seemed to think Andre needed her protection.

They tapped on the door of his dilapidated bungalow. "In here," they heard Andre call out, unnecessarily since the paintless, sagging door hung half open, and in the dim light they saw him standing with a book in hand, marking his place with a finger. "Heard you coming down the road. Watch—"

Anthony tripped over a dumbbell on the floor, catching hold of a threadbare armchair. A box of Tastee Donuts tipped onto the bare wood floor. Andre seemed unaware they'd fallen. He wrapped his book-free hand around Emma in a half hug.

Some time ago, Anthony had received a call supposedly from a parent of a child in the Invokers Youth Development Center accusing Andre of sexual molestation. Emma had proved not only that the accusation was false but that the call had actually come from Pastor Mitch himself in an attempt to blackmail Andre into selling his property to the Riverside Paradise project that he and Bea were developing.

Emma stooped to pick up the box of donuts. She seemed to consider herself Andre's minder. His "head was in the clouds," she'd once told Anthony. To Andre, his property was just a comfortable place where he could read, think, and tie up his dinghy at the river. He didn't think of it as having monetary value, which made him vulnerable to people who wanted to take it from him. This is what Emma said she feared.

The little window by the armchair let in enough light for reading, perhaps, but it took a while before Anthony's eyes adjusted well enough to make out a table stacked with books and a straight-backed chair piled high with empty pizza boxes. He saw that Andre was still in light blue pajamas.

"Maybe we could sit?" Emma suggested. She and Anthony each insisted that the other take the chair. Andre turned over two buckets. Anthony sat on one.

"Tea?" Andre offered. He went through a narrow doorway into what must have been a kitchen. Emma followed. From his bucket, Anthony heard giggling, then Emma saying something like "better just leave him alone."

Emma put the three cups of tea on the window sill and took the chair. Andre took the bucket next to Anthony, a smile on his face and his knee touching Anthony's.

"Um," Anthony said. "About Esmeralda. Apparently, you're her sponsor?" He had his notepad out. "She complained to you about Pastor Mitch's threats?"

"She says the pastor shook her by the shoulders." Andre studied Anthony's face. "Maybe you noticed I got a little rough with him at the church. I shouldn't have, but I couldn't help it."

Anthony looked up from his notes. "Esmeralda doesn't go to his church, doesn't work for him. Any idea why he threatened her?"

Andre put his finger to his temple. "Esmeralda can't imagine. Psychologists say that irrational behavior often results when deep-seated fear triggers the self-preservation instinct, which has been proven to—"

"What do you think the pastor is afraid of?" Emma interrupted.

Andre blinked. Anthony had already learned that it was difficult to derail him from his train of thought.

"Because," Emma went on, "all she told me, he was shouting about 'books and resurrection.'"

Andre grinned. "Are you familiar with *Searchlight*? I'm sure Anthony is. I heard about it from his colleague Pari. It seems that in the modern world, the exchange of ideas has been accelerated by—"

"Right," Anthony interrupted. "And Pari's blog *Searchlight* published the fact that the recently adopted Christianized alt-right textbooks for county public schools are published by Bea and the pastor's RES-RECT, which stands to profit tremendously from their adoption."

Andre nodded. "And this so-called pastor presumes that Esmeralda gave Pari that information for *Searchlight*."

"He can't be serious?" Emma's mouth dropped.

Andre chuckled. "I know. I asked her about it. First of all, she doesn't have a computer. Second, when I asked if she'd seen the 'Blog,' she said, 'I know about the Block, but I never go there. My husband either.'"

Anthony tried to keep a straight face. The City's infamous Block was the location of strip clubs and sex shops.

Emma wondered, "I guess she could have called Pari at the newspaper and given the information to her."

"Esmeralda doesn't know Pari," Andre pointed out. He shrugged.

"I'll ask her, though," Anthony offered. It was possible, he guessed, that Esmeralda was Pari's confidential source.

"Please thank Pari for printing my comments on the advantages of septic systems over sewer lines in the *Ledger*'s Letters to the Editor." Andre cleared his throat. "Letters to the editor can be traced back to the 18th-century in America, earlier in England. Their effectiveness in influencing public opinion has varied over the years. In colonial times—"

Emma put her hand on his shoulder. He covered it with his and kept on going. "... in the aftermath of the Revolution." She tapped his shin with the toe of her sneaker, lightly once, then harder. He scratched his head.

"About the sewer line, Andre." Emma leaned towards him. "We wanted to talk about that."

Anthony added, "Yes, Pari and I are sympathetic to your objection to installing it."

"Pari told me," Andre said. "Up in the tree. An interesting name. Persian, I assume. I've been interested in Sufi poetry lately. The concept of the unity of all creation with its creator is—"

"You're losing me, Andre." Emma gave his shoulder a little shake.

"... which your Pari quite well understood. She agreed that by revering nature as a reflection of the One, we can—"

"Right." Anthony saw a chance to get back to the sewer line. "She didn't put it quite that way to me, but she agrees the county's plan to lay a sewer line would go against, um, what you were just saying."

Emma passed Andre his mug of tea from the window sill, waited for him to stop talking and take a sip, then said, "We have reason to believe the County Executive has bypassed normal procedures and regulations to push this project forward. Also that he's diverted Federal environmental funds to finance it—because he's supporting the Riverside Paradise project with Bea and the pastor." She turned to Anthony.

"Yes," Anthony continued. "And my paper's publisher also seems to be supporting it." He shrugged. "Which is something I need to look into." He couldn't tell if Andre was listening intently or just gazing into his eyes.

"Here's the thing," Emma said. You know the developers have come back as a new limited liability corporation, RESRECT."

Andre nodded, chuckling.

Emma raised her voice. "And yours is the last parcel of riverfront land they need so they can complete the project."

"I won't sell," Andre reassured her.

Emma tapped his arm. "But you might have to. The neighborhood will have to pay an additional tax for the sewer line and a very high frontage assessment fee."

Andre reached for a cake donut.

Emma went on, "So if you can't pay it, you'll have to sell. And so might your mother and the other families who live on the road behind you. They'll have to pay the sewer connection fee, too. Which they can't, I'm sure. They won't have a choice. They'll have to sell their houses to Riverside Paradise."

Andre went to the table, came back with thick document, and handed it to Anthony. "I was hoping the public would reject the sewer line on the grounds of its harm to nature. If you think they won't, here's my analysis of how much it would cost me and my neighbors, along with an analysis of the county, state, and Federal regulations that their method of financing the project seems to be violating." He leaned over to put his tea mug back on the sill, steadying himself on Anthony's knee. "I don't see why they aren't satisfied just having all the land up to mine to build their villas on."

Anthony was sure *he* knew. They wanted the whole riverfront strip, and they wanted it without Andre's ramshackle bungalow standing as an eyesore among their pretentious villas. Yet it wasn't likely Andre even understood the concept of "eyesore." He'd liked the looks of the decrepit fishing cottages that were torn down better than Bea's villa, according to Emma.

Anthony clapped his palm on the thick document. "Thanks. Maybe this will help prove the sewer line is a scam."

"By the way." Andre picked up an envelope from the table. "Would you give this to Pari? She knows what it is."

As they headed back, a yellow school bus passed them on the gravel road. Kids were coming home from school. Anthony pictured Beth, Bill, and Alan climbing to the tree house, telling Andre about their day.

"You're kind of quiet," Emma said.

"Those kids who live near Andre. You think they'll have to move if the sewer line goes through?"

"We need to find a way to make sure they don't."

For some time, neither of them spoke. As they turned onto North-South Highway towards Shady Park, Anthony slowed down. He tended to do this when he was thinking. Now it was about the way Andre touched his knee and looked at him. Determined not to jump to conclusions, he still couldn't help wondering if Andre was gay. He felt his cheeks warm as he realized this was none of his business.

"Andre's gay," Emma said. "Guess you noticed."

A full blush throbbed over his face. Emma was toying with the envelope in her lap, and he hoped she didn't notice.

She held up the envelope. "That reporter Pari," she said. "I can tell Andre likes her. I guess you do, too?"

He nodded. Emma watched him as he slowed for a light. "Andre says she's 'striking.' He assumes she's your girlfriend."

"Yes."

He wondered if Pari had taken seriously Victoria's hint that she and Anthony might get back together. He hadn't seen

Pari since that phone call. She said she needed to "work from home for a while." He gripped the steering wheel in frustration. A horn beeped behind them, and he saw the light was green.

Emma dropped the envelope back onto her lap. "I'm sorry." She pushed her fingers up nervously through her hair. "I have to ask you, Anthony. Is Pari the woman who called asking me to stay away from you. I wouldn't want—"

"No. That wasn't Pari."

"Right. I know you said it was somebody who doesn't work at the paper any more. I just wanted to be sure. Because if you think it's better, I can stay—"

"Please keep working with me, Emma. I need your help. I guess you saw that the *Shady Park Ledger* endorsed Andrew Mauer for County Exec. And Frank Fortunato, the Arm the Teachers guy, for the House of Delegates?"

"We get the officials we deserve. That's what my husband Charles says. Those two are sure to win in our county, with or without the *Ledger*'s support. Their backers don't read the newspaper. They watch TV."

"I'll tell you something, Emma. Sometimes I think of quitting the *Ledger*." He bit his lip.

She twisted in her seat to face him. "You can't, Anthony. It was your reports that got Tran's family released from wrongful detention. Your reports exposed Bea and the pastor for defrauding Andre's neighbors. If it hadn't been for you—"

"My publisher won't let me say anything negative about the County Exec."

"Don't quit, Anthony. If the Exec is behind using an illegal sewer project to get Andre's property, the public has to know."

30

Hot blooded

Jealousy is always born with love
but does not always die with it.
—Francois de la Rochefoucauld, *Maxims*

Sure enough, in early November, Andrew Mauer was re-elected County Executive and Frank Fortunato became the State Delegate for the Shady Park-Nottingham Estates-Bay Hills district. When Anthony got to the newsroom, he expected everybody to be talking about the election. But Emma was right. The results were expected and almost un-noteworthy. Ralph was waiting for him with a yellow sticky note. *Grand Opening of Pet Yoga Salon in Shady Park*. "Going to have to ask you to cover this. Pari called. Can't come in again today. Working on that rightwing curriculum."

"Yeah, she told me."

"She said it's a big story. 'National importance' she claimed." Ralph grinned. "I said OK, keep on it a while longer." He twirled one end of his mustache. "Also, she asked if you'd talked to Victoria."

"She did? What did you say?"

Ralph's magnified eyes observed Anthony through his glasses. "I said I wouldn't know." He seemed embarrassed and looked away, tapping the sticky note. "The place closes in an hour."

Anthony grabbed a camera and took off down North-South Highway. He walked into a shop in the Executive Shopping Center that had a handwritten sign on the window: *Grand Opening. Your Pet Deserves the Best.*

"Anthony! What a surprise." Victoria's friend Jennifer stood at the registration podium, a fluffy white dog in her hands. She immediately forced the smile off her face and lowered her voice. "I was so sorry to hear about you and Victoria. How are you dealing with it? This is my little Maltese. I call him Malty. Say hello, Malty. He so needs exercise, and I thought it would be best to start him off with something not too stressful."

The proprietor, an anorexic looking woman in her early 40s wearing skin tight leggings with a dog design embroidered on one leg and a cat design on the other, walked up to Anthony. "Welcome to the Shady Park Pet Yoga Salon, where we believe the path to enrichment should be open to all."

Anthony handed her his card.

"Oh, thanks for coming." She led Jennifer and Anthony behind a Japanese shoji screen to a room of tatami mats. "Your shoes need to be left here before you go into the asana space, if you don't mind."

Women were on the mats holding their pets—four or five dogs, one cat, and what looked like a ferret—in poses demonstrated by another very lean woman at the far end in front of a mirror. Anthony started snapping pictures.

Jennifer sat on a yellow plastic chair with Malty on her lap waiting for the next session to begin. When Anthony finished taking the proprietor's picture and getting the details for the story, Jennifer patted the chair next to her. "You must be devastated. Victoria is so .... A doll, that's what Chad says. He makes me a little jealous." She bent to give Malty a consoling kiss on the mouth. "Anyway, who knows? Maybe you'll get her back."

"No. That's not going to happen."

"Don't want to get your hopes up, but Victoria tells me when John Rowland comes to her house lately, he talks to the maid more than to her. And he's never *yet* taken her to Sur le

Dessus for dinner with Chad and me like you did." Jennifer sighed. "You have to feel sorry for her. She still acts like she's crazy in love with the guy."

When he got back with the pet yoga story, Pop motioned him into his office, shaking his head. "Anthony, my boy. Need you to do me a favor. It's about Victoria."

Anthony shoved his notepad into his pocket.

"Dumbest thing Britney Grosbeck ever did, getting rid of Esmeralda. She's a straight shooter. No way she'd ever tell a lie, as far as I can see."

Anthony had a feeling he knew where this was going.

"She came to me. I thought she was going to ask for a raise. And I would have given it to her, by God." Pop felt in his breast pocket for a cigar. "Way she tells it, this John Rowland is all over her like a hound on raw meat."

Anthony had a hard time imagining Esmeralda putting it exactly that way.

"So I've decided next time he comes around to tell the son of a bitch he's not welcome in my house." Pop sucked his cigar lit. "Trouble is, it's going to break Victoria's heart." He blew out an exasperated puff. "She worships the guy."

Anthony nodded.

"He's twice her age," Pop boomed. "A womanizer to boot. If I let him keep coming around, you can bet our Esmeralda's going to quit."

Anthony gave another confirming nod. Pop put his hand on his shoulder. "Here's the thing. I told Victoria she was better off with you."

"No, I—"

"She's home right now. How about you go over and at least talk to her?"

"I can't, Pop. I agree John Rowland's no good for her, but there's no way she and I can get back together."

Pop's dark eyes studied Anthony from beneath his massive brow. Finally, he shrugged. "Just tell her what you think of Rowland, then. I'll settle for that."

When Anthony didn't look up, Pop said, "Ah, and something else. That rightwing Christian textbook thing? Turns out you're right to call it a scam. Do this for me, and then I'm planning to give you and Betty—no, Poly, no, you know, the new girl—the go-ahead to expose it. Got to get some ducks in a row first. I'll let you know."

Anthony called Victoria from his car in the *Ledger* parking lot, resentful that she still seemed to have some control over his life.

"Anthony, have you seen the ratings? They're up ten points since I've been reporting. I'm wearing my hair a different way. I guess you noticed." She breathed out a sigh. "It doesn't seem John has."

He waited for her to go on.

"Mothers are calling in to the station, mostly reporting people they think might be terrorists, but a lot of them are praising me. 'That Victoria Whitman really digs beneath the surface.' That's what one said."

Anthony cleared his throat. "But about your reports, Victoria. You realize you need to separate internet rumor from facts, right? Even your dad says he told you that."

"Oh, don't be jealous, Anthony. It's pretty clear that hejab woman fired the shot, isn't it? Willard's gun wasn't fired, and that woman was standing right in front of the teacher who got shot."

"But that's not why people assume she's the shooter. I think it's just because she was wearing a hejab. Anyway, she doesn't own a gun." As soon as he said that, he remembered that Shahnaz's husband had brought home the pistol from work for her protection. "I mean, she didn't."

"Didn't? She has a gun now?"

Without answering, he changed the subject. "You still seeing John, then?"

Victoria forgot everything else. "Anthony, I'm so in love! John is so ...." She paused, and he thought he heard her sniffling.

He tapped his fingers on the dashboard. She needed to know about John Rowland. This was going to be hard. He knew she'd hate him for it. "Vicky, I'm going to come over to talk to you."

"OK. Oh, hold on. John's calling me now. I need to take this. See you soon. Bye."

Victoria's family lived in Bay Hills, an enclave of aging ivy-clad colonial revival houses north of Shady Park. The wide, balanced facades of most of the homes featured covered central entrances and dormer windows. Victoria's house was brick, painted white. Leaves from enormous oaks swirled in the breeze, settling on the deep green grass. A dark-haired man looked up from raking and nodded as Anthony walked up the brick path to the portico.

Esmeralda opened the door. A familiar dog smell hung in the entry hall. Pop's white Borzoi ran up to give Anthony a lick on the hand.

"No. You sit," Esmeralda told Boris. "Do not bother guest." She smiled when Anthony introduced himself. "Please to meet you, Mr. Anthony. Everybody—my friend Natalie, Mrs. Emma—say you are simpatico. So sorry I no wait on the bus stop." She reached out to shake his hand.

In the daylight, Anthony could see why John Rowland might be attracted to her. He said, "I used to visit here a lot. You must have started with the Whitmans recently."

Esmeralda's eyes darkened. "Yes. Mrs. Britney fire me. I work here for now."

He wasn't sure what "for now" meant. In a way, his mission from Pop was to make sure she didn't quit. He needed to talk to her, but not now, so he slipped her his card and said, "I came to see Victoria."

"Of course, Mr. Anthony. Maybe you and me can meet some other time to talk? You can sit in here."

He turned and saw Victoria standing by the French doors to the living room.

The ebony lid of a grand piano was covered with framed photographs of Victoria, ranging from baby pictures to high school and college graduation portraits. Boris circled and flopped down on the threadbare oriental carpet in front of Anthony's chair. Victoria raised her voice. "Esmeralda, no coffee. We need to talk in private." Her eyes were swollen, and she gripped a tissue. She sat across from Anthony, sniffling. When Esmeralda closed the doors, she said, "Anthony, I need to ask you something. How can a girl know if a guy is losing interest in her?"

Her sad face softened his annoyance at still having to deal with her. He got up to retrieve a tissue she dropped. But then Boris got up, too, thumping his long furry tail against Anthony's leg.

"You're leaving?" Victoria clapped her hands. "Sit, Boris." Boris didn't sit, but Anthony did.

"Losing interest, Vicky? You mean John Rowland?"

"Of course. Who else?" She burst out in tears.

Like Pop, Anthony was pained to see Victoria unhappy. At the same time, like Pop, he knew the best thing would be for her to forget about Rowland. Plenty of fish in the sea, Victoria? No, that wouldn't help.

Victoria's mascara was smeared. "Answer my question. How can you tell?"

"Vicky, I'd say if something makes you worried he's losing interest, then he probably is."

She sobbed, "It's that bitch Esmeralda. She's trying to get

him away from me. I'm sure of it." She pulled another tissue from her pocket and blew her nose. "You should see the way John acts around her."

It wasn't hard for Anthony to imagine. He ventured, "But what about her? You're not saying Esmeralda encourages him?"

"I know what these people are like. Hot blooded. Maybe they can't help it. But I don't want her here." Victoria's pearlescent lipstick had smeared onto the edge of one cheek. "I told Mom. She agrees."

"Vicky, I think you're making a mistake. Esmeralda's—"

"You're taking her side? I heard her talking to you just now. *Maybe you and me can meet some other time to talk.* That woman's incorrigible. With her husband right outside raking leaves! She'd better stay away from you, that's all I have to say." Victoria dabbed her eyes. "Anyway, Mom promised me she'd fire her as soon as Pastor Mitch finds a replacement from his Invokers or whatever you call them up at his Northbrook church."

"I don't think it's fair to fire Esmeralda, Victoria."

"See? You are defending her."

Anthony took a deep breath. It was time to tell her what he'd seen John Rowland doing at the bus stop. "Vicky, there's something you should know. It's John who's hitting on Esmeralda, not the other way around." He briefly described the scene.

Victoria stopped crying, tilting her head in disbelief. "Anthony, I guess you're sorry to lose me, but don't tell lies. It's not like you. I'll never believe John did that." She closed her eyes as if to get the picture of John pursuing Esmeralda out of her head.

"It's the truth, Victoria. I'm sorry."

She shook her head. "No. I know the real reason why he *might* be losing interest in me. I'm sure it's because I haven't come up with any 'breaking news' stories for a while."

That didn't seem like the real reason to Anthony, but before he could say anything, her phone rang.

She got up and stepped away. "John, Sweetie. I was just thinking about you."

She listened, visibly shocked by what John was telling her. She began sobbing into the phone, "Johnny, no. Megyn Drumpfer?"

Anthony heard Rowland's voice but couldn't tell what he was saying.

"But, Johnny," Victoria said, "viewers have called in to praise my reports. Why would you replace me with Megyn?"

Rowland spoke longer this time.

Tears rolled down Victoria's cheeks. "That's not fair, John. If there's no news, how do you expect me to—?"

She took a breath and held it, listening.

"Wait, Johnny. Wait. I do have a new scoop. That hejab woman? I found out she owns a gun."

31

Scooped

I doubt not then but innocence shall make
False accusation blush and tyranny
Tremble at patience.

—Shakespeare, *The Winter's Tale*

On the way home, Anthony stopped by the Grab 'n Go for some fried chicken. Kaila thanked him for his *Ledger* article on the fight in the store. "Unfortunately, as you know, it is impossible for facts and logic to change the minds of people who have a strong desire to believe something, and since the audience of certain television news broadcasts consists primarily of those people, it is inevitable that—"

"Yes," Anthony said. "You're right. All we can do is put the truth out there." He didn't want to get into a long conversation now. "I'll just take this chicken and this jar of instant coffee." He liked coffee better than tea, and his tea drinking guest seemed preoccupied with her own project lately.

He was sipping his after-chicken coffee when the early evening news came on his tiny TV.

"John, I'm standing in front of the Northbrook APARTMENTS, where Shahnaz Delpak, the woman suspected by many of FIRING the shot at the School Board hearing lives. Although she was released by the police after first BEING arrested, I have learned that she does OWN a gun. John."

"Victoria, thank you. Do we know if the suspect had the gun in her possession at the meeting?"

"John, we can't say for sure. But one woman who was

STANDING with her on the platform at the time, Beatrice Doggit, reported to the police that she saw Delpak reaching under her clothes just before the SHOT was fired. John."

"Victoria, thank you so much for this exclusive report. As always, WPSK TV will stay on top of the latest developments in this story."

Anthony kicked the table leg, harder than he meant, causing Thumper to give out a single bark down below. He felt sick to his stomach, and it wasn't the chicken. He went to the bathroom but didn't actually throw up. He lay down on the bed, but that brought up thoughts he wasn't prepared to deal with right now.

Pari would be devastated by the report. He called her but the phone rang and went to voicemail. He recorded, "Pari, I need to talk to you." Then he called her parents' number. That phone also took him to voicemail. They had all probably gone to be with Shahnaz.

He called Victoria.

"Anthony. Thanks for the scoop. How did I look?"

"How could you, Victoria? I told you Shahnaz *didn't* have a gun at the time of the shooting. For some time, she's been getting threats because of your reports. That's why her husband recently brought a pistol home from the gas station—for her protection."

"I don't know, Anthony. Maybe she had the gun then, too. She was right in front of the teacher who got shot."

Anthony couldn't deny this. It was looking bad for Shahnaz.

The next morning, Pop was fuming. "How could you let TV scoop us on a story like this? It's the smoking gun, for God's sake. You don't find out about it—but Victoria does?"

"Pop, the woman only got the gun after her family started being harassed. Her husband brought it home from work for protection. I knew that."

Ralph pushed Pop's office door farther open and edged in, but Pop kept Anthony in his glare. "So you were sitting on the fact that she had a gun?"

"There's no evidence she had it at the time of the shooting. I was waiting to ask her husband's employer if he could verify that the gun was at the gas station during the Board of Education hearing."

Pop turned to Ralph. "It was your advice to sit on the story? I hope not."

Ralph said, "Pop, you know we need to get all the facts we can before going to press. Looks to me like that's what Anthony was doing." He turned to Anthony. "A Professor Shandule, Pari's father, I believe, wants you to call him. He says it's urgent."

The carrel phone was slippery in Anthony's sweaty fingers. Pari's father said, "Anthony, I'm between classes and only have a few minutes to talk. Our friend Shahnaz Delpak's house has been searched by the police."

They had no choice after Victoria's report, Anthony realized.

"Pari was very disappointed that the story got out about Shahnaz having a gun in her apartment—and the way the TV news handled it. So I wanted a reporter who deals in facts to know about the search. It'd be great if you could find out what's really going on."

"Sure, Professor."

"Mark."

"Sure." He swallowed. "I guess Pari's already looking into it."

"She's in Syracuse working with her brother on a story. She didn't tell you?"

"Um, no." Anthony didn't allow himself to brood about this. He was in his car heading towards Shahnaz's apartment in minutes.

"Yes? Who is it?" a man's voice called cautiously from behind the graffiti trashed door. When Anthony gave his name, Shahnaz peeped through the crack and let him in.

She introduced her husband Reza. She was breathing heavily. "Lucky the police didn't come until after Jim left for school," she sighed.

The apartment had been ransacked. Drawers had been dumped onto the floor, Persian carpets turned over, couch cushions pulled up. The samovar lay on its side, the gilt trimmed mirror sat on the floor, the pictures on the wall hung askew. And this was only the living room. Anthony asked to look into the other rooms. Mattresses were pulled from the beds, dresser drawers pulled out or emptied onto the floor. In the kitchen, every cabinet door hung open, with the food and dishes scattered on the counter or table. He snapped some pictures with his phone.

"My God, My God!" Reza kept saying. "It is just like in Iran. Like the *Pasdaran*, the Revolutionary Guard. The reason we left."

"I showed them the pistol," Shahnaz said. "But they looked everywhere anyway. I don't know what for."

Anthony asked them for a description of the gun. Reza said, "Little gun. My boss says it is Raven MP-25. Shahnaz said she will never touch. She want me to take it back." He looked at his wife. "Sorry. I should listen. I, too, I do not like gun. It is just, I think this is America so better have a gun."

"I have to ask," Anthony said to Shahnaz. "You didn't have it with you at the School Board hearing, did you?"

"No. No. I have never touched it."

Anthony wrote this down. "Did the police take anything else?"

"Our letters," Shahnaz said. "Our pictures. Jim's laptop.

Our Persian music DVDs."

"And my camera," Reza added. "Same like in Iran." He took Shahnaz into his arms, his fingernails lined with grease. He'd probably rushed back from his job at the gas station. "Maybe we should go live with my cousin in Los Angeles," he said. "I can fix cars now. Maybe get a mechanic job there."

Shahnaz shook her head. "The police said we can't leave the area as long as the investigation is open."

Reza closed his eyes, defeated.

Shahnaz said Reza was a film producer in Iran. When Ershad, the Ministry of Culture and Islamic Guidance, declared their latest film decadent and immoral, the company collapsed, and all their work was destroyed. "Reza was depressed. We came here to stay with our cousins, but they have all gone to LA now."

The county police department was about a mile away. He got there in time to catch his friend Rob going out for lunch. "Need company?" Anthony asked. "How about Java Hut?"

Rob ordered a tuna melt, Anthony a chicken sandwich. Most of the customers were men, red hats with *Mauer for America* apparently de rigueur. As he'd expected, Anthony didn't recognize any other policemen. Java Hut had donuts but they couldn't match the ones farther down the highway at Tastee. He and Rob sat in a corner and talked low.

"We never found the casing," Rob told him. "We have the slug we dug up from the school meeting room. It was smashed all to hell—too deformed to connect to a particular gun. Only thing ballistics could tell us is it's a small caliber." Rob took a sip of coffee. "Not much, maybe. But that's the kind of gun we found in the Delpak apartment."

Anthony felt his throat tighten.

"Serial number shows it was bought by the gas station owner her husband works for. McGinn is questioning him right now. We'll see if he says it was at the gas station at the time of the shooting. Then see if that can be proved. We're questioning everybody who works there. Questioning the woman's neighbors, too."

"I guess you'll examine the gun, see if it's been fired recently."

"Waiting for the ballistics report."

"It's the harassment of his family that made her husband think he should bring the gun home."

"Um-hum." Rob looked him in the eye. "And we know when the harassment started. With Victoria's TV broadcasts. Playing on the viewers' fear. We had no choice. We had to go get the gun when that report came out." He swallowed a bite of his sandwich. "I have to wonder how Victoria found out about the gun. I mean, her 'news' usually comes from your articles, and you didn't write about it."

Anthony gave a self-conscious shrug. He imagined Pari wondering the same thing.

Rob gulped down the last of his coffee. "Want to come back to the station with me? Get the word on fingerprints?"

Anthony was planning to try calling Pari again, but he went along.

"No usable prints," Detective McGinn called over to Rob's desk. He frowned when he noticed Anthony. "You Anthony Mansfield, *Shady Park Ledger* reporter?"

Anthony nodded.

"There's been a complaint against you. Attempted rape."

III

32

Persons of interest

Artificer of fraud …
That practis'd falsehood under saintly shew,
Deep malice to conceal, couch'd with revenge.
—John Milton, *Paradise Lost*

"Do you know Beatrice Doggit?" Detective McGinn had taken Anthony to the interrogation room, Rob following.

"Have you ever been in her house? Were you there alone with her on a day near the end of October? Did you sexually assault her in her Jacuzzi?"

Anthony answered the questions and told his story.

"So she was naked but you weren't? Is that what we're to understand?"

Anthony lowered his head, nodding.

"Would you please say 'yes' for the record."

Rob interrupted. "Listen, Mike. I've known Anthony since we were in high school together. There's no way he did anything like this."

"Still," the detective said. "We take complaints like this seriously. We have to investigate." He squinted at Anthony. "Any reason Beatrice Doggit might want to make up a story like this?"

"I wrote news articles revealing a real estate scam she was running. She hates me."

The detective cupped his chin. "And yet, by your admission, she exposed herself to you and invited you to bathe with her naked?"

Anthony told him about the pastor's threat that Bea would make this accusation if he didn't take down Pari's blog and write an article in favor of the right-wing school curriculum. "By which he and Ms. Doggit stand to make a lot of money," he added.

"Hmm." The detective frowned. "We need to get all this in writing."

Before Anthony could leave, the detective said, "You're not being booked, you understand? But it would be helpful if you let us get your fingerprints."

Anthony's hands trembled as the police sergeant rolled each finger across the inkpad, then over the card. When she finished both hands, she gave him a paper towel and alcohol to wipe off the ink.

"Sign giving your permission," the detective said. "Then go in there. Marge will take a blood sample for the DNA."

What's next? he wondered, pressing a cotton ball to his arm. He wasn't being arrested, the detective said, but it felt like it. In the movies, criminals were allowed one phone call. He would be wasting it to call Pari if she was in Syracuse. He could call his father, he supposed.

"Not planning to leave the county, are you?" the detective said.

So they were definitely letting him go.

"Come on," Rob said. "I'll walk you out."

Anthony's head was spinning. He tripped on the step outside the door and grabbed Rob's arm. "I can't believe this. I've done nothing wrong."

"Chin up," Rob said. "It's a she said, he said case. A detective already went to interview Bea, but she wasn't cooperative. You're not charged yet. If she doesn't come in to do the paperwork, you won't be." He stopped at Anthony's car. "The complaint will stay on the record, though. I'd stay away from Bea from now on, if I were you."

Anthony was familiar with the English Department at Piskasanet Community College, which consisted of a series of small offices along a corridor too narrow for two people to pass side by side. He found Professor Mark Shandule's office halfway down. The door was open, and Pari's father sat hunched over his keyboard, staring at his computer.

Anthony knocked and went in. "I went to Shahnaz's place, Professor, uh, Mark. The police pretty much tore it apart."

"Yes, she called. Mastaneh and I are going over after work to help them put it back together." He shoved some white hair out of his eyes.

"It's too bad her husband brought that gun home." Anthony decided not to mention something that worried him even more, that the slug found at the scene of the shooting came from a small caliber gun like the one they found in Shahnaz's apartment. He only said, "She should probably get a lawyer."

Mark nodded, drumming his fingers on the arm of his chair. "I can't help wondering what the next TV news report will say."

"Mark—and I hope you'll tell Pari this, too—I'm going to do my best to see that Victoria Whitman, for one, doesn't get wind of the apartment search."

From where he sat, Anthony caught sight of "*Searchlight*" on Mark's monitor. He pointed. "Pari's blog?"

"Right. It's mushrooming. You wouldn't believe it. Board of Education officials from across the country. People from the Southwest especially weighing in, telling how the alt-right evangelical curriculum was introduced in their schools." He gave his hair another swipe. "Pari has a 'counter,' she calls it. Over 100,000 comments so far. It's about 60-40 in favor."

"Of Christianizing public schools?"

Mark frowned with a single nod. "But look here." He clicked to another page. "See? Comments on the idea of

Board of Education members having a financial interest in publishing textbooks: 75-25 against. A lot of them claim this is against the law or an ethics code violation in their state. Including ours."

Anthony hadn't looked at *Searchlight* for a while. Bea and her partners must be panicking.

Mark clicked. "Here. This is a list of the passages that right-wing evangelists put into one curriculum in the Southwest. My son Ken and his friend put it together. Pari wants to put out a list for our own county. When the public sees what's going on, things can change."

Anthony gave the list a cursory look. "So, when is Pari coming home?"

Mark's chair squeaked as he swiveled from the screen towards Anthony. "You're not in touch? I thought you two were .... Well, I know she's been really busy. She's thinking of quitting the paper and doing this full time."

Mark's phone beeped. "A message. Excuse me. I better take a look at this. It's from Mastaneh." He bit his lip as he read. "Bad news," he told Anthony. "Shahnaz has been arrested."

He called Rob on his way to the newsroom. "But the police didn't arrest Shahnaz when they picked up the gun. Why now?"

"Ballistics report came back. The gun was fired fairly recently."

When he hung up, Anthony flipped through the pictures on his phone that he'd taken at the Board hearing. Shahnaz was holding a book in both hands in every shot he had of her. He checked the video. He'd focused his camera on the unruly crowd rather than the speakers on the platform. After the shot was fired, he'd held the phone over his head. The video was too shaky to show much, and it was aimed at the gunman by the door.

He scrolled through the contact list on his phone, called Pari's father, and told him what he'd learned from Rob.

"Thanks, Anthony. Reza took off from work. He's home with their son Jim. Mastaneh and I are already on our way to the Northbrook Detention Center. Wish Pari were here."

"Me, too."

Elbows on carrel, head in hands, Anthony ran through some decisions he'd made lately. He'd sat on the story of the police searching Shahnaz's apartment and taking the gun. He'd sat on Bea's accusation of attempted rape. It was news. No denying that. Would the *New York Times* report it even before she filed an official report? Nowadays, probably. He didn't care. Let somebody else dig that up and report it. But an arrest he had to report. It would be on the public police record. He paged to the *Ledger*'s Police Blotter section on his newsroom monitor and typed: "Shahnaz Delpak arrested on suspicion of firing a gun on school property. The investigation is ongoing." He clicked Enter and went home. With luck, that would get slipped into the *Ledger* without anybody noticing it. The *City Paper* had enough arrests of its own residents to report on. And Victoria never went to check arrest records. She was afraid of police stations.

33

A Clean, Well-Lighted Place

It was the light of course but it is necessary that the place be clean and pleasant.

—Ernest Hemingway,
"A Clean, Well-Lighted Place"

As soon as Anthony sat down at his carrel, Ralph ambled out of his office, a cynical twist on his lips. Here it was. Ralph had probably realized the Police Blotter entry should have been reported as a full story.

Instead, Ralph slapped a yellow sticky note onto his screen: *Moms for School Safety, Nottingham Estates clubroom, 10:00 a.m.* Anthony did his best to stifle a sigh of relief. It was possible Ralph had read the Police Blotter but hadn't recognized Shahnaz's name.

"Better grab a camera." Ralph used a whiny voice. "The moms want to see their pictures in the paper."

Nottingham Estates was a neighborhood of McMansions, as Anthony's father called them, east of the highway that split Shady Park into new and old. According to Ralph, the wrought iron security gate was always left open because the residents couldn't keep track of the security code to punch in. Inside the gate, the asphalt road wound through wooded turf, no houses visible from the road, only here and there the stone or brick columns marking the entrance to a driveway. If you stopped your car, you could sometimes catch sight through the trees of a huge brick or stucco mansion that looked like a Renaissance villa or Georgian estate except that it was brand new. Anthony had never been in one of these houses.

He drove past the golf course and found the sprawling community clubroom that overlooked the pool. He sucked in a breath before getting out of the car, hating this kind of assignment.

A tall gray-haired black man in a white jacket held a glass of wine on a silver tray as Anthony walked past into a room as big as a basketball court. Under a wall of windows overlooking the golf course ranged a line of tables covered with hors d'oeuvres. Anthony headed towards a group of chairs at the far end of the room facing a low podium and a movie screen.

As soon as some of the women saw his *Ledger* nametag, they rushed up. Anthony gave each one his card.

"Come meet the person who got this movement going." A woman in a white pants suit took him by the arm up to the front. "Britney, the *Shady Park Ledger* is here."

Britney Grosbeck looked Anthony over. "OK. You again. I was hoping that charming young lady from WPSK TV would be here. The one who interviewed me at Shady Park Elementary/Middle."

"Maybe she'll do a report tomorrow evening," Anthony said. "After she reads about it in the *Ledger*." He stood to the side taking pictures.

Britney put down her glass of red wine on a table that held a projector. "Mothers," she began. "Mothers. As you know, the County Executive held a meeting at the Shady Park Library for signing the Arm Our Teachers petition. Even though it was rainy! Of course, many of you didn't attend." She picked up her glass of wine and drained it. "So now you have another chance to sign. Here in Nottingham, in a more pleasant environment." Anthony wondered if she was alluding to the brawl she'd caused at the library.

The woman in the pants suit passed around a clipboard for signatures.

"Our children's teachers must be required to carry guns to protect them," Britney cried out. "Also. Also, ladies. Another thing. Maybe you know, the State Board of Education scheduled a hearing on school safety for later this month. Yes. But where have they scheduled it? In the City. The City, right? As if any of us are going to take the risk of going there." She paused to let one or two women mutter their indignation. "So you know what? This is our own hearing, in a safe, welcoming place."

Anthony slipped around the room scribbling down names and taking pictures. Britney kept talking but had only a single point to make, which she kept repeating. "We have to protect our children from terrorists." She held up a piece of paper. "I have a message. From Frank Fortunato, who just got elected to the, whatsit, House of something. He's on our side. He says with our support, he'll make sure teachers have to carry guns to protect our children."

As the petition was being passed around, Britney signaled for another glass of wine and drank it. "And now," she said. She knocked on the table for attention. "Now, in case our petition fails—" She looked towards the projector, nodding.

A man Anthony recognized as her husband Derek came to the front. "Concerned parents," he began. "I present you with Evergreen Academy." He signaled to the waiter at the door to dim the lights.

Pachelbel's Canon heralded a slideshow that Anthony assumed was a pitch for a planned private school in the Nottingham neighborhood of Shady Park. The first pictures were of exquisitely-dressed children, all Caucasian, who might have been in the first grade. As the slides progressed, the children got older, and were still impeccably dressed, implausibly neat and clean. And still all white.

The plan seemed to be to build a school for grades 1 through 12. In every slide, the children were smiling, politely greeting each other. Classroom scenes showed them tilting books up on their brand-new desks as if reading. Pachelbel's Canon played on as a deep recorded voice expounded on the advantages of the planned academy. "You will have the satisfaction of knowing your child's classmates have been chosen with the utmost care."

Anthony was waiting for a description of what they would learn, but there was nothing about that. It was all about who your children would associate with in this exclusive school. He thought about his own school days, wondering what he would be like now if he hadn't mixed it up with different kinds of kids, if instead he had been raised from first grade through high school in a walled, protected garden like Evergreen Academy. Could he have become a reporter? Maybe he would have become a reporter like Victoria.

34

Victoria redux

Not to be loved is a misfortune,
but it is an insult to be loved no longer.

—Montesquieu, *Persian Letters*

Ralph was less interested in the text of Anthony's Evergreen Academy story than the pictures and names of the women. In fact, he condensed the article into picture captions of several lines each. The story was no sooner loaded onto the server than Britney called the *Ledger* to ask when it would come out.

"Didn't you tell her tomorrow?" Ralph said.

Anthony nodded. "She can be quite insistent."

Ralph stared at Pari's empty carrel. "Pari not coming in again today? She didn't call in."

"I hear she's in Syracuse working on a blog."

Ralph eyed him as if he were spouting pig Latin.

"It's an internet discussion," Anthony told him. "You know Riverside Paradise and the textbook publisher are both controlled by a corporation called RES-RECT, right?"

Ralph nodded. "Uh-huh. You say 'RES-RECT' is printed on the Paradise pamphlets. Pari says it's printed on the books."

"Well, Bea and her gang deny they own RES-RECT."

"Why?"

"Because Bea is on the Board of Education and she urged them to require the RES-RECT books. It's an ethics code violation if she profits from that decision. And there's plenty of profit."

Ralph narrowed his eyes. "So what's this about a blog?"

"Here, I'll show you." Anthony brought up Pari's blog on his monitor. Ralph pulled up Pari's chair, dropped his glasses down off his head, and read.

"It says 'a witness' heard Bea Doggit, Pastor Rainey, and Derek Grosbeck saying they own RES-RECT and are profiting from the books." Ralph turned to Anthony. "Who's the witness?"

"Pari wouldn't tell me. I've looked into RES-RECT. It's a Delaware shell corporation, designed to make it hard to find out who owns it. That's why Pari's witness is a key."

"She's going out on a limb. I hope she's corroborated her source."

"Me too."

"So when is she coming back?"

"I don't know."

Ralph shrugged. "Oaky doaky, then. Since she's not coming back any time soon ...." He pulled a note from his pocket, grinning. "Here you go, then." *Ribbon cutting at discount shoe store 1:00 p.m.*

Shops opened for business and went out of business regularly in Shady Park. The mattress store he'd covered when it opened had been a taco joint shortly before and a different mattress store before that. The pet yoga place had been a soft serve ice-cream shop previously and a bicycle shop before that. Anthony prided himself on remembering the metamorphoses of all the shops since he was in high school. His favorite: a pet store that became a used clothing shop that became a Chinese carry-out that became a musical instrument shop that became a fabric shop that became lawyer's office that became a novelty shop that became a podiatrist's office that burned down. An antique boutique built on the lot lasted for about a year but had moved out, leaving the building now empty. If it became a pizza shop, Anthony would win $5 from Ralph. He'd have to pay Ralph $5 if it turned into a nail salon.

He thought of the new Discount Shoes that he was on his way to cover as the former Elegant Tiles, Superior Carpets, Bert's Burgers, Doggie Treats, and FedEx drop off. It was always with a somewhat sad heart that he went to cover a Grand Opening or Ribbon Cutting. How long did these entrepreneurs hope to stay in business? What made them think they would be the ones to last? The *Shady Park Ledger* covered their openings, sales, remodelings, and expansions faithfully—and reaped new advertisements each time the building changed hands. They didn't cover the closings.

Anthony's salary depended on these turnovers. When he'd taken the pictures and written the copy for the Discount Shoes ribbon cutting, he bought a pair of shoes. Dockers, or imitation Dockers, to be precise. It was the least he could do.

He put the new shoes on in his car, then called Pari. The message indicated her phone had been turned off. Since he couldn't leave a voice message, he texted *I miss you.* He guessed it was possible she was getting so many calls over the book controversy on *Searchlight* that she couldn't handle them any more. The more he thought about it, the more he believed it.

Ralph didn't have anything else for him to cover that day. He headed home early. There was a lot Anthony was keeping from Ralph. The arrest of Shahnaz. He was hoping she'd be cleared and released before any real story would develop. His own interrogation—for attempted rape. Same thing: he put it out of his mind, hoping it would go away.

The autumn air was chilly and fresh. Clear blue sky. Yellow, red, and orange leaves. He took Thumper for a walk. Nothing like a nonjudgmental dog to cheer you up. As he turned the corner, his phone rang. "Pari," he said aloud, and yanked it from his belt.

But it was Victoria. Sobbing. "Anthony, I need to talk to you. Don't ask what. Just please come over."

A dark green Volvo SUV sped past him on the Bay Hills road. GOLFR, the license plate read. Victoria's mother. By the time Anthony got to the Whitmans', it was already parked in the driveway.

Esmeralda let him in, eyes sparkling with surprise. "Mr. Anthony, you are welcome."

Boris ran up to give him a lick, whimpering faintly, picking up Thumper's scent on his hand. Victoria's mother, Michelle, clomped down the hallway dragging a black plastic garbage bag. "Esmeralda, these are the clothes from the golf club ladies and their friends that Goodwill didn't want. Throw them away, will you? Or you can dig through them and see if there's anything you want to take home. Hi, Anthony. Victoria's up in her room at the top of the stairs to the left. She refuses to come down."

The stairway wall was covered with framed pictures of people Anthony didn't know. He wondered if Victoria even knew who they were—she rarely talked about people beyond her own age. Of course, John was an exception.

Boris followed him, then led the way to the closed door of her room. Anthony tapped. He'd never been in her room before, never even been upstairs.

"Anthony? Come in."

His nose itched from the heady perfume that hung in the air as if emanating from the vivid flowers of the wallpaper. The dresser was whitish blondish goldish with elaborate carvings on the legs. Victoria's vanity mirror was framed by the Justin Bieber bobble head and other mementos that had hung on her carrel in the newsroom. Boris sat in the open doorway, unwilling to come in.

"What's wrong, Victoria?"

"Anthony." She ran and threw her arms around him, sniffling. "It's John. He says he's going to bring Megyn Drumpfer back after all. Even though the scoop about the hejab woman having a gun pushed our ratings through the roof. He says he's going to switch me to research. Research, Anthony? I might as well work for the paper."

The thought of her returning to the *Ledger* was not appealing.

"John doesn't come to see me any more. He doesn't take me to his apartment any more."

Anthony struggled for something to say.

She stepped back, holding her face in her hands. "Oh, when I think what I did when I was there with him—to show I loved him. And what I *almost* let him do!"

Anthony, who had never gotten more than a kiss from her, preferred not to dwell on these details. He said, "Maybe a little training in research wouldn't be a bad thing, Vicky. You can always get back in front of the camera later, possibly with a different TV station."

She dried her eyes on the back of her hand. "I don't get it. My reports stir people up. They've increased the ratings. What more does he want?"

Anthony thought he might know. He said, "You know, there are rumors about John Rowland going from one woman to another. That's all I'll say."

She sobbed gently. "Jennifer told me she heard that." She lifted teary eyes to Anthony's and reached to straighten his collar. "Jennifer thinks I should get back with you. So does Pop. Even Mom, lately." She pursed her lips. "What do you think?"

"No. Pari and I are—"

"Pari? So it's true. I could hardly believe her when I called her about the blog."

"About the blog? When was that?"

"I don't remember. I've only called her once since I left the *Ledger*."

So it was the call Pari told him about the last time they'd been together. His legs wobbly, Anthony looked for a chair. The only two had Victoria's clothes tossed over them. He sat on the bed. "You called Pari about her blog?"

"Yes. Pari's name came up one night when Pop was having a meeting here, everybody shouting. So I called her. I said, 'You're making Pop and Bea and the pastor and Derek furious with that blog of yours. You'd better be careful because, not Pop, but the others are the owners of the book publisher you're bad-mouthing on your blog."

"You heard them say they were the owners?"

"Yes. And that's what I told Pari." Victoria dropped down next to him on the bed. She sniffled and absently ran her fingers through his hair, twisting some of it up. "You've let yourself go since we broke up."

Anthony took her hand away. "Hold on. So it was you who told Pari who owned the book company?"

Victoria folded her arms. "Yes. And I told her something else, too."

"What else?"

"I told her I might want you back some day so she'd better stay away from you."

35

Howls and yelps

Where I have seen corruption boil and bubble
Till it o'er-run the stew

—Shakespeare, *Measure for Measure*

If there was one advantage to Anthony's current predicament, it was that his father would be hard put to characterize his life as 'monkish' these days. On the contrary, the phrase 'girl problems' came to mind. He hated that characterization even more. He headed back to the newsroom to immerse himself in work. There was Andre's tome to go through on the county's violations of State and Federal law in pushing forward the sewer project. That would be a mind-clearer.

But even before he got to the highway, he pulled over and called Pari's house. "Mastaneh, have you and Professor Shandule talked to Shahnaz? Mark said you were going to the detention center."

"We did. I talked to her. She said the police asked her if she had the pistol with her at the Board of Education meeting. She told them no. We all know that's the truth. But the FBI told them to hold her on terrorism charges. A public defender came to talk to her in private. Then we had to leave."

"The police say the gun had been fired recently."

"Fired? That can't be. Her husband put it in the drawer when he brought it home, and it was still there when the police took it."

"Yeah, I guess they mean before that."

He heard Mastaneh gasp.

"I have a contact at the police station, Mastaneh. The police are looking into it, and I guess the FBI now, too. I'll let you know as soon as I hear anything."

Drivers passing by glanced at him. He probably shouldn't stay on the shoulder of the road much longer, but he couldn't help asking, "Is Pari home yet?"

"No. The poor thing seems almost afraid to come back. We encouraged her to write that blog, and now she's afraid she's going to be fired for it. Or worse. She doesn't say what." Mastaneh paused. "Funny she doesn't call you. I could give her a message."

"Would you tell her I'll make sure she's not fired? And, um, that I miss her."

"How about coming over for some khoresh, Anthony? We know you like it."

"Oh, thanks, but I'm going to be working late at the newsroom tonight."

Nora and Sharise were giggling when he walked through the *Ledger* business office. Sharise's eyes were teary from laughing. "A nasty little man was here asking for Ms. Pari. We say we didn't know when she be back."

"You get his name?"

"He wouldn't give it. Little guy. Gray hair. Kind of shiny suit, all wrinkled up."

"Plus his nose," Nora put in. "Blackest mole you've ever seen right on the tip of it."

Anthony got up to the newsroom just as Pop was leaving his office, a sailing gear bag over his shoulder. He knew what was coming. Pop would ask if he wanted to crew on his boat in the Wednesday night race at Colonial City harbor. He'd done it a few times. It was exciting, but it was Pop and a bunch of older men, some of them inclining towards the cantankerous.

"Can't tonight, Pop. I just came from talking to Victoria."

Pop about-faced, dropped the bag on his office floor, and motioned Anthony to close the door.

"She's sad, Pop. It looks like John Rowland has lost his interest in her."

"That's nothing to be sad about." Pop picked up a half-smoked cigar from an ashtray and re-lit it.

Anthony felt he was walking a fine line. He wanted to suggest that Victoria was going to be all right. But he didn't want to give the least impression that he and Victoria might get back together, and he didn't want Victoria to come back to the *Ledger*. "I told her it might be a good idea to move to WPSK research, get away from Rowland, you know?"

"Excellent idea."

Anthony told himself he'd fulfilled his side of the bargain, to warn Victoria about John. Now it was Pop's turn to fulfill his side, to let Pari put a story in the *Ledger* identifying the owners of the textbook company.

Pop looked at him out of the corner of his eyes. "I did have it out with those Riverside Paradise puppies. Turns out there's big money in the textbook business. They howled and yelped when I pointed out the Board of Education code of ethics says a member can't profit directly from a decision the Board makes." Pop chuckled, coughing out smoke. "So, if the public finds out about it, Bea Doggit, the Board member, has to give up her stake in the publisher, RES-RECT. But RES-RECT also funds Riverside Paradise. They chased their tails around for a good while but couldn't find their way out of that."

This sounded hopeful. "So, what are they going to do? Divest from the textbook company? Quit the School Board? Reverse the decision to use the new textbooks?"

"I don't know. Seems to me those are their only choices." Pop slipped his thumbs into his belt. "But let me tell you something, Anthony. The County Executive wants Riverside

Paradise to go through. He plans on having a villa there himself. And he's helping Riverside Paradise get the land they need by approving the sewer line. Maybe that'll work." Pop looked away towards the picture of the island hanging behind his desk. "The Exec is going to help me out on something I want. I can't afford to cross him."

It was time to bring up Pari's *Searchlight* posts. "I guess you know, Pop, Bea's ownership of the book publisher has already been made public."

"Public? We haven't identified Bea in the *Ledger* yet. Maybe we should, but I don't know." He picked up his bag. "As for some internet chatter, I can't see why anybody's worried about that."

"Pop, last time I checked, over 100,000 people have read the blog. It can't be long before the *City Paper* picks up the fact that Bea is violating the ethics code—and prints the story. Bea and her Riverside Paradise lawyers can threaten, maybe even get the blog taken down, but the truth is already out. It's got to be only a matter of time before the District Attorney looks into it."

Pop threw his bag down onto the rug. "100,000 readers? Now I see what made that Riverside Paradise wolf pack howl so loud." He sat down, rubbing his eyes. It seemed forever before he lifted his head and trained his gaze on Anthony. "The code is clear, seems to me. You can't use your position on the Board to guarantee your own profit. Bea's RES-RECT owns the publishing company. Which 100,000 people now know." He slammed his fist on his desk. "They'll just have to come up with another way to get the money they need. Print the damn story."

It was really Pari's story. He called her, but her phone went to voicemail. Instead of leaving a message, he called her mother. "Mastaneh, Pop at the *Ledger* wants Pari to come back and print the textbook story. It's important. Could you tell her that?" The "come back" part wasn't literally true, of course. She could just as easily email it in from her brother's house in Syracuse. "And, um, she can call me for details."

Thumper saw the leash in Anthony's hand and wagged his tail at the bottom of the apartment stairs. Leaves blew off the trees in a strong northwest breeze. Anthony hoped Pop had made it to the starting line on time. It would be an exciting race in the heavy air, and he knew Pop would still be pumped up and talking about it tomorrow.

One thing still bothered him. Pop said the County Executive was going to "help him out on something" and so he "couldn't afford to cross him." But, surely, printing a story that jeopardized a major funding source for Riverside Paradise would be crossing him. He wondered what the "help" from the Exec was that Pop was giving up.

Thumper was on a sniffing spree. He poked his nose into a pile of leaves, causing a groundhog to hurtle out from hiding. He scratched at a heap of weeds and a garter snake slithered out. He was about to see what lay under a batch of sticks around the corner when he lifted his head and sniffed. Anthony smelled it, too. Perfume.

Thumper twisted around abruptly, his ears back. Bea was tottering towards them on stiletto heels. "Anthony Mansfield. Anthony Mansfield, stop. I want to apologize."

He didn't trust her, but he stopped anyway."

Panting, Bea stood so close to Anthony he could feel her breath on his face. Then suddenly she pushed him back away from her and turned towards her car with a face that looked like Munch's *The Scream*. Thumper growled.

"Got 'em," a short gray-haired man in a shiny suit called from across the street. Anthony noticed a mole almost on the tip of his nose as he crossed over, holding up a cell phone. Thumper growled again, and the man reached for something in his jacket.

"Easy, Thumper." Anthony held his collar and patted him. "What's going on, Bea?"

She cowered behind the shiny-suit man. "Shoot that dog if he tries to bite."

"He won't bite," Anthony said. "I've never seen him act like this. What's going on?"

The little man swiped three pictures across his phone screen. The first: Bea pressed up against Anthony, his hands on her shoulders. The second: Bea pushing him away. The third: Bea recoiling with her Edvard Munch face. "That should do it." He gave Bea a single nod.

Bea steadied herself on the little man's arm as she crossed the street back to her parked car. She turned back. "If that fake news blog doesn't come down, young man, the police are going to be very interested in these pictures."

36

Facts are facts

> *I could not but smile to see how industriously they locked the door on my meditations, which followed them out again without let or hindrance, and they were really all that was dangerous.*
>
> —Thoreau, *Civil Disobedience*

Ramen was his comfort food. He sat slurping in front of the monitor on his table, paging through *Searchlight*. Pari's brother Ken in Syracuse had posted an article explaining how national embarrassment had shamed one Board of Education in the Southwest into taking some of the most egregious statements out of the curriculum. Anthony couldn't imagine Bea Doggit being embarrassed at any of these statements, however. In the Weighing In section of Pari's blog, there were now almost 150,000 comments. As the number of comments increased, the percentage objecting to the right-wing, Bible based curriculum also increased.

A sidebar on the main page was dedicated to Pari's own comments. There was a new one on top: "My friend, who made a formal protest against what our local Board of Education calls a 'conservative curriculum,' has just been arrested and may be charged with terrorism." The comment briefly explained Shahnaz's case. Anthony was reading it when Pari called.

"Pari. At last." His voice was cracking and he had to stop.

"I miss you, Anthony." It sounded like she was taking short, sharp breaths.

"Pari, I'm sorry Victoria got hold of that gun story." He

wanted to say she hadn't gotten it from him, but that wasn't literally the truth.

"Yeah. I gave you time, Anthony, but I guess you didn't talk to her? Remind her to get all the facts before reporting? Explain what harm her sensationalist reports are causing?"

"I did talk to her. She doesn't get it. But anyway, don't worry. John Rowland's not interested in her any more. He took her off the air and put Megyn Drumpfer back on."

"Good, I guess." Pari let out an exasperated sigh. "Now you're making me feel sorry for her again."

"You shouldn't." He swallowed. "Pari, I found out Victoria told you a bunch of nonsense. Don't listen to her."

"You still love me? Just me?"

"How can you doubt it? Come home, Pari."

She seemed to be crying. "First, let me tell you. Shahnaz called me from the detention center. She dictated a statement she'd written in Farsi. I translated it. Listen." Pari read it to Anthony. By the time she finished, any thought he'd ever had of giving up being a reporter had vanished from his mind.

Pari asked, "What do you think? Should I post her statement on the blog?"

"Absolutely."

"I love you, Anthony. I'm going to post it, then drive all night and come straight to your place. If you hear a knock on the door before daylight, that will be me."

Letter from the Piskasanet Jail

My name is Shahnaz Delpak. The police have asked me to make a statement admitting my guilt. Against the advice of the Public Defender, I have decided to do so.

Admission of Guilt

I am guilty of wanting my child to learn and value the scientific method so that he knows how to apply reason to the discovery and verification of facts.

I am guilty of wanting my child to learn that historical conclusions, like the conclusions of science, must be based on extensive examination of documents and all other available data.

I am guilty of objecting in public when a school board charged with teaching these principles instead turns its back on them and tries to make children think that facts can be modified to conform to what one wishes were true.

I am guilty of insisting that neither my own religion nor that of any other person should be allowed to present its articles of faith as facts to the children in our schools as if they are ideas that can be accepted with the same assurance as facts that have passed the test of logic and reason.

Notwithstanding the new mid-range, pocketed coil, edge supported mattress—or perhaps because of it—Anthony tossed in bed most of the night trying to fall asleep. He'd left the door unlocked. His mind churned with thoughts of Pari sleeping with him again, here in this bed. He would have to make space for her in his little apartment. They would be a news team, working together on stories, dual bylines like on their very first article interviewing Shahnaz.

He must have finally fallen asleep because he woke to the touch of cold hands on his back, a cold cheek against his. Pari. He felt her cool kisses all over his face and neck. Her laugh rang like bells, the first rays of daylight sparkling in her soft brown eyes.

"That was the longest we've been apart since we met," she whispered.

"I was worried, to tell the truth."

"Silly. I'm the one who was worried. Hold on a minute." She called her mother to say she was back.

Neither of them brought up the topic of Victoria and her newscasts. And there were important things Anthony needed to tell her. But not right now. It wasn't long before Pari fell asleep in his arms.

They didn't make it into the *Ledger* newsroom until after noon. As Anthony sat beside Pari at his carrel, it was hard to start thinking of work. He stared at his blank monitor without turning it on. There was a list of assignments on the desktop, but he didn't read it. He glanced over at Pari. She was talking to her mother again. "How can I help?" she asked. Then she said, "OK. Give Shahnaz's son a kiss for me. Poor Jim. He must be devastated."

The police scanner chirped. Something about trash spilling out of a truck—Anthony wasn't listening closely. Pari didn't seem to have heard it at all. Her computer was on, but she was staring into space, her fingers resting on the edge of Anthony's carrel.

"Mom says Shahnaz's husband is taking unpaid time off to stay home with their son while she's ...." She couldn't finish.

He put his hand down just touching hers.

Pari swallowed. "But since Shahnaz didn't do it, they'll have to let her go, right?"

The sports writer Sam Yeager came rushing in. "State wins the championship. Who could have thought? Hey, you guys. State graduates, right? You must be jumping up and down."

Anthony knew they'd won. Mild satisfaction would be a more accurate way to describe his reaction. Pari said, "Fantastic, Sam. Can't wait to read your report on the game." Supportive. Polite. That was Pari. Even though Anthony knew she didn't care a thing about football.

Anthony checked the clock over Pop's door. "Almost one. What do you think, Pari? Go grab some lunch?"

Pari smiled. They'd eaten Ramen with eggs just an hour ago. "I don't know. You think maybe we should do some work first?"

Sam Yeager said, "That terrorist thing. That's got to be keeping you guys busy."

"Yeah," Anthony said. "I don't know if 'terrorist' is—"

"Right. I read your *Ledger* reports. Just meant, you know, that shooting at the school."

Anthony's mood was dimming from the glow he felt at having Pari back. The shadowy thoughts he'd been hiding in the back of his mind were forcing their way out. There were some serious things he had to let Pari know about.

"Well, well." Ralph came in, observing Anthony and Pari with eyes enlarged by his glasses, slowly nodding his head. "The Bobbsey twins re-enter the workforce."

Pari pointed to her monitor. "I've been working on the

Board of Education curriculum story." She raised her eyebrows. "I don't know what Anthony's been doing."

Glasses down, bending over Pari's shoulder, Ralph looked at the Shahnaz "Admission of Guilt" on Pari's blog.

"Wait a minute. This woman is in jail? We never reported that."

"It's in the Police Blotter section," Anthony hastened to say. "I didn't want to make a big deal of it until I got all the details."

Ralph frowned.

"Because, the truth is, she's a friend of Pari's mother."

Ralph had his hands on his hips, speechless. He took a step back.

Pari spoke up. "I already reported it in my blog, Ralph. We'll print the whole arrest story in the *Ledger* right now. Facts are facts."

Anthony called Rob at the station to check for any more developments in the Shahnaz arrest.

"She's sticking to her story," Rob said. "Doesn't have money for a lawyer, so we assigned a public defender."

"The evidence is just that the gun was fired recently?"

"Yeah, we went through her apartment pretty thoroughly looking for the shell. Came up with nothing. We might have a motive, though. Don't know if you've seen her 'Admission of Guilt' on the internet? She had it in for the School Board, that much is clear."

It was a fact that Shahnaz had a gun in her apartment of a caliber similar to the one that fired the shot. It was a fact that the gun had been fired recently. It was also a fact that Shahnaz disagreed with the Board's decision to change the curriculum. Anthony thought about leaving that out of the article but Pari said to go ahead with it.

Suspect Held in School Board Shooting

Ralph nodded when he read the story. "We need to print this." He flipped up his glasses. "You guys think she's innocent, don't you?"

Pari nodded. Anthony said, "She doesn't seem like the kind of person who'd shoot anybody."

Ralph shrugged. "Who does?"

Anthony closed his notepad. "Call it a day, Pari?"

Ralph said, "Just a minute. Pari, Pop tells me you have a story about this Bea character using her position on the School Board for profit? We going to get that soon?"

Pari pulled up another document on her monitor. Ralph flipped down his glasses and read. "OK, I saw this on your whatchamacallit—blog. 'A witness' says Bea owns RES-RECT? Not named? Any corroboration?"

"There was another witness, too," Pari told him. "Pop himself."

Ralph pushed his glasses up and rubbed his eyes. "I guess Pop knows what he's doing. This isn't going to look good for some people he's been schmoozing with." He gave Pari a pat on the shoulder. "Anyway, as you say, facts are facts."

The fact was already on the internet, but putting it in the paper would be adding salt to the wound. Anthony felt a drop of sweat run down his side from under his arm.

After Ralph went back into his office, Pari said, "Any reason I shouldn't print this story exposing Bea as the book company owner, Anthony? Just asking. You look kind of pale."

Anthony hadn't told her about the attempted rape accusation and Bea's threat to make it public if he didn't retract the claim that she owned RES-RECT. He'd been so happy after Pari came back from Syracuse, he'd put Bea's threat out of his mind. "I guess not," he murmured.

"I know what you're thinking. Get the other side first. I'll call Bea, give her a chance to deny it. The pastor, too, and that Derek Grosbeck guy."

A chill of dread shot through his chest as she clicked the *Ledger* phone pad keys. He had to stand up.

"Ms. Doggit? Pari Shandule from the *Shady Park Ledger*."

Anthony suddenly remembered he had something to talk about with Nora and Sharise downstairs.

37

Wanted

Cry 'Havoc' and let slip the dogs of War.
—Shakespeare, *Julius Caesar*

Pari was silent, looking out the car window all the way back to his apartment. It wasn't until the car stopped in front that she said, "I think you know what Bea told me."

"I'm sorry, Pari. I ... first of all, I want you to know I didn't do anything."

"Of course you didn't try to rape her. I just can't believe you didn't tell me about this."

"I guess, we were so happy after you came back. I didn't want to spoil it."

"Bea says she has pictures to back up her charge."

He explained the pictures the best he could.

"And she says she's going to give them to the police if I write the article." Pari bit her lip.

Anthony's feeling of guilt for keeping quiet about this soon turned to anger. "Let her do it. I don't care. I can fight this. Write the article, Pari."

Board of Education Member Uses Position for Profit

It was short, a statement that two witnesses had heard Bea and others say they owned the company that sold the Bible based textbooks the county Board of Education had voted to use. The article pointed out that this was an ethics code violation and gave an estimate of the large amount of money the company was set to gain from the Board's decision. It also said that Bea, the pastor, and Derek Grosbeck denied partial ownership of the company.

Soon after the article came out, Pari got a call at the *Ledger* from the District Attorney's office asking for the names of the witnesses mentioned in her article. She put her hand over the receiver. "Anthony, should I tell them?"

"You told me one of them was confidential."

"No. I was just teasing you."

"Uh-huh. Anyway, I know it was Victoria. She told me herself."

"And Pop didn't say not to give his name when he told you about it, right?"

"No. He was mad. He wanted the story out."

She gave the District Attorney's office the two names. Anthony waited for the next shoe to drop. He didn't have to wait long. His phone lit up. *Detective McGinn, Piskasanet County Police.*

"Anthony Mansfield? There's been a new development in the charge against you. We'll need you to come in for further questioning."

Pari went with him. She'd never been to the police station before and sat in wide-eyed silence until Anthony turned into the parking lot.

"Help you?" Picking up a pen, the busty cop at the desk gave them a piercing stare. Pari asked if there was some way she could speak to Shahnaz Delpak. "Your name?" When Pari gave it, the response was "She's at the Northbrook Detention Center. You'll do best to call ahead, see what the visiting hours are. Anything else?"

"Anthony." It was Rob coming down the dim hallway. Noticing Pari, he smiled and gave Anthony a quick thumbs up.

The desk cop was shuffling papers. "Just a minute, Miss."

To Rob she said, "Detective McGinn has Ms. Pari Shandule on his interview list."

"Somebody call me?" The detective came out of a gray door in the gray-painted concrete block wall. "Pari Shandule? We tried to get ahold of you. Your mother said you were visiting ... your brother, was it?" He glanced at Anthony. "I'll talk to Ms. Shandule first if you don't mind waiting. Rob, if you'd come along, too."

Anthony sat on the gray metal bench across from the desk cop, staring down at the gray vinyl floor. He assumed Bea had told the detective she had incriminating pictures. The bench was hard. He stood up, stretching. *Wanted* posters were tacked to a bulletin board along the wall. With a nervous chill, he scanned them. One drew his attention. He stepped up to take a close look and read the description: "Wanted for child support non-compliance."

Rob came out of the interview room with Pari. "I'll keep her company while she waits for you. Down the end of the hall. You know where it is."

Detective McGinn nodded at a metal chair by a metal table. "First of all, let me ask you the same thing I asked Ms. Shandule. Have you ever seen Shahnaz Delpak in possession of a gun on her person?"

"No. She says she's afraid to touch a gun and never has."

"Right. Can you confirm how it was that the police found a gun in her apartment?"

"She says her husband brought it there from work for her protection. Her son says the same."

"Did anyone in the family fire the gun that you know of?"

"They say they didn't. I believe them."

The detective slid open a drawer on his side of the table and took something out. "OK, Rob wanted to make sure I saw this before I questioned you." It was a copy of the *Shady Park Ledger* folded with Pari's article exposing Bea on top.

"You and Ms. Shandule work together on the paper, I take it? And so this news report might make Ms. Bea Doggit angry at you even though she's listed on the byline, not you?"

"Yes."

"OK, point taken. But she now says she can provide evidence that you are sexually harassing her. Pictures, she says."

Anthony described Bea approaching him while he was walking Thumper. "I think it was a setup."

"And what makes you think this?"

"She had a man with her, on the other side of the street, with a camera phone. When he took the pictures, he said something like 'Got 'em. That should do it.' And then Bea threatened me, as I told you."

Anthony kept waiting for the detective to pull out the pictures. His cheeks felt hot just thinking about it. Instead, McGinn asked Anthony if he'd seen them.

"Just a glance."

"Tell me what you saw."

Somehow Anthony felt like he didn't have to answer this question. But he said, "Me holding Bea off when she leaned into me."

"Hmm," McGinn said. "That's a tough one. Who's pushing who, you know what I mean?"

"It was a blackmail setup, Detective. The man who took the pictures? He came into the *Ledger* office looking for Pari right after her blog identified Bea and her partners as owners of the company that's profiting from—"

"Yeah, I understand. You witnessed this?"

"No, but Nora and Sharise at the *Ledger* did."

Detective McGinn took some notes, then looked up. "Blackmail's a serious charge. Assuming you can't tell me who this mysterious man is—"

"Actually, I can. He's the man on one of your *Wanted* posters out there with a mole right at the tip of his nose."

When they got back to the apartment, Anthony still wondered if the police really had Bea's pictures. Pari did her best to lift his spirits. She sat on his lap. "Cheer up, Buddy. I'll come visit you every day in jail."

He hugged her. "Not a chance, Doll. I'll be on the lam, and you with me. I have connections in Guatemala, see?"

38

A hole to crawl in

Hell is empty and all the devils are here.
—Shakespeare, *The Tempest*

Anthony's car was having the brakes relined, so he rode with Pari to the newsroom. She stopped at Mahmud's Econo-Gas station on the way. Mahmud, Reza Delpak's boss, was a big swarthy man with hairy arms. Pari greeted him in Farsi. He brushed her cheeks with his mustache and said, "Fill 'er up, *Junam*?"

Pari switched to English to ask him about the gun. He shook his head. "Nothing more I can say. I told police the gun was in drawer under cash register. Stayed there since I buy the station. Nobody never touched it until Reza borrowed it. That was after they paint bad words on his door."

"How about the other workers? None of them used it?"

"Police asked everybody. Reza, no. Bill, no. Carl, no."

"Wasn't there a kid who worked here once in a while on Sunday evenings?"

"Daryl. A student. He started getting bad grades. I said he better quit for a while and study."

The gas nozzle clicked off.

"Did you tell the police about Daryl?"

"No. He quit just before the shooting. They asked who was working here now. I didn't think about Daryl."

Pari handed Mahmud her credit card.

"No charge. Please. For Mastaneh and Mark's daughter, gas is free." He put his hands in his pockets.

Pari stuffed some bills into his shirt pocket. "One favor, though. Can you give me Daryl's phone number?"

On the way to the newsroom, Anthony asked what Mahmud had called her. "Sounded like *junam*."

Pari laughed. "Yeah, *jun* or *junam*. It's ... it's like 'Hon.' You know how people in the City call each other 'Hon'? My mother calls me *jun*, too."

Sharise and Nora were standing by the stairs to the newsroom when Pari and Anthony arrived. "Lordy," Nora said. "Trouble upstairs. We can hear it all the way down here."

Sharise shook her head. "That Doggit woman, that Pastor Mitch, and another man. They come stomping in. We're going up, see if everybody all right."

Anthony led the way, all of them following. Ralph was hunched by the closed door of Pop's office, listening. Something banged against the door. "All right in there?" Ralph called.

Pop's voice rang out like he was calling hounds off a scent. "No. I back your damn Riverside Paradise. But I can't back fraud. We stand by our story because it's true."

A woman's voice said something, but it couldn't be heard. Pop boomed out again, "Bea, it looks to me like the District Attorney's on your tail, and you with no hole to crawl in but one. Give up that damn Board position. Let them take another vote without you on it."

Indistinct murmuring, then the door flew open. Anthony and the others backed to the corridor walls, forming a silent gauntlet of disdain for the visitors to pass through. Bea caught Anthony's eye and waved a finger at him. Next came the pastor, his lips shut in a wide seam over his jutting chin. Finally, Derek Grosbeck, staring down, face flushed.

Pop stood in his doorway, his brow furrowed with anger, watching until they left the newsroom. He looked at his employees as if first noticing them, then shot Ralph a glance.

"Go ahead with that 'Letter from Jail,' Ralph. Time to let people know what's going on." He took a breath and buttoned his jacket. "I'm going sailing. Anybody want to come with me? Sharise? Nora? Take a day off? Little cruise up the river and back?"

Sharise had gone with him before. She said, "Come on, Nora. It'll be fun. Pop needs to cool off."

Shahnaz's "Letter from the Piskasanet Jail" appeared in the Opinion section of the next paper. The response took the *Ledger* staff by surprise. Letters to the editor poured in, overwhelmingly in favor of Shahnaz's point of view. Some knew the Christian curriculum was Bea's work and asked how she'd gotten on the Board. Anthony and Pari recognized one of the letter writers: Andre Smyth. He talked about separation of church and state without actually mentioning Shahnaz or her predicament.

Pop walked down the corridor, cigar in mouth. "Well, well. It looks like we're finding out what people who *read* think." He squinted at Pari. "Let's get a statement from the Board of Education."

Pari wondered under her breath if the chairman of the Board of Education was one of these people who read and think. She looked up his name and made an appointment for her and Anthony to interview him that afternoon.

They found his office on North-South Highway next to Pet Supply World. The sign said *Doctor Reginald Bland, Podiatrist.*

"Just call me Reggie," he insisted. "No need to be formal. We can talk back here." Plastic models of foot bones and illustrations of the pink, red, and orange insides of feet took up most of the wall space in the narrow room. Dr. Bland tapped an open copy of the *Ledger* on his desk. "I'm happy to see that the press is interested in the education of our children."

"We wanted to get your reaction to Mrs. Delpak's letter," Pari said.

Anthony was taking notes.

"It's a fine letter. Very well written." Dr. Bland's beady eyes shifted around the room as if looking for help.

"We were wondering if you agree or disagree with what it says."

"Agree or disagree. This is a hard one. Of course, there are many opinions on how education can be improved." He turned his hand one way, then the other.

"Whether public school textbooks should present the beliefs of a particular religion as facts, for example. Can you give us your opinion on that?"

"Well, as chair of the Board, I make it a point to listen to all sides of a dispute. I am always willing to be persuaded by a strong argument."

Pari didn't give up. "On the question I put to you, then, which side of the dispute do you personally find more persuasive?"

"Actually, I see my role as a peacemaker. I find it helpful to support the will of the majority."

"Then, can you tell me how you would vote if the Board were tied on that question?"

A glance to the left, then to the right. "It's hard to say."

"All right. Can you tell me, have you heard from any Board members since ...?" She pointed to the newspaper.

"Several called. Yes. Some feel that they were deceived. They didn't know the vote would directly benefit one of our members. Others say it doesn't matter. It's the curriculum our children should have."

"I see. And what do you think?"

"Well, my opinion might not be important. The State Department of Education believes that we've violated a Board ethics code. They say we have to meet and rescind our vote to use Bea Doggit's books.

"I see. Any idea when that will happen?"

"By the end of next week, the Education Department is insisting. Otherwise, they'll file for an injunction with the Circuit Court to stop us from using her books."

When they left the office, Pari observed, "You definitely can't call the good doctor opinionated."

"You think?" Anthony flipped his hand left and right.

Pari wondered, "Can Bea build Riverside Paradise without the textbook money?"

"I doubt it. The project was dead until RES-RECT was formed and started selling books to the county."

Anthony's phone rang. *Derek Grosbeck*. "Anthony Mansfield of the *Shady Park Ledger*? There's a story I think you should cover."

39

The Horsey Invokers

If he have need of thee, he will deceive thee, and smile upon thee, and put thee in hope; he will speak thee fair, and say, What wantest thou?

—Ecclesiasticus, 13.6

Out beyond Bay Hills stretched miles and miles of rolling grassland edged by white paddock fences. Old stone farm houses and white barns dotting the hills were now joined by a growing number of huge, imposing homes built within the past few years. Thoroughbreds grazed in the fields or carried riders in velvet helmets and jodhpurs trotting along dirt race tracks. This was the home of the Horsey Invokers. And here in the Bay Hills branch of the Church of the Invokers of Jesus was where Bea was going to make her "important announcement," according to Derek.

Anthony had called Emma before going. She said the Bay Hills branch of Pastor Mitch's church was a key to the continued success of Riverside Paradise. "Got that from Britney Grosbeck," she told him. "Derek has some hope that the money flowing in to Riverside Paradise from this mega church could help to keep the project alive even if Bea's right-wing evangelical books are voted out."

"Why do they support Riverside Paradise?" he'd asked. "I don't see what they'll get out of it."

"They don't know Pastor Mitch is diverting their money to the project. A lot of it, anyway. Got that from my friend Natalie who works at the Northbrook branch of the church and helps with the records."

The big shindig of the week was on Wednesday evening, Emma had told him, so the Invokers wouldn't have to miss out on their kids' weekend games and lessons or on the men's Sunday TV sports. That's the night Derek had asked them to come.

Pari had fretted forever over what to wear.

"You could ask your mother," he suggested. "No. Maybe not. Or you could call my mother. No, that wouldn't help either."

Pari flicked her fingers across the clothes she had hanging on a CATV cable Anthony had strung from the dresser to a window frame. "I think I'll wear what I usually wear."

"Good choice. Me, too."

The road wound to the top of a wide grassy hill overlooking the bay. They could see gray and white gulls circling down below them. At the edge of the hill was the church, darkened stone forming its center portion, which must have originally been a farmhouse, and bright new stone on each side widening the original building to ten times its size. Atop the center was a metal structure shaped like a cell phone tower with a giant gold cross on top.

White-uniformed men directed traffic from the approach road into a semi-circular asphalt lot, where other men in uniforms waved vans to one area and cars to another. Anthony heard a whistle and saw a man in white agitatedly waving his arm at him to hurry up.

Heavyset Latino workers unloaded sound equipment from cargo vans parked at a side door of the building. Others carried a kettle drum, a double bass, three tubas, and a mass of assorted string, brass, and percussion instruments. Pari started snapping pictures from the car window.

The Invokers ambling towards the church from the parking lot definitely seemed to be wearing what was comfortable. A few women wore tennis sweaters and skirts, some were still in riding breeches and boots, and one or two men had on plaid golfing pants and floppy hats. Two women in polo shirts and jeans carried billowy blue robes draped over their arms. Most of crowd, however, were dressed pretty much like Anthony and Pari.

Strolling unhurriedly towards the church and chatting to everyone within earshot seemed to be part of the liturgy, as was smiling. The words *Jesus*, *Lord*, *God*, *bless*, *blessed*, and *pray* punctuated everything they said to each other. It was as if they had to say the words to establish who they were. "I belong. I know your tribal language. I'm like you. Accept me." Anthony dropped his head, hoping no one would speak to him.

Holding hands seemed to be encouraged. Anthony took Pari's. He liked this part of the liturgy. A woman with rhinestone blue hair nodded at them, smiling. "God bless you. What a lovely couple."

Anthony managed a smile. It was a very kind sentiment, and it made him feel good. But he couldn't come up with anything to say in return. He never felt like it was his place to comment to strangers on how they appeared to him.

A welcome line of men in suits and women in fluffy dresses greeted each person who entered. Inside was a lobby reminiscent of the outer area in a family restaurant where kids can play video games while their parents talk over coffee. In fact, there were kids playing video games, quiet ones, not the kind Willard Scherd played. Anthony stepped over to take a closer look. Some of the screens did feature characters in Middle Eastern robes, but the idea wasn't to blast their heads off, apparently.

Banks of cushioned benches rose in a semi-circle to the ceiling. The musicians were taking their places and tuning up on a wide stage that completed the circle. Soon trumpets were sounding, drums were pounding, and everyone was on their feet, waving their hands in arcs like rock music groupies, singing a song they knew by heart but which Anthony and Pari had never heard. It contained a lot of the above-mentioned words plus "hallelujah" quite a few times.

Anthony was surprised that Pastor Mitchell Rainey was not the first to come on stage. The first speaker was a muscular man who looked like a football player standing for an interview. Frank Fortunato was his name, he reminded the congregation quite a few times. He was newly elected to the House of Delegates on a platform of "making schools safe for our children."

Fortunato was followed by a series of men in suits who each gave either a brief motivational speech—"with the Lord's help, each and every one of you can achieve your dreams"—or a brief feel good about yourself speech—"the love Jesus has for you is unconditional." Anthony was most interested in a man in a pale blue suit and white shoes who described in loving detail the plan to build Riverside Paradise along the Piskasanet River. He finished his description of this earthly paradise by saying, "I have found the place where Jesus wants me to live." Anthony never found out who he was although he'd seen him talking to Bea earlier and suspected he was her flunky.

After each speaker had worked up the audience, the band broke out in a song. It was only after the loudest banging on the kettle drum and shrillest blaring of the trumpets that Pastor Mitch came on stage. He opened a Bible and read a quote he said was from Proverbs about giving freely and thereby growing richer. The opposite of giving freely was withholding what you should give and ending up with nothing. The audience seemed quite familiar with this message, many of them punctuating it with shouts of "hallelujah."

Pastor Mitch spread his arms and looked around the building, a stiff smile plastered above his squarish chin. "Behold," he crooned. "Behold this house of God. Not many years ago it was a crumbling farm house. But we planted the seed, and we have grown." He stretched his arms to the rafters. "Our prosperity reflects the glory of Jesus!"

A thunderous mixture of amens and hallelujahs broke out. Pastor Mitch let it go on for quite a while before lifting the mic and, with a feedback squeal, announcing, "And now ... and now .... Let us hear now from a sister in Jesus, a woman graced with the bounty of the Lord."

Cheers broke out as Bea, in a white low-cut satin dress minced across the stage in black stiletto heels.

"She looks like a movie star about to accept an oscar," Pari whispered.

"Let's see how well she can act."

A few whistles rang out as Bea took the mic in one hand and raised the other, palm outwards, towards the faithful. "Jesus," she moaned. "Dear Jesus, I have heard your call. I accept the sacrifice you require me to make. Let me be a witness to the power of your word." She threw her head back with a gasp as if breathing in that power.

Anthony rolled his eyes sideways to see if Pari also noticed how much of Bea's breast was exposed as she heaved in the power of the Lord. Pari's open mouth told him she did.

The Lord had called Bea to resign her position on the Piskasanet County Board of Education. A murmur rumbled among the Invokers when she made this announcement. Bea put her hand on her breast. "No, brothers and sisters. Do not question the call of Jesus. He has shown me that this is the way I can best serve."

A few hallelujahs rang out.

"Yes, hallelujah, I hear Jesus calling me to see that our children receive his word in their schools. I cannot question the Lord when he tells me I can do this best by serving apart from the Board of Education."

Bea filled her lungs and let her breath out in quivers. She took her time before turning to the main point of her performance. "Brothers and sisters in Jesus, you can help. The Lord is calling you as he called me. His work can be done with your help."

Anthony noticed activity among the musicians behind her. A conductor dressed all in black rose and faced the band, arms raised, turning his head to watch Bea for his cue.

"Jesus needs you to tell our Board of Education it must continue with the Christian curriculum and materials they have recently adopted. Call them. Tell them to reaffirm the godly education program I brought to our county. Tell them this is a Christian country. Tell them we must educate our children as Christians."

She threw out both arms. Drums thundered, trumpets blasted out, the whole building vibrated. The Horsey Invokers rose, singing:

Stand up, stand up for Jesus! ye soldiers of the cross;
Lift high His royal banner, it must not suffer loss:
From vict'ry unto vict'ry, His army shall He lead,
Till every foe is vanquished, and Christ is Lord indeed.

The newsroom was empty when Pari and Anthony sat down to write their article. Dr. Bland had sent a text responding to a few more questions from Pari.

Board of Ed Set to Rescind Vote on Books

Anthony watched as Pari typed in the story. The Board was scheduled to meet at 7 p.m. on the following Wednesday at the Education Complex in Colonial City. Pari quoted Dr. Bland saying the Board had "become aware of an ethics code violation" in their vote approving new textbooks for the schools and that they would meet to declare that vote invalid.

She explained that the ethics code violation occurred because Ms. Beatrice Doggit, a Board member, was the primary owner of the company that profited from the book sales to the schools.

Dr. Bland was quoted saying he didn't know yet if any further business would be on the agenda.

"OK. Now what about Bea's announcement in church?" she asked Anthony.

He leaned over the keyboard and added a one-sentence paragraph: "Ms. Doggit recently announced her intention to resign from the Board."

"Let's leave it at that," he said. "The *Ledger* doesn't need to publicize her request for people to lobby the Board to reaffirm their textbook vote now that she's resigned."

40

Home alone

In the hollow Lotos-land to live and lie reclined
On the hills like Gods together, careless of mankind.
—Tennyson, *The Lotos-eaters*

For decades the county's method of choosing Board of Education members had been controversial. Until recently, a Nominating Commission made recommendations to the governor, who largely ignored them and made his own appointments. Now the county was transitioning to a direct vote, and any sudden vacancy would be filled by a vote of the Board.

"Marco," Mastaneh said. For some reason she always called her husband Marco instead of Mark. "With that Doggit lady gone, you could reapply for a place on the Board." Without asking, she spooned another huge helping of khoresh onto Anthony's plate just after he'd managed to get the first plateful down.

"Great idea," Pari agreed. "Is there any way you could be appointed next Wednesday?"

Her father laughed. "No, that's the emergency meeting to rescind the vote on Bea Doggit's books. I'll definitely be there, though. Guess you *Ledger* reporters will be there, too?"

Pari took Anthony's hand under the tablecloth. "Wouldn't miss it."

When the time came, Anthony drove to Pari's house to pick the three of them up. He didn't see Mark's car in the driveway.

"Mom and Dad already left," Pari told him. "They're old,

you know. They like to be early."

Anthony checked the time on his phone. There was no need to leave for at least half an hour.

"Well." Pari's brown eyes beamed excitement. "I'm the hostess now. Would you like some tea?"

"Um—"

"Or anything? Come into the kitchen. I made flan. My mother loves it. Here, sit in this chair. I'll get you some."

She put plates of flan on the table and sat across from him, something that wasn't possible at the little table in Anthony's cramped apartment. "Mom and Dad eat breakfast here. It's more convenient than using that low table in the dining room. If I had a house, I'd probably—sorry, I'm babbling. Would you like a beer? My dad drinks beer. Pistachios?"

They split a beer, and he chomped on some pistachios. Pari asked him to help bring a box down from her bedroom. "Some more things I want to bring to your place."

The stairs in the old house squeaked, and the air got noticeably warmer as they went up. She led him down a dim hallway, the dark-stained floor creaking under their stockinged footsteps. She clicked a loud switch and a light came on far up on the high ceiling. Now he could see the walls were a dark green, the woodwork varnished, not painted. She took his hand. "In here."

The mahogany door opened to a room brightened by the last rays of day coming through a window. "It's an old house," Pari said. "I painted the walls white in here to cheer the place up. What do you think?"

The walls were bare except for a worn travel poster of Iran's Persepolis, a large pencil sketch of the front of the *Shady Park Ledger* building, and a blown-up photograph of Mrs. O'Leary's house with Thumper sitting at the foot of the steps to Anthony's apartment. "Nice. Interesting artwork."

"Mom and Dad carried that poster all over Iran and Europe before they settled here. Mom did the *Ledger* sketch from a picture I took. See that little car with the roof rack?"

He stepped closer. "Mine?"

She gave a wide-eyed nod.

The stark look of the room highlighted the elaborate Persian carpet under their feet. "My mom and dad know the man who drew the design for it. He lived in Semnan, not too far from Tehran. Tehran is where Mom and Dad met."

"Your desk, bookcase, bed—they look like they're all from Ikea?"

"I put them all together by myself." She led him to the window. "See over there?" It was the hill they'd stood on at the edge of the Piskasanet Community College parking lot. "Remember?"

She turned to face him. "Can you believe it? We're alone in my room."

He kissed her, and the world of Board meetings and local politics faded away. They kissed again. Before he knew it, Anthony was holding her naked body against his on the bed. Time had stopped.

Even after the peak of their passion, they lay motionless, entwined, oblivious of everything but the present. Anthony felt himself sinking into the warmth of her eyes—and let himself go. "Pari," he whispered. It was all he wanted to say. They lay not in sleep but in languorous contentment. Neither seemed willing to break the spell.

"Oh." Anthony opened his eyes as his hand touched something soft under Pari's pillow. She kissed his eyes closed, but the spell was fading. He pulled out what he'd touched. It was his light blue Laser Regatta T-shirt, the one he'd lent her to wear after they sailed to the island and her clothes were wet. "You still have this?"

"I wear it every night at home. Even took it to Syracuse with me. Sorry. I should give it back to you."

Anthony felt a constriction in his throat. He waved his hand No.

"I'll give you something of mine, then." She slipped the shirt over her naked body and took something from her desk drawer. "It's agate. Made in Esfahan. My mother gave one to me and one to Ken. Let's see if it fits on your finger."

The School Board meeting had obviously been in progress for some time when they got there. Pari's father caught her eye, questioning, and she held her hand apologetically over her heart as they slipped into the back of the meeting room behind an unusually large number of excited public observers.

Something important had happened, Anthony realized, but he couldn't concentrate. He kept glancing at the ring on his little finger, twirling it, touching the stone. He checked to see if Pari was taking notes. But she wasn't. She was smiling at him.

The Board chair tapped his gavel, and Anthony looked up. "Now that our mistaken vote on the curriculum has been rescinded," Dr. Bland said, "and now that the Board has accepted the resignation of Ms. Doggit—"

"Vote again on the books!" a woman in front of Anthony shouted. Others shouted agreement. A clean-shaven Board member with a bow tie spoke up. "I hear you, and I move that with Ms. Doggit no longer on the Board, we take a new vote on the curriculum to assure a proper conservative focus on our children's education." More shouts rose up from the onlookers, some in favor, some against.

Dr. Bland took off his reading glasses and wiped them on his sleeve. When the shouts only increased, he gave the gavel another tap. "I remind Reverend Blatchford," he said, indicating the bow tie man, "that according to legal counsel we are prohibited from taking a major vote if there are vacancies on the Board."

"Bring back Professor Shandule," someone shouted. Anthony saw it was Emma's husband, Charles. "Bring back common sense," Charles called out. Emma herself stood and said, "Yes. We want Professor Shandule."

"So that's Emma?" Pari whispered. "And her husband. My mother says she knows them."

Another woman stood. "Our county has become a national laughing stock," she declared nervously. "We've just voted the flawed texts out. Why would we bring them back?" It was Ms. Ernst.

Pari grasped Anthony's arm. "Let's hope there's no gunfire at this meeting."

Dr. Bland might have been thinking the same thing. He rapped his gavel three times. "Ladies, gentlemen. Thank you for your comments. We have scheduled open hearings over the next two weeks. That is the time to hear from and discuss the merits of applicants for the vacant Board position. Not now. Then, only after the Board is at its full capacity can we take up the matter of textbooks again." He banged his gavel and declared the meeting adjourned.

"You two caught the most interesting part, at least," Pari's father said. "If you don't count Bea Doggit's tearful, Jesus invoking resignation."

41

Good cop, bad cop

'Tis pleasant purchasing our fellow-creatures.
—Byron, *Don Juan*

School Board Rescinds Vote on Texts

Pari's article noted that the Board could vote to reinstate the "rejected materials" as soon as the vacancy had been filled. She said the Board chair expected such a vote, if held, to be close.

Ms. Ernst called Anthony's desk phone. "I have to thank you and Pari for continuing to let people know what's going on." She giggled. "To tell you the truth, I was afraid you weren't going to make it to the last meeting."

"Oh, we, um—"

"Anyway, I found out there are enough standard books and materials in the Colonial City warehouse to put back into the schools immediately. So let's hope for the best."

Ralph called Pari and Anthony into his office. "Look." He had brought Pari's *Searchlight* blog up on his monitor without help. "My son says blogs are 'where it's at.' I think he might be right. I've read everything on *Searchlight*, all the comments. I told Pop. I said I think the paper could add a blog like yours to its website. I told him it could stir up interest, maybe increase ads. What do you say, Pari?"

"I'm not sure I—"

"Could you add a blog to the online *Ledger*? And, you know, manage it?" When she didn't say No, he took her downstairs to talk to Jerry.

Anthony's desk phone rang. It was Derek Grosbeck, angry. "You were at the Invokers service in Bay Hills. Pastor Mitch saw you. Yet you didn't print a word Beatrice Doggit said."

"We reported she was resigning from the Board."

"That wasn't the story. She asked the congregation to call Board members demanding they support the Bible based curriculum. We expected the paper to broaden that request, help us reach out to people outside the church."

"You say 'we.' I assume you mean RES-RECT, the corporation that sells the books?"

Without answering, Derek said, "Listen, there's no need for the press and business to be at odds. We need to meet."

Derek and Britney Grosbeck's house in Nottingham Estates had bronzed concrete lions reclining on plinths at the entrance to the driveway. Anthony parked his car on the circular drive in front of what seemed to be a replica of a chateau in the Loire valley.

"Maria, the door!" Anthony recognized Britney's voice. "That's your job, you understand?"

Emma always used a quote-unquote tone of voice when she called Britney her "friend." According to Emma, Britney had fired Esmeralda simply because she wanted to take some time off when her husband was sick. The new housemaid opened the door.

Britney's voice echoed in the two-story hallway. "Maria, where are you going?"

"Mr. Derek, he say tell when visitor come."

"I'll tell him. Go clean up the mess in Chelsea's room before she gets home from school." She turned to Anthony. "I need to talk to you before Derek does. In the den."

They sat at a walnut table with an intricate veneer pattern. "The rape," Britney said. "I know about the rape."

Anthony put his phone on the table. "Do you mind if I record this conversation?"

"It's your funeral."

Britney's eyes narrowed as he turned on his phone and opened his notepad. She said, "Listen, I can get Bea to drop the rape charges."

Anthony stared at her. "I'm not sure I understand—"

"Oh, you understand. Bea and I got a little tipsy here one night, and she let it all out. She told me you raped her."

"I didn't. That's a lie." His notebook paper was curling from the sweat of his hands. He checked to make sure the blinking red recording light was still flashing on his phone. He didn't really have a plan for what to do with the recording. It might come in handy if he had to prove he was being blackmailed. But if it came to that, the rape attempt accusation would already be out there.

Britney said, "If you support Guns for Teachers in the *Shady Park Ledger* and write in favor of bringing back Bea's curriculum, we can keep this rape between ourselves. If not, WPSK TV will hear that you're a rapist."

A wave of heat passed over Anthony's face and neck. He couldn't control the blush, which he knew Britney would take as an admission of guilt.

"So. Do we have a deal?"

Before he could answer, she said. "Oh, and another thing. You have to see to it that the *Ledger* helps publicize the Evergreen Academy we're planning."

Anthony spoke over a catch in his throat. "I'll never write anything in support of teachers carrying guns or the Christian Right curriculum. You can forget that. As for publicizing Evergreen Academy, you could place an ad in the paper. I can give you Sharise's number."

There was a timid tap on the den door. "Mrs. Britney, Mr.

Derek say he need talk visitor now."

In seconds, Anthony was sitting across from Derek Grosbeck instead of his wife. Derek's angular chin and crooked nose had replaced Britney's puffy face and pouty lips. He wondered if this were bad cop replacing good cop, or the reverse. When he was nervous, Anthony sometimes had to suppress a giggle, and the light flashing on Derek's bluetooth earpiece didn't help.

"I'm a businessman," Derek began, tossing a manila folder onto the table. "Let's cut to the chase. I and my partners could make a lot of money on Riverside Paradise or lose a lot of money on it. And your articles in the *Shady Park Ledger* have hurt. Because of your articles last summer we had to disband INVOKIM and restructure our loans. Now, just when the new financing through RES-RECT starts coming in, your articles seem bent on cutting that off, too." He slapped his palms on the table. "I'm a simple man. When I do something, I do it for a reason. And that reason's usually money."

Anthony squirmed in his chair, and Derek wiggled his finger on the flashing bluetooth receiver to tighten it in his ear. He peered into Anthony's eyes. "I can give you money."

Anthony shook his head, and Derek tapped his earpiece in tighter. It seemed to be kind of a compulsion. He said, "I'm not talking about a bribe, you understand? I believe you have talent that we can use. What Riverside Paradise needs is a public relations director." He put his hand on the manila folder. "I'm offering you a job." He narrowed his eyes. "Six figures. A generous six figures." He opened the folder, slid it across to Anthony, and tapped near the top of a contract.

The salary next to his finger was a quarter of a million dollars.

"What do you say, young man? Quit the paper and come work for us."

It surprised Anthony to find himself sitting there without

being able to utter a simple No.

"Look," Derek said. "Andrew Mauer is on our side. He's facilitating the sewer line construction. And that is going to get us the rest of the properties we need. It can't be stopped. It's a done deal."

Anthony found his voice. "But the people who still live there will have to leave."

"Don't worry about Andre Smyth and the other holdouts. We'll take care of them."

"But don't you need the RES-RECT book proceeds to finance the construction?"

Derek slowly nodded. "That's right. And we need a good PR agent to help make sure we get back that publication contract with the county." He pulled a gold pen from his coat jacket and dropped it on the contract.

So far, nothing about rape. Anthony wondered if it was possible Derek hadn't heard about it. Or maybe bribery was his thing, and he wouldn't actually sink to blackmail.

Derek stood. "Take some time to think about it. I hope you join us. But we're determined. Riverside Paradise is going to be built one way or another."

42

The Happy Patchers

Too poor for a bribe, and too proud to importune;
He had not the method of making a fortune.

—Thomas Gray, *On His Own Character*

The light blue Laser Regatta shirt hung loosely over Pari's body, dropping to just above mid-thigh. She wore it constantly in Anthony's apartment even now that the weather was cold. He would catch himself admiring her smooth legs—and stroking them when she sat on his lap. If giggles were a good indication, she liked it.

He had told her about Britney's threat to accuse him of being a rapist. She cried. It reminded her that Shahnaz was in jail falsely accused by people like Britney. Pari had been so sad Anthony had forgotten to tell her about Derek's offer. Maybe now was the time.

"Derek wants me to quit the *Ledger* and become the Public Relations director for the Riverside Paradise project."

"You never told me."

"Yeah, for a salary of $250,000."

Pari laughed. "Will you have to kill?"

"Probably not. Just steal people's property away from them and ram Bible based instruction down children's throats."

"You're serious. He really offered you a job?"

He nodded. For some time, neither spoke. Then, as he said, "He needs to be stopped," at the same time she said, "*Pedar sag*!"

"What?"

"It's what my mother says. *Father dog*. Son of a bitch."

Anthony was quiet for a while. She asked what he was thinking.

"How to stop him. How to stop all those Paradise crooks."

"Me, too. Well, we've cut off their main money source, unless the Board votes their texts back in at their next meeting."

"Pari, you've got to convince your father to apply for the open position."

"He already did. I have an idea they'll choose him. The Board members like him, even the ones who voted for Bea's books. He taught some of their children at the community college."

Emma called Anthony a few days later to say the construction of the sewer line was beginning. A backhoe and two bulldozers were digging up Andre's front yard, piling up huge mounds of dirt blocking his front door.

"I'm on my way. I'll take some pictures. How about coming with me?" It was as if Anthony thought of Emma as Andre's interpreter.

River Road wasn't as green in winter as in summer, but the pines and holly still gave it a peaceful, rural look. The now-abandoned yards that had been cleared of their houses in preparation for building Riverside Paradise villas were starting to be overgrown with green and purple henbit, as if nature were reclaiming the riverside.

As they approached Andre's house, they felt the road vibrating and heard diesel engines roaring. Sooty exhaust hovered above the road. Behind heaps of dirt, only the roof of Andre's little bungalow was visible.

His driveway was blocked by a ditch, and they had to park in the turn around at the end of the road next to Andre's car. It had a large dent in the front fender that Anthony hadn't noticed before.

They climbed over a long mound of clay that rose between the road and Andre's house.

"Sorry," Emma said, grabbing Anthony's arm to steady herself.

"Watch it. Slippery here," Anthony warned. They were following a path made by Andre's footsteps leading from his car to the back of the house, ignoring a worker in a yellow jacket and hard hat trying to wave them away.

Andre stood at the open kitchen door, grinning. "Pardon the mess. As they say, there's no stopping progress."

"Andre," Emma sighed. "They're tearing your property apart."

Anthony was incensed, too. "All those empty lots along the road—and they had to start at this end, right in front of your house?" He apologized that he hadn't printed anything yet about the sewer line construction. "I wanted to check some things out first. I thought I had more time."

Their comments didn't seem to register. "Come in," Andre said, raising his voice to talk over the diesel engines and pounding backhoe. "You're in luck. I have donuts."

They left their muddy shoes outside. It was quieter when Andre closed the door. "So Pari didn't come," he observed. "I was hoping to get a reaction from her."

Neither Anthony nor Emma understood.

"The Persian love of classical poetry is well known, of course, but I was hoping that my amateur effort at composing—"

"What in the world are you talking about, Andre?" Emma shook his arm.

Andre reddened—and, surprisingly, stopped talking. He bit at what was left of a fingernail as they sat at the green formica kitchen table. "I understand she might have been too busy to look at it yet." He bit a different fingernail. "Or hesitates to be critical."

"The envelope!" Emma exclaimed. "It's still in my backpack in the car. I forgot to give it to Anthony. I brought it today and forgot again." Then she told Andre, "Pari hasn't seen it yet."

Andre put a finger on his temple as if it was all starting to make sense.

There was a lull in the bulldozer and backhoe noise. It was replaced by the whining of an electric saw and the rapping of a hammer somewhere out behind Andre's house. Andre grinned. "Mateo," he said. "Esmeralda's husband. Whenever the Whitmans don't need him for lawn care, he's down here helping build Old Man Grayson's new house. Building it practically all by himself."

Old Man Grayson was one of the residents who'd been cheated out of their houses by Bea and the pastor, then compensated for the property after Anthony reported what they'd done. His riverfront property now belonged to Bea and her Riverside Paradise project, but luckily Grayson had another piece of property back from the river that he could build a new house on.

"I'm teaching Mateo and Esmeralda to drive," Andre said.

Emma asked the same thing Anthony was thinking. "Is that what explains your car's crashed fender?"

Andre chuckled. "Ah, the fender problem. Yes. After that accident, my mother bought them a huge old car to practice in—lots of metal all around them. We keep it in her yard." He chuckled again. "Their son Juan can't start driving for another year. If I survive teaching the parents, I'll teach him, too."

Anthony wanted to go outside to take some pictures of the sewer line construction. Emma stayed in the kitchen finishing her tea with Andre.

He squatted low to get a shot revealing the height of the clay mound blocking off the house and the excavation equipment now parked for the day in the road. He shot the whole neighborhood, including Andre's mother's house and all the remaining fishing bungalows. Using the *Ledger* camera's zoom lens he snapped a picture of Esmeralda's husband building a house far back beyond the others. Two Latino men were working with him. Anthony was surprised how far along the house had come. He smiled to see that the design replicated that of Andre's little house almost exactly, except it was new.

A crunching sound made him look up. A black Mercedes sped down the gravel and oyster shell road, skidding to a stop in front of Andre's house. Bea and the pastor got out.

"Well, look who it is," Bea cried. "Our licentious news reporter."

"Funny," the pastor said. "I had you pegged for a heterosexual, yet here you are in front of—"

"Oh, no." It was Emma calling out the front window.

"She's here, too?" Bea grumbled. "Jesus, give me strength." She eyed the mound of clay blocking off Andre's house and froze.

"Coming to see Andre? This way," Anthony said, starting up the slick path over the clay. "Watch your step."

At the back door, Andre said, "Pardon the inconvenience. Mind leaving your shoes outside."

Bea and the pastor refused. "We'll talk here," Bea said. "I hope you're beginning to see how determined we are to construct Riverside Paradise."

The pastor added, "And we want you to know our generous offer for your property still stands."

Andre only glared at him.

"Pastor! Pastor!" an old woman was shuffling down the dirt road towards the house. "I saw your car. What a surprise. I have something for you." She was carrying a casserole dish.

"Your mother, Andre?" Emma smiled.

Andre nodded.

Mrs. Smyth was out of breath. "Pastor, I want you to have some of my scalloped potatoes. It's the least I can do."

Anthony had heard from Emma that the pastor tricked Mrs. Smyth into accepting a $30,000 loan against her house that she thought was a gift. His plan was to foreclose when she couldn't pay it back. Somehow Emma had forced the pastor to forgive the debt. "Maybe one day I'll tell you how," she'd said.

Pastor Mitch stood awkwardly holding the casserole, looking for somewhere to put it. But he was undaunted. "How very thoughtful," he gushed. "You know, Mrs. Smyth, I hate to see you living all alone in that ramshackle house." He tried to hand the casserole to Bea, but she wouldn't take it. He went on, "Someone your age, I believe, should be living in a warm climate. Florida, for instance. In a condominium with zero maintenance required."

Andre's mother put her hands on her cheeks. "You would do that for me?"

"That and more. We can offer you close to half a million dollars for your house."

"Oh, my," she said. "Oh, my. Thank you."

Bea said, "Praise the Lord. We can go back to your house right now and sign the papers."

"All right," Mrs. Smyth said. She looked at Andre. "It's a very kind offer, don't you think, son?"

Andre had been observing all this with a calmness that puzzled Anthony. Having his mother sell her house to Riverside Paradise was obviously the last thing he wanted.

"Yes, Mom," Andre said. "Very generous."

She nodded to the pastor. "My son agrees. I'll do it."

"Only," Andre said, "I do wonder about the Happy Patchers."

In an instant, his mother's face lost its color. Her jaw dropped. "God forgive me," she said. "I forgot about the

Happy Patchers. The quilting guild ladies love so much to meet at my house. They love to walk down onto the pier and watch the ospreys and gulls, even in cold weather."

The pastor said, "Mrs. Smyth, I understand this would be a transition you'd have to adjust to. To help you along … I said half a million." He glanced at Bea. "I'm sure we can do better than that."

"I'm sorry," Mrs. Smyth said. "Pastor, I hate to turn down your offer, but I just can't disappoint the Happy Patchers."

43

Snow jobs

Time shall unfold what pleated cunning hides:
Who cover faults, at last shame them derides.
—Shakespeare, *King Lear*

Anthony and Pari double checked Andre's research and used it to write a series of articles on the sewer line project. The first, featuring Anthony's photos of the backhoes, ditches, and mountains of dirt in front of Andre's house, tied the project directly to Bea and included this:

Local Realtor Behind Controversial Sewer Project

> … The sewer line will run along the part of River Road where Ms. Beatrice Doggit of Executive Homes and her partners are seeking to purchase the remaining properties to clear the way for construction of their planned community of luxury houses to be called Riverside Paradise. Current residents have complained that the underground sewer will endanger the environment and will impose a burdensome tax on low-income property owners.

The second article focused on Andrew Mauer's role in pushing the project forward:

Sewer Project Bypassed Regulations

> . . . The *Shady Park Ledger* has confirmed that installation of the sewage line along a stretch of River Road was begun under the orders of the newly re-elected County Executive Andrew Mauer without the feasibility and impact studies required by the county and state and without funds allotted for it in the current budget. Mr. Mauer could not be reached for comment.

They saved the most shocking for last and included photos of additional outrageous and unnecessary digging that Andre emailed to them:

Federal Grant Illegally Used to Fund Sewer Line

> . . . Sources in the county public works department confirm that the River Road sewage line was financed by diverting money from a Federal environmental grant on the orders of County Executive Andrew Mauer.

It had been Mauer's illegal use of Federal money that swayed Pop. He considered himself betrayed. "I support the guy, he gets re-elected, and he makes me look like a fool by breaking the law." Pop slumped behind his desk, avoiding eye contact with Anthony. "There's a difference between using your influence, leaning on people—between that and violating Federal law." Pop got up, went to the wall behind his desk, and took down the picture of the island. "Screw it," he had said. "Print the damned articles."

Anthony was reading through the huge batch of letters to the editor that the articles had produced, and Pari was writing replies to comments on her *Searchlight* blog when Victoria called.

"Anthony. So good to hear your voice."

"Hi, Victoria." He noticed Pari give him a glance.

"I never should have let you go, Anthony."

"Oh, I don't know. It's better this way."

"They put me in research at WPSK. Can you believe that? I hate it. Pop says why don't I come back to the *Ledger*?"

"No. You'd be bored to death." Anthony shot a glance at Pari, now engrossed in scribbling some kind of doodle in her notepad.

"Boring, I know," Victoria said. "Lately it's all about School Board meetings and sewer lines and stuff like that. That's all Pop talks about. You should hear what he says about Andrew Mauer."

"Oh?"

"I guess you know Mauer promised Pop he'd get that island in the Piskasanet River taken off the Nature Preserve list so he could buy it?"

"What!"

"He did. A year ago. And Mauer was going to get the zoning changed so Pop could build a house there. I heard Pop tell Mom. Now he says Mauer's sure to be kicked out of office."

"Why is that?"

"I don't know. Something about signing a contract."

"Contract?"

"To buy Lot 2 in Riverside Paradise. That's what I heard Pop tell Mom. He's going to get it cheap." She breathed out a sigh of boredom. "Anyway, I really miss being on TV."

"I'm sure something else will come up."

"Actually I did a screen test for WCTY TV. I'm expecting a call today."

"Good. Good."

"You know what else I miss? Going to Sur le Dessus. That man—I can't even say his name—never once took me there."

Anthony held his breath.

"So … what about it, Anthony?"

"What do you mean?" He knew what she meant.

"We could meet Jennifer and Chad there."

"No."

"Just no? You used to be more of a gentleman. That's actually kind of rude."

"Sorry, but—"

"Never mind. Jennifer said you wouldn't go. Forget it. Sorry to bother you." She hung up.

Anthony hooked his phone back on his belt. Pari's doodle was enormous now. He took the pencil out of her hand. "That was Victoria."

"Uh-huh. How's she doing?"

"They put her in research."

Pari's eyebrows rose. "Seems like a just punishment. Making her look for facts."

Anthony laughed, then turned serious. "I got an idea from something Victoria said. I need to call Andre."

Andre's baby blue bantam car with its bashed-in fender sat in the parking lot. The air was warm enough for a light jacket, but Anthony felt a few dry flakes of early snow tickle his face. Inside Tastee Donuts, everything—walls, tables, menus—was colored pink, orange, and white. In the glaring fluorescent light, Andre sat with droopy eyes, looking as if he'd just gotten out of bed.

He waved two fingers to the woman behind the counter. "Both plain?" the woman said. They seemed to know him at

Tastee.

Andre said the digging in front of his house had stopped, but the ditch was filling up with water now. The backhoe and bulldozer still blocked his front yard.

"The Riverside Paradise gang are probably waiting to see if their Bible based textbooks get voted back in by the Board of Education," Anthony guessed. "Waiting to see if they have the money to continue."

"I suppose there's nothing we can do but wait."

Anthony told him Andre Mauer had a personal stake in seeing that the sewer line went through. "He wants to buy a house there himself—at a big discount. If we could prove it, that would make it bribery. Mauer would be removed from office. The scandal would probably kill the Paradise project."

Andre bit a fingernail.

"Here's my idea. If you could call Bea's office and say you're interested in buying Lot 2 in Riverside Paradise ...."

When Anthony finished explaining, Andre grinned with a slow-motion nod.

They made the call in the privacy of Anthony's car. Andre easily got Bea's office assistant to say Lot 2 was reserved for Andrew Mauer, the County Executive. "Well, that's the only lot I'm interested in," Andre told her. "If it happens to become available, would you give me a call?"

"That was great, Andre."

"I hate to lie. Maybe I *will* buy Lot 2 if it becomes available."

Pari was still downstairs in Jerry's online office when Anthony got back.

"Getting lots of comments?"

"Ugh. I don't know why I started this."

"Pari thinks she needs to correct the spelling, grammar, misused words." Jerry laughed. "I say forget it. The comments are no more illiterate than our President's Tweets."

Anthony looked at the monitor. "Yeah. Why not just leave them to speak for themselves?"

"Hold on," Jerry said. "I want to check the weather." He turned up the TV.

"Now! WCTY TV Weather with Chief Meteorologist Roger Charla. Roger, what can you tell us about the snow we've seen falling?"

In a tight-fitting suit, Roger moved in front of a weather map. "Ashley, the City's emergency vehicles and crews were out early this morning prepared for action. But thankfully the amount of snow was less than predicted. We have Victoria Whitman standing by at Monument Square to report. Victoria, what is the snowfall like there?"

Victoria stood with her blond hair flowing over a thick red muffler. In a shiny yellow storm coat and matching yellow boots, she held a mic in one hand, the other hand lifted palm up. "Roger, it's a very light snow, hardly visible, actually. There's nothing on the ground, but if you LOOK closely at my hand, you can see a white flake settle down on it now and then." She held out her palm for the camera to get a close-up. "There you have it, Roger. I'm not sure you could see the FLAKE touch my hand. Despite the snow, I can report that the roads are clear. Roger."

"Victoria Whitman reporting on the snow in Monument Square. Thank you so much, Victoria. And stay warm."

"Hey," Jerry said. "That's your girlfriend, isn't it? Pop's daughter?"

"No," Anthony answered. "Pari's my girlfriend."

44

A Bland hero

Do not cast away an honest man
for a villain's accusation.

—Shakespeare, *Henry VI, Part II*

The eleven School Board members had met twice in the past two weeks with open hearings on applicants to fill Bea's position. At the first hearing, only one applicant besides Pari's father had showed up, and only Pari's father could give meaningful answers to their questions. At least, that's what Pari and Anthony thought. For the second hearing no other applicant showed up. Mark, Pari, and Anthony were there as observers. Rather than waste time holding another meeting, the Board decided to take an immediate vote. Pari's father was chosen.

A day later, the Board met on its regular biweekly schedule. They sat at a long raised table facing the public observers. Dr. Reginald Bland gave a soft tap of his gavel to bring the meeting to order and introduce the new member, Professor Mark Shandule. There was a light, subdued applause from the packed room.

Pari's hand slid over to grasp Anthony's. Hers was damp.

As soon as the Board approved the minutes, Dr. Bland read the only motion on the agenda, to "mandate that all county schools use the texts provided by the RES-RECT corporation."

Even though there were cops stationed at the Education Complex outer and inner doors and a squad car in the parking lot, Anthony couldn't help looking around to see if anyone was brandishing a gun. Willard Scherd was out on bail until his trial, but Anthony's news articles had made sure the public knew what he looked like. Besides, Anthony reasoned, there was no "haji" at this meeting. Shahnaz was safe in jail.

Each member of the public who wanted to speak for or against Bea's books was given three minutes. Anthony took pictures as they spoke. If the message was only "Bible good. Christians good," three minutes provided plenty of time to express that point of view and allowed for a considerable amount of repetition. Ironically, this simple message was the one that elicited the loudest shouts of agreement from the observers. Arguments based on Constitutional separation of church and state and arguments based on the importance of historical accuracy got some light applause but also some dramatic yawns and one loud moan of "Boooring."

Bea rose among the observers to speak, and Pastor Mitch tried to pull her back into her seat beside him but was unsuccessful. The word "Jesus" floating from her mouth at steady intervals, she brought up a feature of her Bible based curriculum that hadn't received much attention yet—complete replacement of "so-called" sex education with lessons on sexual abstinence. "Do you want your children performing unnatural sexual acts, taking part in sexual orgies? Because that's what they're being taught to do in our schools right now." She lifted her hands and gazed up at the ceiling. "I can hear Jesus crying. I hear him crying for his righteous curriculum to be adopted."

No one offered to speak after that. Dr. Bland called for a vote. He stared at a sheet of paper in front of him, marking responses as each Board member said "For" or "Against" re-adopting Bea's curriculum. When Pari's father was called on to vote, Dr. Bland looked up at him.

"Against," Mark Shandule said.

Dr. Bland marked his paper and repeated, "Against."

Pari whispered in Anthony's ear. "Dad says he taught Bland's son. Helped him transfer to State."

The vote was 5 for Bea's books, 5 against. Beads of sweat lined the top of Dr. Bland's eyebrows. The tally paper shook in his hands.

"I ... that is ... of course, there is much to be said on each side ... I ...."

The other Board members glared at him.

"The chair votes ... while appreciating both points of view ...." He wiped his forehead with a handkerchief. "Against," he said in a rattling voice. "The motion to re-adopt is defeated."

It was an Iranian-American style celebration at Pari's house. Beer for Anthony and Mark, tea for Pari and Mastaneh. Pretzels and potato chips for the American men, persimmons and figs for the others. Pari's brother Ken called from Syracuse. Pari jumped for the phone.

"Let your father tell him," Mastaneh said.

"Oh, right." She handed Mark the phone.

"No, I think you should, Pari," Mark said.

"Here. I'll tell him," Mastaneh said. "Ken *jun*, slaves will be called slaves again in our county schools. The earth is again more than 6,000 years old."

They heard Ken's loud "Woo-hoo" over the phone. Then Pari grabbed it and had to tell him the whole story of the vote, step by step. She included details Anthony hadn't noticed, and he started to take out his notepad to add a few notes but stopped himself. Pari kept saying, "Yeah, I know ... Yeah, I know." Then she laughed, "Right, I guess the junior high sex orgies will begin again. Oh, well."

The mention of sex made Anthony wonder if Mark had heard a comment Bea made to him in the parking lot after the meeting. She'd brushed against him and said, "Rapists like you win the day."

When Mark now asked him how well he knew Bea, Anthony decided he *had* heard her comment. Mark asked what kind of person she was, what dealings he'd had with her in the past. "Of course, I read your news articles," he said.

Pari hadn't heard the "rapist" comment, he was sure. She and Mastaneh were already in the car at the time. But Pari spoke up now. "Dad, I'm sure you know Bea is a real estate scammer. A liar and a cheat."

Mastaneh seemed uncomfortable with the way the conversation was heading. "Let's have some flan," she said. "Pari made it herself."

For Anthony and Pari, the celebration continued even after they returned to his apartment. Before they fell asleep, they lay side by side, Anthony's hand under the Laser T-shirt and resting softly on Pari's breast. Pillow talk.

Anthony said, "I think your dad overheard Bea say something in the parking lot. She called me a rapist."

"So that's why he was asking all those questions. I'll straighten him out."

"Problem is, once you hear an accusation like that, you can't get it out of your mind. It's really hard to believe it's a total lie."

"Not for me." Pari tapped her fingers on his arm as if to get his attention. "And not for my dad. He's like me."

Pari had a way of making him feel better. He was relieved, and yet he found himself waiting for her to say one more thing.

"Don't worry, Buddy."

45

Rail meat

There never was a great man yet
who spent all his life inland.

—Herman Melville, "White Jacket"

Ralph called Anthony into his office. The reports on the sewer line scam had caused a blip in circulation. "Readers love scandal," Ralph said. "Pop should be pleased, but something's wrong. He seems depressed."

Since Ralph might not know Pop had been expecting Mauer to get him a zoning exception to build a house on the island, Anthony said cautiously, "Andrew Mauer seems to be on shaky grounds lately, Ralph. Maybe that's worrying Pop."

Ralph squinted. "I never understood why Pop was such a supporter of his."

So Ralph didn't know. The only reason Anthony knew was because Victoria had blurted it out to him.

Pop sauntered past Ralph's doorway, a frown carving a single line on his forehead. He didn't look in or say hello.

"How about you go talk to him about sailboat racing," Ralph urged. "That usually cheers him up."

Pop sat behind his desk, his chair swiveled sideways, staring down at the picture of the island now propped on the floor against a chair. He didn't look up when Anthony came in.

"Pop, did you catch Victoria reporting on the snow the other day for CTY TV?"

Pop looked up with a weak smile. "My wife saw it. Victoria says she might start training to be a meteorologist for the station now. Or *meter-ologist*, as she and the weather guy pronounce it." He snorted. "Don't know if that's less than an actual meteorologist. Apparently, the main qualification is a pretty face and blond hair."

"Anyway, she looked happy."

Pop nodded. "And no mention of that scumbag John Rowland lately. That's the best part. Nothing like getting your face on TV to cure a broken heart, it seems."

"So," Anthony said. "The Colonial Yacht Club series is almost over. I checked the results so far on the website. Looks like you have a chance to take first place."

The single-line frown reappeared. "Only way I could lose is by a No-Show in the final race tonight. And that's what's going to happen."

"You're not going to show up?"

"All my crew are sick or away in the Caribbean. All except Drill Man."

That was the dentist who always showed up for the winter series looking like he was dressed for an arctic exploration.

"I'll go with you tonight," Anthony offered. "All we have to do is show up and sail the race, right? Maybe I can find somebody else, too."

Pop stood and patted his jacket pocket for a cigar. "This is ... you .... All right, young man. Meet you at the dock."

Anthony had always meant to see if he could get the sports reporter Sam Yeager to put something in the paper about sailboat racing. The problem was, Sam didn't consider sailboat racing a sport.

He found Sam down on the first floor joking with Nora and Sharise. "Final race of the winter series tonight, Sam."

"Ah."

"Pop stands to win the series. How about writing an article on it? Pop would love it. You could come along, see it first-hand."

"In a boat? Are you crazy?"

"I mean you can bring your camera to the Yacht Club dock to record the finish from the pier. Get Pop crossing the line. I'll write the captions for you if you want."

It was a deal.

Sharise heard them talking. "When Pop came in this morning, he told me he didn't have any crew but Drill Man to handle *Dynamo* tonight. Going to be windy, Pop said, all forlorn." She chuckled. "I said I'd be glad to come along as 'rail meat' if he wanted. To help hold the boat down."

"What'd he say?"

"He just gave me a hug and said he wasn't going to sail."

"Well, he is now. Meet you at the dock at 5:30, OK?"

Then he thought of Pari. Why not? She'd been on a sailboat once.

Sharise was already on board when Anthony and Pari got there. Pop had her in red foul weather gear and was zipping her into a life jacket. The wind blew her hair into a black tangle on top of her head. Pari was wearing the Laser shirt under everything, for luck, she said. Sam Yeager yelled from the dock and snapped a picture. "Is that the starting line out there?"

Pop motored out behind the line, cut the engine, and headed up to the wind. Sharise had sailed with him a few times on pleasure cruises around the harbor and knew how to help Drill Man raise the main while Anthony went forward to attach the jib halyard. Pari stood on the bow to help Pop "watch for traffic" as thirty boats maneuvered for position at the line. The five-minute warning gun went off.

"*Avenger* heading towards us on starboard," Drill Man shouted.

"Ducking," Pop said. He eased the main, dipped behind *Avenger*, and tacked immediately. "Starboard," he yelled, now in control to windward of his rival.

Dynamo and *Avenger* were both 40-foot boats with the fastest handicap ratings in the fleet. To win the race, they had to complete the course well before the others. It looked like there were maybe fifteen people on *Avenger*, some truly with no function other than to counter the heel of the boat with their weight when sailing upwind. Rail meat.

"Jib up," Pop yelled. Drill Man couldn't move very agilely in his outfit, and Anthony came to help.

Pari came back to the cockpit and held Pop's stopwatch. "Thirty seconds till the start," she called.

Pop was in his favorite spot at the pin end of the line, farthest from the race committee boat. He sailed down the line steadily on port, sails eased slightly, ducking any starboard tack boats, and tacked onto starboard right at the committee boat just as the starting gun went off. Drill Man trimmed the main. Anthony and Sharise trimmed the jib.

"Know how to read a compass?" Pop asked Pari. He gave her the job of calling out "header" when the wind shifted away from the mark and "lift" when it aimed them closer.

"OK," Pari said. "Well, um, 'header.' We're sailing five degrees farther away from our original—"

"Hard alee," Pop yelled, tacking onto port. Sharise and Anthony were working as a team with the jib now while Drill Man managed the mainsheet.

After a few minutes, Pari called out, "Now we're down five degrees going this way. So 'header,' I guess."

"Hard alee," Pop yelled, tacking back onto starboard just below his rival. They eased sails a bit to gain speed, then headed up sharply as soon as they pulled past *Avenger*, taking his wind.

"Hold your ears," Anthony yelled to Sharise and Pari. "There's a lot of cussing on that boat over there right now."

Everyone except Pop climbed to the high side of the heel-ing boat and sat facing outward with their legs over the rail, arms over the lifelines. The wind increased even more. Thin whitecaps formed on top of the waves, and foam splashed their faces as the boat plowed through. Because of its greater amount of "rail meat," *Avenger* began to catch up. Pop pinched closer to windward to try to keep in front, but that slowed them down even more.

Pari sat facing forward with only one leg over the rail and one arm hooked around the lifeline. "Header," she called. "Maybe ten degrees."

"Can't tack," Pop said. "He'll T-bone us."

"Fifteen degrees," Pari called out. A huge puff of wind dipped the boat's leeward rail into the water. Pari slid down the deck and would have dropped into the water if Pop hadn't stepped across and stopped her with his leg. Drill Man eased the main, and the boat righted enough for her to climb back to windward and grab a life rail stanchion.

"You OK, Pari?" Anthony shouted.

"Yeah," she said. "That guy tacked so shouldn't we—"

"Hard alee." Pop tacked, and soon they were even with *Avenger*, twenty yards to windward. Anthony could see the pin they would turn around in the windward-leeward course. They reached the layline and tacked back onto starboard. "Ready with the spinnaker?" Pop shouted.

"Not in this wind," Drill Man said. "Not enough crew to handle it."

Anthony knew it was good enough for Pop just to finish the race in order to win the series, but now he really wanted to beat *Avenger*. "We can do it," he shouted and raised the pole to windward, calling on Sharise to cleat the topping lift and uncleat the jib halyard so he could pull the jib down just as they rounded the mark. Pop took over the mainsheet, easing it all the way out. The boat leveled, surging ahead. Drill Man hoisted the huge blue, green, and yellow spinnaker while Anthony went from side to side, first cleating the guy to set the windward corner of the sail, then pulling the sheet to send the spinnaker billowing out in front of them. The rush of water along the sides of the boat doubled. *Avenger* was just turning the mark and having trouble setting their spinnaker. There was a lot of yelling.

Now came the hard part, threading their way through the fleet of smaller boats still making their way to windward. They all had the right-of-way unless they were on port tack and *Dynamo* was on starboard. "Starboard," Pop yelled at a port-tack boat in his path. It didn't tack out of their way. "Starboard," Pop yelled again, and the little boat responded by tacking onto starboard itself, now with the right-of-way.

"Jibing," Pop called to his crew. "Sharise, Polly, everybody, heads down. Anthony ran to free the spinnaker from the pole, and the huge mainsail shot across the deck and all the way out the other side.

"Her name's Pari," Sharise yelled to Pop.

"Looks clear on this course," Drill Man said. But Anthony hadn't been able to attach the pole on the new windward side, and the spinnaker was floating up wildly, rocking the boat from side to side. Still, they were moving fast. The leeward mark was coming up. Anthony pulled the twings on both sides to give some control over the spinnaker, then looked to the top of the mast to check the wind direction.

"Pop, the wind will still be broad enough after we round the mark to carry the spinnaker all the way to the end of the course. I can put the pole back on as soon as we jibe."

Pop jibed around the mark, Anthony clipped the pole back on the guy to starboard, and the boat heeled and picked up even more speed. The Colonial Yacht Club and its pier were on the right, a crowd of members lined up sipping cocktails to watch the boats cross the finish line, which was at about midpoint along the pier. Ahead, about 50 yards beyond the finish line, was a closed drawbridge, too low for a sailboat to pass under. They would be sailing full speed under spinnaker right up to the bridge.

"Girls," Pop shouted. "Get ready to pull the spinnaker into the cabin as fast as you can as soon as we spin around. Anthony and Drill Man, get ready to douse."

Pop kept up the speed as they passed the finish line on the pier. The yacht club cannon went off, making Pari shriek, and a line of smoke coiled into the air. The crowd on the pier cheered. First boat to finish.

Pop spun the boat up to windward just in time to avoid crashing into the bridge. His crew raced to shove the spinnaker down and into the hatch and furl the mainsail. With a flip of a lever, Pop started the engine, and they motored in front of the excited crowd back into Pop's slip. *Avenger* was far behind. It hadn't even reached the mark for the final turn yet.

Sam Yeager came up to them in the clubhouse, beaming. "Look, guys." He showed a picture of them crossing the finish line with a wisp of the signal cannon smoke in the foreground. "I got lots of other shots, too, with the telephoto."

Sharise and Pari gave each other high-fives. "Your hair!" Pari said. "*Your* hair!" Sharise said.

"Ladies," Pop said. "You can freshen up in that room. Then come out for drinks and hors d'oeuvres."

Club members gathered around Pop, Drill Man, and Anthony bringing Manhattans in plastic glasses, toasting the winners of the series. "New crew Harold? Where'd you get those ringers? This is an amateur sport, you know."

Sam had his notebook out and his phone recorder on, asking questions. It was the first time Anthony had been the interviewee rather than the interviewer. He described the whole race in detail, Sam asking a million questions. "I'm going to make a whole spread covering this in tomorrow's paper," Sam told Pop. "I'm almost convinced sailing is a sport."

A handsome man about Anthony's age in a suit and tie snaked through the crowd around Pop and asked, "Harold Whitman, any relation to that stunning new TV reporter, Victoria Whitman?"

"My daughter."

The young man introduced himself. "Tim Hathaway. Clarence's son. *Stardom*? I work for my dad. Hathaway Broadcasting Agents." He gave Pop his card, and Pop fished out one of his, adding. "Victoria's single, by the way."

Anthony looked towards the hors d'oeuvre table and noticed Sharise and Pari surrounded by a group of men, some still in sailing gear just back from the race and some in sport jackets and slacks. Half of the men had at least a touch of gray in their hair. They seemed to be competing for the attention of the two pretty newcomers.

Sharise rolled her eyes somewhat uncomfortably. Pari smiled, giggled, laughed at their comments—enjoying the attention a little too obviously, Anthony thought. A man with a white moustache took a half finished Manhattan from her hand and exchanged it for a fresh one. A younger man waved his arms, probably describing an incident from the race. A bearded man with a cap that said *Captain* gave each woman his card.

"Drop it, my puppies," Pop told the men, edging in between Sharise and Pari. "Nobody's snatching up my star crew."

46

Slugs and shells

"To bed, to bed, to bed!"

—Shakespeare, *Macbeth*

Anthony and Pari collapsed onto his bed that night and immediately fell into a deep, passionless sleep. When Anthony finally woke up, Pari wasn't there. He picked up the *Ledger* from his landing, and there it was.

***Dynamo* Takes Race Series with *Shady Park Ledger* Crew**

It was a special two-page insert with eight pictures. Sam had gotten the details right and made the race sound actually exciting. Anthony hoped Pop would be more pleased than embarrassed.

Pari came in with a bag of groceries and kissed him. "I went to get gas. Mahmud says Daryl's coming back to work."

"Who?"

"The kid who worked there on Sunday evenings, remember? He quit for a while so he could pull up his grades. That was before the shooting, but he's the only person the police haven't questioned about the gun. I called his number a couple of times and didn't get an answer. But Mahmud says he'll be there Sunday.

It was a self-serve gas station with a snack and coffee shop and car repair bays. They didn't need gas, so they parked in front of the shop door rather than at the pumps. A bell hanging from the glass door rang as they walked in. The lights were on, but at first it seemed that nobody was there until they noticed a freckled, curly haired boy behind a bullet proof glass panel looking up from a book. He seemed scared.

They walked up to the enclosure, which had a narrow opening only big enough to pass money or a credit card through. "Which pump?" the boy asked.

"We don't want gas," Anthony said.

The boy bent below the counter rummaging for something. He was breathing hard.

Pari said, "Don't worry. We're not trying to rob you or anything. You're Daryl, aren't you. I'm a friend of Mahmud. I've been trying to get in touch with you. We just wanted to ask you a few questions."

Slowly, Daryl slid back onto his stool, eyeing them cautiously. "OK. We always worry about robberies."

Anthony said, "This could be a dangerous job, I guess."

"Maybe. On Sundays not so much—not many customers. We don't keep much cash on Sundays."

"Do you have anything for protection?"

Daryl's pale face reddened. "We did." He looked at Pari. "I don't know if Mahmud would want me to tell—"

"We're close friends," she said. "He told me he keeps a gun for self-defense, right?"

Daryl looked worried. "Except it's not here now."

Anthony tried to sound casual. "Would you know how to use it anyway?"

Daryl seemed hesitant to answer.

Anthony chuckled. "I guess not. You're probably too young."

"Well, yeah, I know how to use it."

"Come on." Anthony gave him a skeptical squint.

"Don't tell Mahmud, OK? I shot a rat with it one night. I mean I didn't hit him, though."

"Where was that?"

"In the far repair bay. I kept hearing something in there. I saw this huge rat gnawing on a piece of peanut brittle on the shelf."

Anthony laughed as if this was just some funny story Daryl was telling him. "Then what?"

"So then I tiptoe in. I hold the gun in two hands like the cops do on television. The rat is up on two legs, looking me in the eye. I squeeze the trigger. Pop! It wasn't any louder than a tire popping onto a rim. I did jump a little, though. I saw the rat run. Didn't get him, but he never came back again."

"You remember when that was?"

"The last day I worked here. This is my first day back." He scratched his head. "And the gun's not here. I don't know why." He searched through some shelves under the counter. "I know I put it back. Now I'll have to tell Mahmud it's gone."

Pari told him not to worry, and that his story would be very helpful to her friend Shahnaz.

"Shahnaz? I know her. Reza's wife."

"She's in jail." Pari told him the whole story of how she came to be arrested. "So, Daryl, if you would tell the police what you told us ...." She reached through the slot and put her fingers on his. "She's being held as a terrorist. A totally innocent person."

"Sure. Sure. I will." Daryl pursed his lips, and Anthony imagined he was wondering what might happen to him when he did. Anthony didn't know, either.

"Here's an idea," Anthony said. "After your shift, go home. Tell your parents first. And then call the police. Make sure you tell them you just found out about all this."

"Will they arrest me?"

"I'm not a lawyer, but—"

"My dad is."

"They won't arrest you."

The next day, Anthony called Rob at the police station. Rob said they'd taken Daryl's written statement with his father standing by. They took Daryl's fingerprints. And they went to Mahmud's gas station to look for the bullet. It was there, lodged in the wood frame of the shelf. "These little pistols," Rob told him, "they eject the casing after they're fired. We found the casing, too. In the crack where the bay door closes. Swept there, it looked like."

Anthony wondered if anybody had heard the shot that night.

"We asked everybody in the area, and one guy at a gas station across the street remembers hearing something at about that time. He thought it was a tire being inflated and popping onto the rim."

So it was confirmed that Mahmud's gun was fired on the Sunday before the school shooting. That was good.

Rob said, "I know what you're thinking. But the gun could have been fired again in the school."

"Was the gun clip, or whatever, missing more than one bullet?"

"No. Just one. That's something. But there's no way to prove another one wasn't put in afterwards. See what I mean? The District Attorney isn't ready to drop the charge yet."

Back in the newsroom, Pari wanted to get the story out so people would at least know the police now had some doubt that Shahnaz was the shooter.

"Careful, though," Anthony said. "Daryl is just a kid. We don't put kids' names in the paper."

"I know. 'Police are examining new evidence that may indicate Mrs. Delpak is not the shooter at the school hearing.' How about that?"

Anthony tapped his pencil on the carrel. "Rob didn't actually say that. Maybe we should give them some time to dig around a little more first."

Pari flipped her notebook shut and sighed. "You're right. I'll wait."

Anthony stood behind her, his hands on her shoulders, and whispered, "You know, since the race, we've been so tired at night we ... I mean we haven't … Let's go home early." He checked the clock over Ralph's door. "Let's go home now."

47

Lack of evidence

> *"Not a particle of evidence, Pip," said Mr. Jaggers, shaking his head and gathering up his skirts.*
>
> —Charles Dickens, *Great Expectations*

The ringing of Anthony's phone caught him in flagrante delicto, so to speak, although he felt it was the interruption that was the crime.

"Don't stop," Pari breathed. "Don't answer that."

Later, he saw it was Emma and called her back. Esmeralda was at her house and had brought something strange to show her. "I think you should see this."

Pari sighed when he told her. "Ugh, I feel like rubber. I just want to lie here. Can you go by yourself?"

It was Esmeralda who opened the door. "Mr. Anthony. I am so glad you come."

He recognized Emma's son Todd sitting at the dining room table with a girl his age. Todd jumped up. "Hi, Mr. Anthony."

The girl said, "I'm Fran. We moved here from Riverside Village."

"I showed Fran the article you wrote about my science project," Todd said.

Fran beamed. "It's so cool. I know somebody who's famous."

Esmeralda took his coat and looked for a hall closet, but there was none in Emma's house. She draped it over the bannister. Emma came out of the kitchen taking off an apron.

"Thanks for coming, Anthony. I was just talking to Charles. He'll be working late at the hospital tonight. Guess what? He says a friend of ours who works there has a daughter named Pari. So we know Pari's parents and didn't realize it."

The little hallway, living room, and dining room were basically a single open area. "If you could come into the kitchen a minute," Emma said. There was a man's pinstripe suit coat hung over one chair and the trousers over another. Emma lowered her voice. She seemed not to want Todd and Fran to hear. "Esmeralda, show Anthony what you showed me."

"Is from Ms. Michelle Whitman," Esmeralda explained. "She collect clothes from friends, give to the Goodwill. If Goodwill no want, she tell me throw away. Or I can keep anything I want." Her deep brown eyes seemed to darken even in the bright kitchen light. "This man suit I take. Almost new. I know it. It is from Mr. Derek, I used to work for. Same size as my husband. Beautiful suit, but after I take it, I find ...." She stopped and looked to Emma for help.

"Look." Emma lifted the trousers and showed him a hole ripped into the right pant leg. Both women looked at him for a reaction.

"A hole," Anthony said lamely.

"Jes," Esmeralda said. "Then I look in pocket." She glanced at Anthony and slowly slipped her long fingers into the pocket. One finger came through the pocket and out the hole. "Hole is from inside pocket," she said. "And something I find." She pulled out a small brass bullet casing and dropped it onto the table as if afraid it might hurt her. "I know what is this," she whispered. "In my country, is too much killing. Is why we run to America. I am so afraid."

Anthony held open the pocket and looked inside. The inside hole was smaller than the hole that went through the pant leg. Emma handed him a little flashlight. "We used this to look." He shined the light in and saw some of the fabric was blackened.

Emma said, "What else, Esmeralda? Tell Anthony what you told me."

"I'm afraid," she said. "I don't want get in trouble and get send back again."

Emma took her hand. "We're your friends."

Esmeralda was sniffling. "Is from Mr. Derek gun. I know. Very little gun. He have little 'hol-ester' and carry in pocket most of time. Keep in dresser drawer. Ms. Britney, she have little gun, too."

Anthony frowned. "He carried it in a little pocket holster?"

"Jes. The suit was no damage when I work for them. Some time after I working for Ms. Michelle this happen. I never tell anybody about it except Ms. Emma."

Anthony said, "I think the police need to see this."

Esmeralda gasped. "Police? No, please. I am afraid of police."

Anthony racked his brain to find a way to protect Esmeralda. Any number of things could go wrong if she went public with this. The President had the whole country in a panic over "criminal illegals bringing violence across our border." Esmeralda was here legally, but that didn't seem to matter these days—to the general population, the Justice Department, or Immigration and Customs Enforcement.

He or Emma could take Derek's suit to the police, but the police would need to hear the story directly from Esmeralda. And there was one more problem. Derek Grosbeck was a prominent figure in business and politics. Anthony's reports on the textbook scam might have damaged his reputation recently, but that was only by implication. It was Bea who got most of the blame, and rightly so, since the Bible based curriculum was her idea and the book publishing company belonged mainly to her. Derek was only a partner who went along with it. Anthony imagined the authorities would be unwilling to charge or prosecute Derek without indisputable evidence.

He asked if Esmeralda would let Emma keep the suit for a while. "There's something I'd like to check on before we go to the police." Like Pop, he wanted to "get his ducks in a row" first.

Anthony and Pari found Ms. Ernst on duty as lunch monitor in the multi-purpose room, now being used as a cafeteria. A long skirt hid most of the bandage on her calf. She smiled at them, and a drinking straw wrapper flew up and landed on her head, followed by a roar of student laughter.

"Now you see why it's a good thing teachers aren't armed," Ms. Ernst quipped.

Another straw paper circled in the air and dropped at Anthony's feet.

He bent to pick it up and noticed that a single tile had been removed where they were standing. The gap beneath it was covered over with duct tape. He asked Ms. Ernst, "This is about where the first row of chairs was set up for the Board of Ed hearing, isn't it? About where you were sitting?"

She nodded. He showed Ms. Ernst some pictures on his phone. "These are the people who were sitting near you in that first row. It's taken from the back, but I wonder if you recognize any of them."

"That's Mr. Derek Grosbeck sitting next to me. I recognize him even from the back. He's wearing a pinstripe suit and has a bluetooth thingy in his ear."

"Are you sure? How do you know him?"

She blushed. "That's Mrs. Britney Grosbeck next to him. They're the parents who complained about me giving their daughter an F for plagiarism."

"The same lady who said she and her husband were carrying guns?"

"Yes."

A bell rang to signal the end of lunch period. Ms. Ernst had to go back to her classroom.

Anthony found his friend Rob behind the police station intake counter.

"What are you telling me?" Rob held two pictures of Derek and Britney that Anthony had printed out, one taken from the back as they sat at the Board of Education hearing, Nicole Ernst next to Derek, and one from the front that he'd taken at the Evergreen Academy promotion. "You're saying these guys are terrorists?"

"No, Rob. Like I said, there was a gunshot, right?" He pointed to Britney in the pictures. "This woman announced she and her husband were carrying guns."

"You realize that doesn't prove anything."

"It's just that the slug hit the floor right next to where Derek was sitting. I saw where the police removed the damaged tile."

Rob took him back to tell everything all over again to the Detective McGinn, who was handling the case.

"Do you realize who this man is?" the detective asked him.

"It's Derek Grosbeck."

"Right. The chair of the state Republican Central Committee."

Anthony met his gaze steadily. He said, "And a close friend of the County Exec. But you could maybe see if he and his wife really do own and carry guns. Check their guns out against the slug you found. See if Derek's gun has been fired recently." He added, "They live in Nottingham Estates" and gave the address.

The detective looked annoyed. "You don't have to tell me

how to do my job. Listen, a lot of people carry concealed guns. We can't question every one of them whenever there's a shooting." He stood up, and it seemed like the discussion was over.

Anthony said, "So you're not even going to question Derek?"

"You have something against this guy? Oh, that's right—he's the partner of the woman who says you tried to rape her."

Rob broke in. "We just need more reason to consider Derek Grosbeck a person of interest, Anthony. That's all."

"There is something else," Anthony said.

48

Lawyering up

"Has he come armed, then?" she asked anxiously. "Has he brought a pistol or a sword?"
Ian shook his head, his dark hair lifting wildly in the wind. "Oh, no, Mam!" he said. "It's worse. He's brought a lawyer!"

—Diana Gabaldon, *Voyager*

Esmeralda walked into the Piskasanet County police office with a protective phalanx of supporters—her husband Mateo, Emma, Anthony, Pari, Andre, and Edward Donnelly, a lawyer with shaggy gray hair and a rumpled suit who was hired by Andre.

In the parking lot, Anthony had heard the lawyer tell Andre, "You realize I'm not a criminal lawyer." Andre had replied, "Esmeralda's not accused of a crime. We just want to make sure she's not deported illegally." The lawyer had smiled. "That I can handle."

They were ushered into a waiting room, but the lawyer was the only person allowed to accompany Esmeralda in to be interviewed. She carried with her a black plastic bag that had been examined at the intake desk.

Pari introduced herself to Emma. "My mother knows you and your husband. Mom says you tutor at the community college."

"I can't believe we've never met," Emma said. "I really appreciate the things you've written for the paper." They started chatting as if they'd known each other forever.

The rest of Esmeralda's entourage sat silently, Anthony,

at least, wondering how to start up a conversation. He asked Mateo, "How are the driving lessons going?"

"Ah," Mateo said. "The car is in repair shop."

"Andre's? I saw it in the parking lot."

"No. Ours."

Andre spoke up with an explanation. "Although I often deride the first world for the insignificant things we consider to be problems and refer to the real problems of the third world by way of contrast, I've observed that third-world drivers are not only worse than our own but often a real menace on the highway." He looked at Mateo. "The problem does not seem to be lack of skill in manipulating the vehicle but an intense, uncontrollable desire to get in front of everybody else."

"My mother doesn't drive like that," Pari said.

"Yes," Andre replied. "The problem does seem to be at least partly hormone related."

Detective McGinn walked Esmeralda and the lawyer out and called Emma in.

Mateo and Esmeralda talked in Spanish. She seemed more at ease than when she'd gone in. It was probably because she did come out. Anthony listened closely to what they were saying and caught the words *evidencia*, *testimonio*, and *jurar*. That looked bad for Derek Grosbeck. He heard nothing that sounded like deportation.

Eventually, Esmeralda and her husband were joking with each other. She laughed, gave him a gentle elbow in the arm, and said something like *No obtendrás esse traje*, which Anthony took to mean "You won't be getting that suit."

Then Emma was brought out and Anthony was taken in. Detective McGinn had changed his tune. He asked simple questions to verify when Anthony had first seen the damaged suit and the bullet casing and what Esmeralda had told him at that time.

"Actually," Anthony said, "I do remember Mrs. Whitman dragging a bag just like that one down the hallway of her house and giving it to Esmeralda to dispose of. I remember hearing her tell Esmeralda she could keep anything she wanted from the bag. I never saw what was in it, though."

The detective said, "That lawyer she brought. What the hell was that about?"

"An abundance of caution," Anthony suggested. "She was deported not long ago in an immigrant roundup."

"Um-hm. The police don't deport people, I guess you realize."

"Right. But Andrew Mauer and his Riverside Paradise friends think Esmeralda was the source of their recent bad publicity in the *Ledger*. She wasn't, but she's afraid Mauer can get her deported again. It was Mauer who called on his Federal contacts to stage that previous roundup."

The detective put down his pen. "That's all for now."

"OK." Anthony couldn't help adding, "About the attempted rape charge against me—"

"Bea Doggit refused to do a rape kit, and she hasn't come in to file a written complaint yet." McGinn raised his eyebrows. "Don't worry. We'll be in touch."

"I guess you haven't found her factotum, the man on the Wanted poster?"

McGinn just stared. "We'll be in touch."

Back in the parking lot, the lawyer took a little camera from his pocket and asked Emma to take a picture of him standing next to Esmeralda, then another of him standing between her and her husband. He checked the pictures and asked her to take one more of him with Esmeralda. "*Hasta luego*," he said. "Always ready to help."

That evening Anthony called Rob. Rob said Detective McGinn had gone to Derek's house to question him and talked to his wife Britney instead since Derek wasn't home. "She seemed 'hyper.' That's how McGinn put it. He asked if she and her husband had guns. 'We have to protect our children,' she said. 'We have licenses.' And she showed McGinn the derringer in her purse. Derick had his gun with him, she said. So McGinn talks about gun safety and asks where Derek keeps his gun in the house. She takes him to the bedroom to show him a pocket holster in the dresser drawer. And, guess what? It had a hole shot right through it."

Anthony was writing this down. "Hole shot through the pocket holster?"

"Happens a lot when people try to pull the gun out," Rob said. "Carrying a gun that way is crazy dangerous."

Anthony kept writing.

"But this is confidential," Rob insisted. "Until we see if the District Attorney actually files charges against Grosbeck."

As Anthony ended the call, Pari came out of his shower wrapped in a thin white towel, smelling like the lavender soap she'd brought to his apartment. Anthony didn't get around to telling her about Derek and the police until later.

49

Lobsters and pabulum

A stupid man's report of what a clever man says can never be accurate, because he unconsciously translates what he hears into something he can understand.

—Bertrand Russell,
A History of Western Philosophy

The police sent out a brief statement that the District Attorney and FBI had dismissed all charges against Shahnaz, which had included terrorism, attempted murder, firing a weapon on school property, and illegal possession of a firearm. No reason for the dismissal was given.

Anthony knew the release of a "terrorist" was sure to outrage the public unless he could show them that her arrest had been a mistake. He called Rob before writing the story.

"No, you can't say Derek Grosbeck is now under suspicion. His lawyer is negotiating with the District Attorney." Rob cleared his throat. "And you can't even write that."

"What about the evidence against Shahnaz Delpak, then? You must have found something to rule that out?

"OK. Here's what you can say. The gun found in her possession had been fired to kill a rat. The police are looking for a gun of a slightly smaller caliber in connection with the shooting."

"Looking?"

"Come on, Anthony. I'll call you as soon as the District Attorney gets through with Grosbeck and his lawyer."

And so he had to make do with a brief article that never mentioned Grosbeck.

Charges on Delpak Dropped
Gun Seized Was Not Used in School Shooting

His article focused on the gun being fired at a rat. Aggravated assault, gun caliber, residue of various combustion products—these required serious attention to comprehend. Shooting at a rat was something the readers could sink their teeth into.

As for Pari, her family, and Shahnaz's family, they didn't care about Grosbeck. They were happy just to have Shahnaz back. Anthony went along with them to Shahnaz's apartment. Her husband Reza had painted over the graffiti on the door, and Mastaneh had pretty much put the rooms back in order. The samovar was bubbling. They celebrated with tea and pistachios.

Shahnaz couldn't stop hugging her son Jim. They all acted as if Pari and Anthony had stormed the prison to set Shahnaz free. Reza kept bowing, holding a hand over his chest. He and Shahnaz kept calling Anthony and Pari something she said meant "liberators."

Mark Shandule discretely put an envelope on a bookshelf. Objections in Farsi burst from Reza before he changed to English. "No need any more, Professor Mark. I can go back to work tomorrow."

Mastaneh said, "Now no more talk about moving to California, I hope."

Reza and Shahnaz glanced at each other without answering.

Pari joined in. "Don't move away, Reza. If you stay here, I can translate your screenplay into English."

His eyes opened as if he'd never thought of that.

"Good idea," Jim said. "You can produce the film here. You'll be famous, Dad." He took his father's arm. "And maybe I can get back on the Northbrook High baseball team next spring."

Anthony was happy that Shahnaz was out of jail, but that wasn't enough. He wanted her vindicated in the eyes of the public. He wanted to vindicate Jim, too. The kids at school had to stop calling him a terrorist. And that meant Derek Grosbeck needed to be exposed as the person who shot Ms. Ernst. An accident, yes, but he'd been the shooter. He shouldn't have been carrying a gun on school property.

Rob had given him plenty of information, so in the newsroom the next day Anthony started working on an article about Derek. All he needed to know was what plea bargain Derek would be able to make. He sat on his article a day and a half until Rob called, then wrote it.

State GOP Chair's Gun Fired at School Board Hearing

The shot that wounded a teacher at a School Board hearing in September came from a gun brought to the meeting by state GOP Central Committee Chair Derek Grosbeck, according to police.

District Attorney Randolph Keene said Mr. Grosbeck has admitted accidentally discharging a firearm on school property. The police have confiscated his weapon, and Mr. Grosbeck has agreed not to contest the revocation of his license to carry a gun. In return, the District Attorney has agreed to drop all charges against

Mr. Grosbeck except failure to possess a gun license on his person while carrying a firearm.

Mr. Grosbeck's lawyer, Benjamin Starkezahn, said his client was attempting to defend himself and others from a gunman standing at the door when the small pistol he carried for personal protection accidently went off. "It was Mr. Grosbeck's quick action that prevented excessive violence at the hearing," Mr. Starkezahn said.

Witnesses recalled Mr. Grosbeck's wife announcing at the meeting that she and her husband were carrying guns. The gun, police believe, went off as Mr. Grosbeck attempted to pull it from his pocket. The bullet hit a teacher, Ms. Nicole Ernst.

After the shot, Mr. Grosbeck and his wife immediately fled the room while three unarmed women subdued the gunman standing at the door.

The teacher shot by Mr. Grosbeck's gun is expected to recover from a wound to her leg. She said she does not intend to file a civil suit against Mr. Grosbeck at this time.

> Mr. Grosbeck, along with Pastor Mitchell Rainey, is a partner in the Riverside Paradise project. The county Board of Education was found in violation of its ethics code when it voted for purchases that benefitted that project while another partner, Ms. Beatrice Doggit, was on the Board.

Ralph read it. "Won't be as effective as *Shahnaz didn't do it; Derek did*. But fine." He wiped his glasses. "Writing a complex article for the newspaper in order to inform the public—it's like offering a lobster to a baby."

"Huh?"

"It's simply not something he's equipped to eat. He finds a bowl of pabulum and scoops a handful of that into his mouth instead."

This time there was no question of Pop vetoing the article. First of all, he'd already had to give up his dream of building a house on the island when he allowed Anthony to report that Bea and the others owned the RES-RECT publisher. But just as important, he was still basking in the glory of his victory over *Avenger*.

Anthony wasn't willing to let Derek and the Riverside Paradise gang off as easily as this, however. He wanted to make sure they were put out of business. He called the District Attorney's office and got an interview in Colonial City.

The young assistant District Attorney—his nameplate said Jeremy Black, LLD—sat behind a desk piled with papers in a stuffy room of the Courthouse Building. Anthony gave him his card. The attorney remembered reading Anthony's articles on INVOKIM, the corporation Bea, the pastor, and Derek had previously set up to purchase tax liens, seize the houses of Andre's neighbors, and turn them over to Bea's Executive Homes, which was developing Riverside Paradise.

"INVOKIM is dead, but RES-RECT has risen in its place," Anthony told the attorney. He told him everything he knew.

Jeremy Black retrieved a folder from a filing cabinet and paged through it. "Hmm. We've already started looking into the connection between the two." He reached the end of the file. "I see. We're waiting for confirmation of something from Delaware."

Anthony tried to read his expression.

"I have your number," the attorney said. "I'll call you when we have something definite for the public."

It wasn't long before Anthony got the call. Pari grinned over his shoulder as he typed up the story.

Riverside Paradise Declares Bankruptcy

The District Attorney's office confirms that the corporation primarily funding the Riverside Paradise project has dissolved, declaring bankruptcy. An assistant at Executive Homes, the real estate company owned by Ms. Beatrice Doggit, said their Riverside Paradise project has now been abandoned.

According to the District Attorney's office, Ms. Doggit and Pastor Mitchell Rainey, partners in RES-RECT, LLC, filed to dissolve the corporation and declare it bankrupt when a third partner,

Mr. Grosbeck, announced his intention to leave it.

The Investors Bank of Dover holds the primary mortgage on the Riverside Paradise properties. Bank officials could not immediately be reached to comment on their plans for the property.

50

Victims and liars

Anger is a brief madness.

—Horace, *Epistles*

A white SUV jerked to a stop in the *Ledger* parking lot too close for Anthony to open his car door. What the hell? he thought. Drunk driving in the morning?

Britney Grosbeck slid out and banged her fist on the hood of his car. "Who do you think you are, young man? Get out of that car and face me. You've finally gone too far."

He had to work his way over into the passenger seat and get out that side. She was waiting for him with glassy eyes. Anthony remembered Rob saying the detective thought her "hyper" when he interviewed her. It was cold, but she stood there sweating, shifting from one leg to the other. He'd seen this in teenagers he'd interviewed for a story on Adderall abuse. That might be it. Some of the kids said their mothers stole the drugs from them. "Trying to get thin," one girl explained.

Britney yelled, "You retract those fake news stories on my husband. Understand? If you don't, I'm going to broadcast your name on TV, put it on Facebook and Twitter. Let everybody know you're a rapist. Don't think I won't."

"Fake news? But your husband admitted it was his gun that went off."

"Not that. There was something else in your articles that Derek didn't like. I forget what it was. I didn't read them, but I'm sure you know what it was."

"I wrote that Riverside Paradise used an unethical procedure to get money. Is that what you—"

"Ethical blah blah blah. Fake news. You take it back." She was breathing heavily.

Anthony realized it would be hopeless trying to reason with her. He used his calmest voice. "You seem agitated, Mrs. Grosbeck. Would you like to come in to the waiting area and sit down for a minute?"

She gave a dramatic lurch back as if he held a knife. "Sit down with a rapist? Oh, that's a good one. You're a danger to ...." But she seemed to lose track of what she wanted to say. The word "danger" must have thrown her, and she veered onto what Anthony recognized was her main obsession. "A danger to our children, danger from terrorists, danger from the ragamuffins in their classes bringing drugs into the schools."

Anthony scanned the parking lot, grateful that nobody was watching.

Britney took a breath and went on. "You liar. I thought you were going to help promote Evergreen Academy. A couple of pictures—that's all you're going to put in the paper?" She seemed to have totally forgotten the articles about her husband.

"If you send me an update on the Academy progress, Mrs. Grosbeck, I'll—"

But Britney had turned around and was climbing back into her car. Music blared out the open window. He recognized it. *Animal Instinct,* by the Cranberries. She backed out of the parking space and slammed on the brakes just before hitting a car passing behind her, then sped forward over the sidewalk and into a brick wall. Her airbag went off, trapping her behind the wheel, the horn blaring.

Anthony called 911. He and the man she almost backed into stood by until the ambulance arrived. Britney tried to refuse help from the paramedics, but they asked, "Have you been taking any drugs, Ma'am?" and insisted on taking her to City Hospital to be checked out.

City Hospital was where Pari's mother worked as a nurse. Emma's husband Charles worked there, too—as a counselor. Maybe they could work some miracle and straighten Britney out.

Anthony passed by Nora and Sharise on his way up to the newsroom. Obviously, they hadn't heard the confusion outside. Both were beaming at him.

"What?" he said.

Nora pointed to Sharise's desk. A tall pewter trophy inscribed with a sailboat gleamed in her reading light.

"Pop said we can take turns keeping it for a week." Sharise whisked some imaginary dust off it with a tissue.

"Hold on," Anthony said. He clicked a picture with his phone.

"Good idea," Nora cried out. "We'll hang up a picture of each one of you with it on your desk."

The police and fire scanner was chirping in the newsroom. Anthony listened, in the mood for something like a cat rescue or car stalled in traffic to take his mind off the kinds of things he'd been writing about lately. "Ambulance 259," he heard. "Accident victim dazed, no obvious signs of injury. Transporting to City."

Pari came in, looked left and right, and kissed him on the cheek. She put a plastic bag on her desk.

"You've been shopping?"

Her cheeks reddened. "Yeah."

"What'd you buy?"

"Oh. This." She took a book from the bag. *Elements of Sailing.*

Anthony's desk phone rang. Nora. "Wanted to give you a warning. Mole Man is on his way up to see you."

"Thanks, Nora. Do me a favor. Wait a few minutes, then

call the police. Tell them I asked you to report that a man wanted for child support violation is here. He goes by lots of names, but one of them is George Wilson. Say his picture is on a Wanted poster at the station, would you?"

The mole man tapped Anthony on the shoulder. He introduced himself as a "special investigator" working for Mr. Grosbeck. "If we could speak in private, please."

Ralph was out, and Anthony took the man into his office. They sat at Ralph's table. "What do you want?"

"Mr. Grosbeck is, uh ...." The investigator found a page in a notebook he took from his suit pocket. "... is willing to renew the offer of employment he previously made to you. The amount of remuneration will be increased by $20,000 per year." He studied Anthony's face. "With certain provisions."

"Go on. May I record this?"

"No. Turn that off."

"I'll just take some notes, then."

"You will need to sign a contract of employment exclusively with him. You will agree not to publish anything in the future without his permission." He checked his notebook. "And you will agree to begin by writing an article explaining that the report that he was a partner in ...." Another look in the notebook. "... in RES-RECT was in error and that he has never been involved in the Riverside Paradise project."

Anthony shrugged. "I'm afraid it's too late for that. Two witnesses heard him say he was a partner. One of those witnesses was called to the District Attorney's office to testify to that." He didn't mention that it was Pop.

The mole man said, "If you will let me finish. You would also agree to write an article supporting Mr. Grosbeck's claim that it was his gunshot that stopped the assailant."

"No. I'm satisfied with my job here. Tell him thanks anyway."

The investigator flipped to another page in his notebook. "In that case, I'm instructed to tell you that Mr. Grosbeck will offer the services of his lawyer to Ms. Bea Doggit to help her bring her accusation of attempted rape forward and formally file her complaint." He looked up. "As you know, I myself have pictures showing that you sexually harassed Ms. Doggit."

Anthony slid his phone off his belt and snapped a picture of the Mole Man sitting at the table in front of his notes. He quickly snapped a second close-up of the notes themselves. Just in case he needed them.

There was a loud knock on the door. "Police." Two cops came in and checked the Mole Man's identification.

Anthony handed one of the cops the legal pad he's been taking notes on. "This man threatened to falsely accuse me of a crime if I didn't comply with his employer's demands. These are the notes I took of what he said. Would you give them to Detective McGinn, please. I also have a recording of Bea Doggit threatening me, if he thinks that would be helpful."

As soon as the police confirmed the man's identity, they handcuffed him. "You are charged with violation of a child support order over a period of five years. You have the right to remain silent—"

The mole man waved his hand. "Don't bother. I know it by heart."

When they were gone, Pari rushed into the office and held Anthony in a hug. "I heard every word. I was listening at the door." She wiped away a tear. "Oh, Anthony, I'm scared. Is Bea really going to insist they charge you with this?"

"From what Rob tells me, it's not likely."

But Pari was still worried when they were back in his apartment that evening. "What if Bea and her lawyer do get the police to file an attempted rape charge?"

Anthony cracked two eggs into the Ramen he was cooking, staring into the steam rising from the pot. Pari put her hand on his back. "Sorry. I don't mean to upset you. I'm worried, that's all."

He turned around and they kissed. "I love you, Pari."

"I love you, too, Anthony. Turn off the stove. I'm not hungry."

They lay on the bed talking. Pari said, "We could run away if Bea gets them to press charges."

Anthony grinned. "You'd run away with me? Where would we go?"

"I don't know." She ran her fingers over the cover of the sailing book still on the edge of the bed. "I like living here."

"Me too."

"I got it," Pari said. "I'll say you were with me at the time that Bea claims … you know."

"You'd lie for me?"

"Of course." There were tears in her eyes. "No. I guess you're right. I wouldn't be able to."

Anthony's phone rang. "OK," Rob said. "Here's where we stand. The guy we arrested works for Beatrice Doggit and recently for Derek Grosbeck. When we started to file misdemeanor charges against him for years of violating a child support order, he said he'd pay up and admitted the pictures he took of you and Bea were a set-up. He also said he'd helped set up another person Bea accused of the same thing a couple years ago, a real estate competitor. Same charge, same staged pictures. She dropped that accusation when the guy gave up claim to his sales commission. We called her and told her what we have. She's going to drop the complaint against you."

"Drop the complaint? Meaning—?"

"Give us a written statement she'd been mistaken."

Anthony still felt uncomfortable. "Sounds like what victims do when they've been paid off."

Rob said, "Yeah. Or liars when they've got what they wanted, or when they've been caught in the lie. That's our job, separating the victims from the liars. If they try this more than once like Bea, they definitely get thrown into the liar category."

Anthony ended the call, pausing to take it all in.

Pari held her hand over her mouth. "What? Anthony, tell me. What did he say?"

Like a mist slowly dissolving over the river, his worries gradually faded. "We won't have to be criminals on the run, Pari," he laughed. "We can stay here. And keep being reporters."

She held her head against his chest. "And lovers," she added.

51

Yaldā

The true morning will not come,
until the Yaldā Night is gone.
—Sa'adi, *Bustan*

"What do you do for Christmas?" Pari wondered. "Go to your parents' house? We always had a tree, but not a real Christmas. Not like in the movies."

"Yeah, we usually have Christmas at my parents' house. This year they're going to Florida, though. On a trip they won."

"Oh. You must be sad."

"Yeah. It's only this year, though."

She rested her hand on his chest, twirling her fingers. It was what she did when she was thinking. "I have an idea. We can celebrate Shab-e-Yaldā."

"Huh?"

"The winter solstice. The longest night of the year. We stay up all night. Or try to. You'll see." She jumped up, excited. "I could tell you about it. My mom could tell you more. But you know who could explain it better than anybody, probably? Andre."

The bulldozer and backhoe were gone. The ditch had been filled in, and the mound of dirt was gone. Anthony and Pari stepped along a board leading to Andre's front door across a flat area covered with straw. It looked like the county had covered the clay with topsoil and planted winter grass seed. The crooked door opened, and Andre stood in a yellow bathrobe, sleepy-eyed, grinning.

"So," Anthony said. "It looks like the county changed their mind about the sewer line." He felt cocky that their reporting had stopped the construction, and he didn't mind showing it.

Andre responded with a little clap of his hands like a child who'd been given a present. He said, "The press, when exercising its function as a watchdog of the public, has often managed to see that dishonest officials are held to account for their actions. In the late 18th century—"

"Um, I wonder if we could come in, Andre?" Pari teased.

He looked at her expectantly. "I'm guessing you finally got it."

"Got it?" Pari slipped off her shoes inside the doorway.

"The envelope."

Anthony smacked his forehead. "No, Andre. Actually Pari doesn't know about it. Emma keeps forgetting to give it to us."

Andre's blue eyes dimmed. "I see. Well, never mind. I'll bring some tea."

"Envelope?" Pari said. "What's in it, Andre?" But he had already gone into the kitchen. She gave Anthony a silent palms-up, open-mouth look.

As Andre gave each of their teacups a dollop of honey, Pari invited him to a Yaldā celebration at her mother's house.

His eyes brightened. "This is wonderful. I've always wanted to attend a Yaldā ceremony. The night that light slowly overcomes the darkness. The triumph of the spirit of truth and good over the spirit of falsehood and evil. The victory of Ahura Mazda over Ahriman."

Anthony raised an eyebrow at Pari as if to say, "You've started him off now."

"The ancient Zoroastrian religion," Andre went on, "teaches that we must protect the earth, fire, air, and water from the destructive force in the universe. We do this through good thoughts, good words, and good deeds. There is only one true path, the path of truth."

"I'm for that," Anthony said, but Andre didn't seem to hear.

"And the Yaldā celebration—the word is probably related to our word *Yule*, as in Yule log—features the color of fire and the sun to symbolize the cosmic victory of light as the longest night of the year comes to an end. Friends gather until the rising of the sun to—"

Pari said, "Sorry to interrupt, Andre. I need to give you my address. You're coming, we hope." She added, "We can't stay long."

As they drove home, they saw women in gray business suits hammering in notices on the empty lots along the river. Anthony slowed down. FORECLOSED. PROPERTY OF INVESTORS BANK OF DOVER. There was a phone number to call. The same sign stood in front of Bea's villa. Anthony hit the brakes and gawked for a moment. He and Pari gave each other high-fives. All the way home, Pari couldn't stop bouncing up and down in her seat.

Pari's mother had invited Shahnaz and her family. Pari had invited Anthony, Andre, and Ms. Ernst, the teacher who'd been shot in the School Board incident.

"She's so nice," Pari said. "And she seems kind of lonely."

They all sat on cushions placed on the floor around a low table set with candles, pomegranate and winter watermelon slices—red symbols of fire and the coming light—and all kinds of nuts and fruits. Andre had brought donuts with red sparklers and slipped the box onto the end of the table.

Ms. Ernst had to grip Andre's shoulder as she stretched her wounded leg out on the Persian carpet. She didn't know him and seemed embarrassed.

Mastaneh said, "Welcome, Ms. Ernst. So glad to meet you. Our friend Shahnaz says you're a wonderful teacher."

Shahnaz's husband held his hand over his heart. "Yes, we thank you for defending our son Jim in your class."

Andre sat next to Ms. Ernst. "I was very sorry to hear about your injury," he said. "I guess you've heard? Frank Fortunato's Guns for Teachers bill didn't get enough support to come up for a vote."

"Yes," Ms. Ernst said. "I read Anthony's report saying the House of Delegates speaker described that proposal as, what was it?"

"Dumber than distributing free opioids to cure opioid addiction," Andre said. He passed Ms. Ernst the box of donuts. "Let's hope it's a long time before the idea raises its head again."

Ms. Ernst smiled at Andre, holding up a hand to refuse a donut. "I always make sure to read Pari and Anthony's articles even if I skip everything else."

"Then you know Amanda Winwright has been chosen to replace Derek Grosbeck as state GOP Central Committee chair." Andre eyed the bandage on Ms. Ernst's leg and breathed a deep *tsk*. "You must be pleased. Winwright's a strong supporter of gun control."

Ms. Ernst gave a shy nod. She looked around the table as if hoping someone would steer the conversation away from her.

Pari's father said, "And as for our gun-promoting County Executive, Pari and Anthony report that the District Attorney has referred his case to Federal authorities on suspicion of misusing Federal funds. It looks bad for him."

Mastaneh clinked a paring knife against a plate. "Enough about politics. Now, everybody, Pari has a poem she'd like to read."

"What? No, Mom."

"The one that was in the envelope you got from Andre. You looked pleased."

Even in the candlelight they could see Pari was blushing. She shifted her eyes sideways towards Andre. "Mom, Andre probably wouldn't want—"

"I don't mind," Andre spoke up. "It's a ghazal I wrote modeled on the one in Pari's Happy Thoughts blog. I can say it by heart." He straightened up and recited:

The sacred earth below speaks to the truthful heart.
Winds blowing through the trees delight the earnest heart.
I watched in rippling waves as white gulls soared above
Her soft dark hair and eyes, her earnest, truthful heart.

"Bravo," Mastaneh sang out, and everyone applauded. Pari's face was as red as the pomegranates. But there could be no doubt that Andre was pleased. "I followed the rhythmical pattern of—"

"Tea, Andre?" Mastaneh said, and Pari looked relieved.

Mastaneh recited some poems of Hafez. Anthony noticed Shahnaz's son Jim yawning, which made him want to yawn, too. He appreciated the cultural significance of the event, but was it really going to go on until dawn?

Mastaneh put on some Persian music. Reza was talking to his son about baseball. He asked why Jim's friend Juan wasn't on the high school team.

"He didn't want to attract attention because his mother was here without a visa. But now they have visas. Next year he'll try out for it."

The women talked about their families and their jobs. Pari went to the hallway to telephone her brother. Anthony crunched down on a wedge of pomegranate, picked the seeds from his teeth, and sneaked a look at the time on his phone. Andre was talking to Pari's father, whose chin was beginning to droop onto his chest.

There was some singing. Shahnaz turned out to have a beautiful voice. More fruit, more nuts, more Persian poetry. The night wore on, the talk softening more and more to quiet murmurs. That was the last Anthony remembered.

He awoke lying on the floor with someone's leg draped over his. Pari's. The room smelled like burned out candle wick and was dark except for a thin crack of dim light coming beneath a window shade. He listened. No talking, no music. "Pari," he whispered in her ear.

She rubbed her eyes. "Anthony?" He felt her breath on his cheek. "I was asleep. Is everybody gone?"

"I don't know. I was asleep, too."

There was a soft snoring from the other side of the table. Pari sat up. "Looks like Shahnaz and her family have left. Everybody else is asleep."

Anthony whispered, "It's not quite day yet. I don't know what the protocol is, but do you think we could—"

"Sneak out? Yes, come on."

Daylight was starting to break as they walked down the long gravel driveway towards his car. In the dry, clear air, powerful rays of sunlight forced their way through the trees behind the house.

"It's cold, but you can feel the sun on your skin," Anthony said.

"It's Ahura Mazda, the creator, driving evil away, bringing good back to the earth."

Anthony gave her a look.

"Anyway, that's what they say."

On the way to the apartment, Pari said she was hungry.

"Watermelon and pumpkin seeds didn't fill you up?" Anthony teased. Since there was nothing in his little refrigerator, he pulled up to the Grab 'n Go. "We'll get some fried chicken nuggets. It's a traditional American dish. Hope you like it."

It was Saturday. Tran had just come on duty. "Mr. Anthony. So glad to see you. So beautiful morning. Very blight."

"Bright, yes." He introduced Pari. "You look especially happy today, Tran."

"I am happy, yes. Work hard. Save money. We open restaurant soon. Vietnamese."

"Congratulations." Anthony gave him his card. "When you open, call me. We'll put a story in the *Shady Park Ledger.*"

Tran couldn't stop talking about what dishes they'd serve, how they'd decorate the restaurant. His wife Thieu would cook. The restaurant was going to open in a former paint supply shop on North-South Highway. "Ze American deream," he said. "Is right?"

"Right," Pari and Anthony said together.

Nuggets bagged and paid for, they walked out arm in arm. Anthony said, "The Zoroastrian creator aside, it really does feel like the force of good is returning to the earth."

Pari leaned her head on his shoulder.

They walked past a gray car with a red fender that had pulled up directly in front of the store. A young man with a buzz cut in a camouflage jacket sat at the wheel, looking at pictures in a magazine called *Combat.* Anthony looked more closely. It was Willard Scherd.

www.ingramcontent.com/pod-product-compliance
Lightning Source LLC
Chambersburg PA
CBHW020300030826
48979CB00026B/1583/J

* 9 7 8 0 9 9 8 3 8 0 5 7 5 *